OPTICAL ILLUSIONS

A Romance of the Art World

Philip Hook

OPTICAL ILLUSIONS

ISBN 1 85863 042 8

Second Impression 1994

First Published 1993 by
MINERVA PRESS
2, Old Brompton Road,
London SW7 3DQ.

Printed in Great Britain by
Antony Rowe, Chippenham, Wiltshire.

OPTICAL ILLUSIONS

A Romance of the Art World

When Evan Conrad finds himself unexpectedly thrust into a leading international auction house as head of the Impressionist department, his life takes on a bewildering new dimension. His rise and fall are charted in this hilarious comic novel, which is both a biting satire on the intriguing world of dealers, auctioneers and museum directors, and at the same time an ingenious mystery story involving the rediscovery of a 'lost' nineteenth century painter.

Philip Hook, a former director of Christie's, has worked in the London art trade for twenty years, and appears regularly as picture expert on BBC TV's Antiques Roadshow. He is the author of *Popular Nineteenth Century Painting* (1986). This is his much admired first novel.

"Very funny, very clever, and delectably scurrilous" - William Boyd

Optical Illusions

ONE

The man in the immaculately cut suit and Hermès tie pushed an elegant but purposeful path through the throng of students. He moved with confidence, his clothes and manner striking a note of discreet superiority to the array of jeans, tee-shirts and leather jackets which surrounded him. Graciously he paused to accept a paper cup of foul Spanish wine proffered by a bearded youth with pebble glasses, then negotiated a knot of architectural historians exchanging earnest theories on Bauhaus design. A moment later he reached the girl he had noticed across the crowded room.

"I don't think we've met. My name's Ewan Connard."

"Renata Crum." She frowned with unexpected hostility, as if she begrudged him the information. Close to there was no doubt she possessed a gamin attractiveness, accentuated rather than obscured by the severity of her close-cropped blond hair. As she leant forward to put her paper cup down on the window ledge next to her, he sensed a tantalising undulation to her figure beneath the ungainly sack-like coat in which she chose to envelope herself.

"And what subject are you working on?" He flashed his most charming smile, the one calculated to blend irony with intimacy in the most intoxicating proportions.

She addressed him with disconcerting steeliness of eye. "Penises," she replied.

Ewan Connard paused, adjusting himself to the revelation. A youthful 38, he bore more than a passing resemblance to the young Yves St Laurent, or so he had once been assured by an effusive lady admirer met at a drinks party in Camden Town. It was a compliment which he had affected to receive with polite disdain, a fractional elevation of the eyebrow being enough to suggest that an art historian of his eminence had no point of contact with a mere fashion designer; nonetheless, he had not forgotten it the next morning as he inspected his clean-cut features in the bathroom mirror and ran his hands through his thick dark hair, allowing it to bounce back across his forehead with an élan of which Yves himself might have been proud. Ever since the comparison had been made, it had nestled reassuringly in his subconscious, even influencing occasionally his mannerisms and deportment. As he bent to inspect some appetising little early Bonnard, he had taken to fingering his designer spectacles with the same mixture of apparent diffidence and real power which he imagined characterised a St Laurent appraisal of one of his own creations. Now he smiled urbanely and said:

"Really? What particular aspect of the penis are you studying?"

"I am researching the way the penis dominates nineteenth century literature." She looked at him impatiently, as if the answer was too obvious to need stating.

"Does it dominate nineteenth century literature?"

"Of course it does, it's all there if you look for it, you only have to read the material with a modicum of perception. You don't imagine that Dickens or Dostoievsky or Stendhal would have written what they did in the way that they did if they hadn't had penises. Their attitude to various issues - to women in particular - is conditioned by a whole set of appallingly unbalanced male-rooted assumptions. These men were victims of their own sexual stereotyping."

"So the penis is mightier than the sword?" smirked Ewan.

"You may find that sort of puerile comment clever and amusing but I happen to be undertaking a serious and fundamental reappraisal of some devastatingly prejudiced and outmoded attitudes."

Connard blinked. Normally students hung on his words, laughed gratifyingly at his every joke. Even at London's premier institute for the study of Fine Art, where he taught, his views were treated with almost oracular respect. He had already published two well-received books on aspects of Post-Impressionism, and, equally important, had himself been born with sufficient social pedigree and private income to move naturally in the circles of the very rich owners of the pictures about which he wrote with such authority. He enjoyed the limelight, being conspicuous at private views and exhibition openings. Certainly he had his critics: some found him arrogant and others were irked by the smoothness of his manner and the glibness of his judgements, but these criticisms tended to founder on the rock of his seemingly unassailable scholarship. Connard was used to success. He was unmarried, but not, through some rare chromosomatic malfunction, homosexual. He enjoyed social life and went to a large number of parties. Indeed this was the one indiscriminate area of an otherwise fastidious life, his voracious acceptance of invitations. But it was explained by the fact that he relished the company of women to the point where the opposite sex was an obsession, and he found parties a useful means of meeting them. This was the reason why he had now descended, both literally and metaphorically, to the basement common room where he was attending a drinks party for the first-year research students of the Institute. He came in hope that this year's crop might include one or two young women of potential; indeed it was not impossible that some girl here, if she played her cards right, might end up enjoying a late-night private view of the intriguing collection of old master drawings in his elegant flat in Manchester Square. At a distance he had suspected that Renata Crum might be that girl. Now he was not so sure.

"Yes, of course," he said pacifically. "I'm so sorry. But I wasn't aware that this institute cast its net so wide for subjects for MA theses."

"God, you don't think I belong to this archaic and elitist set-up, do you? Not bloody likely. It's the sheer irrelevance of most of art history that gets me. Just answer me this: why aren't more art historians working on Artemisia Gentileschi? It stands out a mile that she's the one worthwhile subject left in the seventeenth century. That's what I'd be doing if I were here. But I'm not, thank God. I'm reading Women's Studies at St Ethelreda's."

Connard reminded himself that he had lunched that day in the exquisite surroundings of one of the West End's smartest restaurants. His companion had been the fabulously wealthy Californian widow who was Chairman of the Board of Governors of the San Pietro Museum of Fine Arts, an establishment whose directorship was about to fall vacant. He had shone, he had sparkled; and he had basked in unstinted appreciation. Did he therefore need the present tirade, or its squalidly abrasive perpetrator? He concluded that he did not. He announced, with a patrician politeness intended to re-establish a sense of decency and order: "Well, it was a great pleasure to welcome you here this evening. I'm delighted you were able to come along."

"I'm only here because Evan Conrad persuaded me to come with him. Where's he got to? Evan, over here!"

At the sound of his name being called a fresh-faced young man in his late twenties turned away from the group gathered round the table with the paper cups and the bottles of wine and obediently made his way towards them. He blushed vividly when he caught sight of Connard. "Oh, Dr Connard, how nice to see you. You've met Renata then? Renata, Dr Connard is my Director of Studies...."

"So he's the berk responsible for your absurd thesis subject." Renata Crum turned to Connard with a renewed aggression. "Why the hell did you get him all fired up on this irrelevant French pointillist when he could have been working on someone genuinely significant? I mean I accept that Artemisia Gentileschi might be a little outside his period, but what about all those incredibly underrated female artists of the early twentieth century? Kathe Kollwitz, Paula Mohderson-Becker, even Gwen John or Vanessa Bell?"

In some embarrassment Evan Conrad stepped in. "Please, Renata, it's a bit much for you to start lecturing Dr Connard like this...."

"No, no, not at all." Connard decided that dignified retreat was now the best course of action. He found it hard to imagine Renata Crum ever responding positively to a late-night invitation to Manchester Square. "I've been most intrigued to hear about your work, and it's always refreshing to hear strongly-held views expressed with conviction." He gave a self-deprecating little laugh suggestive of profound urbanity and worldly-wisdom, and, nodding to Evan, moved on.

What now? He looked about him with some distaste. Recently one of the quality Sunday supplements had run a series entitled "My Favourite Room" in which various eminent authorities were invited to expatiate on the most lovely interior they had ever experienced. Ewan Connard had contributed the flawlessly beautiful library of a little known but utterly ravishing Palladian villa in the Veneto where he had stayed as a private guest on more than one occasion. Unfortunately the Institute Common Room would not have finished high on anyone's list of lovely interiors. It was painted in an unappealing colour which had pretensions towards Pompeian red but succeeded only in conveying an effect of widespread rust; the plaster was crumbling at intervals and the walls were half-heartedly decorated with posters advertising long-gone exhibitions by obscure Colombian print-makers and Rumanian post-constructivists. Lighting was provided by rows of fluorescent tubes set starkly in the ceiling. For a moment his eye alighted on an anaemic-looking young woman with a shock of self-consciously Pre-Raphaelite hair. There was a possible diversion. But on the other hand he did have that book review to finish. Perhaps he should cut his losses for the evening and go back to the flat. Christ, this wine was disgusting. Undecided, he circled the room once more, and then dived in for a brief attempt on the Rossettian girl.

Meanwhile Evan Conrad contemplated Renata Crum and wished that she wouldn't be so aggressive. It wasn't the first time it had happened, of course. And in a way he was vaguely conscious that her strength of will might be part of her attraction. But to find her laying into Dr Connard of all people, abusing his own Director of Studies, that was unacceptable. It could be his own career that was endangered here. Yes his career, for God's sake. He would be loathe to admit it publicly, but there was a strand of Evan Conrad that was ambitious, fiercely and materially ambitious. Beneath a diffident exterior he harboured fantasies about his future that included not just academic renown but occasionally even dreams of wealth too. The horizons of his suburban, non-conformist upbringing had expanded dramatically at provincial university. Now here he was in London, embarked on post-graduate research in art history, catching glimpses of even more alluring possibilities. And yet it wasn't quite as simple as that. He still hadn't quite been able to jettison the idealistic left-wing mental furniture which was standard issue to most of those undergoing British Further Education, even some art historians. The balance between Conscience and Ambition still swayed uncertainly within him. Now, however, it tipped momentarily in favour of Ambition and, goaded by the possible damage Renata might have done to his prospects, he decided to remonstrate with her.

"Look, love, why can't you be a little more polite to people?" he pleaded.

"Why should I be? It did him good to hear a few home truths."

"Ewan Connard is someone I particularly admire, as it happens. He's also a man who could be useful to me in the future if I go into the museum world."

Renata was unimpressed. "He's an oily ponce. The worst sort of sexist bigot."

"I think you're being a little unfair, you know."

"And what's so wonderful about the museum world, for God's

sake? You're so blinkered about your future."

"What do you mean, blinkered?"

"You're so set in your ways. You should be more flexible, more adventurous, you should think about doing something more relevant for a few years."

"Like what?"

"There's a bloke in my college who's taking a two-year sabbatical to go and live in the jungle and fight despoliation of the Amazon Rain forests."

"But I'm an art historian."

"Don't be so pathetic."

"Where are you going?"

"I'm getting out of here. This place makes me sick." With a gesture of scorn she flung her scarf about her and in so doing knocked several dozen paper cups to the floor. Evan struggled ineffectually to retrieve them, abandoned the attempt, then hurried out after her, running up the basement steps to the pavement. It was a lot colder outside.

"OK, I understand: you're upset about something. Why don't we talk about it? I'll stand you a Chinese take-away and we can eat it back in the flat."

"Not bloody likely. I told you already, I've got this vital Women Against Carnivorism meeting at 8.30, and I'm not going to miss it. You can ring me later in the week."

There was no arguing with Renata in this mood. She was unappeasable, possessed by some fury which drove her to wreak indiscriminate verbal vengeance on any male who might venture within her orbit. Perhaps he should try to be unpleasant back to her; but to be honest he disliked unpleasantness and was not adept at handling it. Defeated, he watched her unchain her bicycle from the Institute railings and pedal off into the night. It looked like a lonely bus ride back to Earls Court. And a solitary Chicken Chop Suey.

Half an hour later he let himself into the squalidly unprepossessing apartment, a room of which he rented from a squalidly unprepossessing Australian dentist called Roger Brady, and was relieved to find that at least his landlord wasn't at home. He entered the tiny kitchen in search of a plate from which to eat the Chinese meal which he was clutching to him, an evil-smelling lukewarm brown paper parcel. He sat down on the sofa in the living room and ate meditatively, abstractedly forking in large mouthfuls of fried rice and bean shoot. His thoughts wandered to Renata's recent observations. Was there any justice in them? Was Ewan Connard an oily ponce? Was a career in the museum world not a fit calling for a man of action?

There were certainly aspects of Ewan Connard which, if Evan was truthful, did not entirely appeal to him. There was his excessive smoothness, for a start, and the scent of privilege which clung to him. But at the same time these shortcomings also had their fascination. They were symptoms of a state to which Evan himself inspired, the state of success in his chosen field of Art History. In many ways he wouldn't mind changing places with Ewan Connard. There was much to be envied in his life and achievement.

Evan pushed away his empty plate and reached for his books. There was time for an hour or two's work before bed, he decided. And, his mind still lingering on the question of Connard, he admitted the academic debt of gratitude he owed to his director of studies. That couldn't be denied. It had been Connard who had first inspired then encouraged him along the line of research which he was now pursuing. The starting point of his thesis was an article Connard had written in the Burlington Magazine entitled 'Claude Hartier, The Forgotten Neo-Impressionist'. The pretext for the article had been the coincidental appearance on the art market of a colourful pointillist landscape signed with the initials C.H., and the discovery of a previously unpublished letter in the Bibliothèque Nationale from Georges Seurat himself, the Father of the Movement, to Hartier. The dramatic resurfacing of an artist of the stature of Hartier was a stimulating event as delineated by Connard. The brief but suggestive correspondence between the two - reproduced for the first time in Connard's article - confirmed the high opinion in which the young Hartier had once been held by the leading pointillist painter of all time. Evan picked up the now familiar text and experienced once again the original thrill of excitement as he re-read it:

Paris, 22 June 1884
My dear Hartier

It was truly a great pleasure to visit your studio this

> morning and I thank you for showing me your work as one artist to another. I hope you will not misinterpret what I say, but I have to confess that it was something of a shock to see the progress you have made. I do not exaggerate when I tell you that you have developed ideas, at least in theory, which are in many ways in advance of my own researches into colour. Certain of your landscapes seem to achieve goals at which I myself have been aiming without complete success for the last few years. I salute and congratulate you, rejoicing in the knowledge that we are partners in working this same challenging field.
> Your friend,
> G. Seurat

Yes, Evan had felt at the time of that first reading, yes, here was a subject with enormous potential. Here was a thesis worthy of his steel, a thesis to capture his imagination, a challenge which would open up his own academic future before him. He would labour diligently until he had uncovered the entire corpus of Claude Harrier's submerged oeuvre. He would piece together the man's artistic development. He would re-establish him on a pinnacle of eminence of equal if not superior height to Seurat himself, both as painter and as theorist. There would be many pictures to trace, and perhaps even writings. It was all tremendously exciting.

And then he had come down to earth. Perhaps Connard was already working on the enterprise. It wouldn't have been surprising, given the crucial first steps he had already taken in the form of the Burlington article. Hardly daring to hope, Evan had taken his project to Connard earlier that year. Was there any contribution he could make to Hartier studies? A catalogue raisonné, perhaps? Why not, Connard had said. Good idea. Connard's own workload in other directions was currently too heavy for him undertake the commitment. Evan could do the research, under Connard's supervision of course. And Evan had been delighted, grateful for this unexpected generosity.

So Evan had set to work enthusiastically. The first two months of his research to date had been occupied with preparation, reading round Seurat and his followers, investigating the theories of Neo-Impressionism, and scouting about for further works either by or attributable to Hartier. So far there were five: not a wealth of material, it was true, but a start. And he had high hopes of further leads when he was due to visit Paris next month to meet Dr Louis Ranchec, the French art historian who had first unearthed the Seurat letter to Hartier and shown it to Connard. Admittedly Ranchec had been strangely reluctant to reply to any of Evan's letters to date, and his telephone appeared to be out of order, but Evan had every confidence that when he actually went to Paris he would track his man down and swiftly overcome what was doubtless nothing more than a severe case of Gallic scholastic reserve.

This evening Evan's work went well. Two hours later he laid down his pen having covered three sheets of foolscap with tightly-packed notes on late nineteenth century colour theory. He stretched and yawned: he felt ready for bed. Withdrawing to his room, he stumbled about between piles of dirty laundry and unwashed coffee cups before finally sliding between the sheets and switching off the light.

He felt a sudden wave of loneliness. He lay on his back and considered Renata, or more particularly the absence of Renata. He was very attached to her, but there was no denying that she was difficult to manage. Her strongly held and forcefully expressed opinions made her an uneasy companion socially; her political commitments made her difficult to pin down privately; but nonetheless on those rare occasions when she consented to spend the nocturnal hours between a Lesbian Sweatshop Theatre Evening and a Green Women's Working Breakfast in bed with him, her guard could momentarily slip and she would betray glimpses of a tenderness and sensuality thrillingly at variance with her normal manner. It was that other Renata lurking within who tempted and tantalised him. Yes, he was attracted to her partly because of her elusiveness. But that didn't mean that he necessarily agreed with some of her judgements about his own career. What was so wonderful about the museum world, she had demanded? This was dangerous talk, not to be encouraged. The museum world was the one for which he was being prepared, and that was that. If he himself also felt the occasional twinge of yearning for a more glamorous and dynamic element in his future, it was for the time being better suppressed. And there was one thing he was quite sure about: he would not be seeking that element of glamour and dynamism in the Rain forest of the Amazon jungle.

He was drifting towards a troubled sleep when the peace of the flat was abruptly shattered by an explosion of noise. A succession of antipodean oaths interspersed with little shrieks of hysterical female laughter announced the inebriated return of his landlord, and his landlord's current girlfriend Glenda. Roger Brady's only hobby was drinking. Fair enough, thought Evan. But did he also have to come home in the small hours and fall over the furniture? On mornings after the night before Evan would contemplate the dentist's bleary eye and shaking hand over the breakfast table and he wouldn't envy Roger's 9.30 am patient. There was nothing shaky about Roger now, however: Evan listened with a horrified fascination as the pair of them withdrew to Roger's bedroom (which adjoined his own) and engaged in an uncompromisingly direct coupling scarcely five feet away from Evan's left ear. On balance he found it difficult tonight to welcome this reminder of how straightforward and uncomplicated human passion could be.

Ewan Connard was also prey to a certain dissatisfaction that evening as he sat at the elegant desk in his supremely tasteful study in Manchester Square. He had abandoned the Lizzie Siddall look-alike fairly swiftly on discovering that she suffered simultaneously from both a bad nose cold and an insatiable desire to discuss Victorian industrial architecture to the exclusion of all else. He had taken a light supper at home and settled down with a glass of claret to the book review for the London Art Digest whose deadline was imminently approaching. But he found it hard to concentrate on the mass of verbiage which he encountered as he turned the pages of 'Towards Opticality: Studies in Syntheticist Impressionism' by Professor Vern G. Throg, Emeritus Fellow in the History of Art at the Carl Snead University, South Dakota. What drove American academics to write in such a dense and unrelenting style? He let his eye fall to a sentence at random:

"The painterly: linear interface, a nodal point in the tensity between form and content when prismatically perceived, predicates color modes which synurge towards opticality as opposed to opticalism, the distinction energised by awareness of the infinitely variable interstrands of chromatic response."

Dear God, he hadn't the patience for much more of this. His

thoughts drifted away from the outpourings of Professor Throg and back to the events of the evening. The memory of the abortive and somewhat sordid drinks party in the Institute Common Room unsettled him. He found himself taking stock for a moment, contemplating what the future might hold. At 38, the years of promise were almost over. He was approaching a watershed. A more substantial role, an added gravitas would befit him now. And perhaps a little less chasing after deceptively ferocious feminists hardly half his age might not be inappropriate. What a dreadful woman Renata Crum had turned out to be. And what a lunatic his student Evan - what was he called? - yes, Evan Conrad, must be to get involved with her.

Evan Conrad. A strange name, he mused: but for a couple of letters, the same as his own. There, he fervently trusted, the resemblance ended.

TWO

Three men sat in the elegant surroundings of the panelled boardroom of one of London's leading auction houses. Rokeby's was by general consent the oldest established in the land, and had for some time past discreetly canvassed a claim to being the most successful; not, of course, in terms of turnover, as they were overtaken by larger rivals, but in terms of the quality of items offered. There was some truth to this boast as the firm had traditionally kept close ties to the old families of Britain, many of whose idiot sons had regularly broken fine Chinese vases in Rokeby's vaults when therein employed (to cement links) as porters. Rather like a Conservative cabinet of an earlier generation, the Rokeby's board was dominated by Etonians, with all the unspoken areas of mutual experience and comforting network of common connections that this implied. Nonetheless, the grim realisation that times were changing was beginning to impinge, the awful suspicion that new methods were called for was beginning to take root. The three men who sat in the boardroom personified in their different ways the varied strands of tradition and innovation which now characterised the business.

They were an uneasy amalgam of forces and intelligences, not natural bedfellows in a business, or any other sense. However, they all shared one thing in common, an acute awareness of the looming if somnolent presence of old Mr Terence Rokeby, the 74 year old chairman of the firm, dozing ineluctably in his capacious office next door. Was he or was he not compos mentis? There were varying theories on the question; but he had let it be known that he intended to retire at the end of March, and that his successor would be appointed from one of the three gathered together now. In the meantime they were to form a triumvirate to run the firm on a day to day basis, pulling together for the good of the company but at the same time uncomfortably aware that their individual performances in this context would determine who won the victor's crown when the prize was finally bestowed.

The Honourable Freddy Fairbanks found it hard to believe, in his heart of hearts, that he would not be the one who triumphed in the end. He was a tall, blond, good-looking man with a tendency to floridity after a good lunch. He had been educated as a member of the ruling class, brought up on a family estate where forelock tugging by employees was not discouraged, and while he realised that the same degree of subservience was not always a viable proposition from the Rokeby porters, some of whom hailed from Romford and other such unfeudal areas, nonetheless he was used to giving orders and to being obeyed. Not that the Rokeby porters concerned him too closely. It was his proud boast that he was not a man to be bogged down by detail: he saw things in the broad sweep, looking down as he did from the top of the mountain. His strength was the charm he could bring to bear on the recalcitrant owner of a Velasquez on a shooting weekend, on the widowed inheritor of a Braque met skiing in Gstaad. He preferred to leave industrial relations, management structures, computer technology, and indeed filing systems of any sort to the plodders, the nuts and bolts men whose sad and unromantic metier they were. These were the mechanics who looked after the engineering of the racing car which was Rokeby's, while Freddy was the driver, flamboyant, daring, his scarf flying after him as he accelerated into the straight. He glanced across at Ron Wheale, the second member of the executive trio sitting across the table from him, busy with a pocket calculator. There was the mechanic par excellence: if only the bugger didn't have ideas above his station. Just because he could talk with a spurious fluency about management bases and work-load parameters, he imagined he could take the reins of the whole company. It was patently absurd for old Terence even to consider such a possibility. But time would tell. He, Freddy Fairbanks, would ensure that nothing untoward came about. He wanted ideally for Rokeby's to be built into a company in the Fairbanks image: stylish, relaxed, flexible. In fact he prided himself on his flexibility. There was no problem of such complexity, no tight spot of such awkwardness, that could not be negotiated somehow with the aid of his famous charm. He had some standards, though: he never accepted shooting invitations for Wednesdays as it was difficult to decide which weekend to tack them on to. And he never dipped his pen in company ink; at least not since last year when Harriet had caused all that absurd and unnecessary trouble and had had to be transferred to New York.

Freddy glanced round at the other two and decided that the

moment had come to assert himself. It didn't do any harm to take command now and then. "Right," he said firmly, "shall we make a start? I know there are several important items on this week's agenda, but the most pressing is..."

"Just hold on a minute, Freddy," interrupted Wheale, looking up from his calculator and an infuriatingly neat file of papers.

"I think it would be wrong for you to go on until I have these interdepartmental budget ratio forecasts up to date." Wheale poked buttons decisively and self-importantly, took a gold pen from his jacket pocket and made a swift notation in his file, conscious of the fact that he was engaged in arcane and mysterious rites beyond the scope of the other two. He was a small dark man, immaculately groomed, who tended to favour shirts which were a little too studiedly tailored to the contours of his thickening torso, and chose ties suggestive of mid-Atlantic meritocracy. He lived in Hemel Hempstead and had been educated at a grammar school. However, his children were at fee-paying schools and while he was acutely conscious of the gap between himself and a man like Freddy, he worked constantly to narrow it, and sought frequently to remind Freddy and others like him in the upper echelons of Rokeby's of the indispensability of Ron Wheale and his management talents to the success of the firm. In this respect his attitude was ambivalent: on the one hand he admired and aspired to the condition of those patricians who appeared to move effortlessly through life to claim its prizes as of right; and on the other he was confident that his own abilities in certain areas were such as to put his rivals in the shade, so he was not prepared to be patronised. The accoutrements of social life at a rarefied level intrigued and attracted him. In time attendance at Ascot, even membership of White's, were goals which he planned to attain. He looked forward to the day when he too was invited shooting to the great houses of Britain, and to that end was secretly taking private lessons at a local establishment with a prolific supply of clay pigeons. Meanwhile he had recently ordered a suit with four buttons on the cuff. The only reservation he felt about these aspirations consisted solely in the possibility that they might be construed as admissions of any sort of inferiority on his part. He would not yield an inch to the others on that basis.

The third man in the room stared meditatively out of the window and raised jaded eyes heavenwards in a somewhat camp gesture of annoyance at the delay Wheale was imposing on proceedings. Endymion Luce ran the furniture department at Rokeby's and did so rather well. He felt strongly about furniture: he liked pretty rococo pieces, certainly, but his most passionate feelings were reserved for examples whose line and stance were strong and virile. He was fond of telling intimate friends of the occasion on which a particularly masculine late eighteenth century desk had given him an erection. Endymion Luce was an expert specialist, unlike his two rivals. He was looked up to because of his expertise in a particular field. This was both an advantage and a handicap in the race for the chairmanship: his brilliance was an asset, but it tied him too closely to one particular department for him to be universally accepted as the overall boss of every one of them. But he was certainly ambitious for the crown, and to that end tried to keep his occasionally colourful private life as discreet as possible from his professional duties. That he had not been entirely successful in this aim was attested by the fact that his secretary, a nice girl from Gloucestershire called Amanda Fyffe-Knightley, had recently taken to rinsing his coffee mug with Dettol every time she handled it, after reading an irresponsibly alarmist article on the subject of Aids in the women's section of a national newspaper.

"Do you mind, Ron? I have a rather pressing engagement at 4," said Luce, who had arranged to have his hair cut.

"Ready to go now," said Wheale briskly, snapping shut his calculator. "Let's get cracking. You were saying, Freddy?"

"Yes, right. I was saying that there are several important items that need our attention today, but the most pressing is the question of the Impressionist Department." Endymion turned his chair back round to face the table and gave the matter his direct attention. Ron reacted less languidly to flick open another file, remove an elaborate looking graph, and lay it out precisely in front of him.

"Snap!" he cried. "I was going to bring that very matter up myself. I have figures and diagrams here that prove in a world market context..."

"Yes, yes, Ron," continued Freddy, refusing to yield centre stage, "we can all have the pleasure of looking at those very impressive bits of paper later. But the essential point is, for the purpose of this meeting, that since Denzil left us six months ago things have not gone well in the Impressionist Department. We have fallen back. We thought we could get by without taking anyone new on to replace Denzil, but quite frankly I am afraid that Eric Steward hasn't proved up to it. You were going to have a word with him, Endymion, last week. How did that interview go?"

"It was a bit of an ordeal. I am afraid the poor dear started weeping."

"There you are. Can't have that. The net result of it all is that our market share has declined considerably."

"On a direct seasonally-adjusted base comparison reduced from 20.9% to 14.3%," interposed Ron quickly.

"In fact," observed Endymion, "if it hadn't been for the great improvement in the furniture and decorative arts sales in the summer season, we'd all be up shit creek as my old nanny used to say."

Ron looked askance at him. Mention of nannies, butlers or stables simultaneously fascinated and unnerved him.

"We all realise what a debt of gratitude we owe to the unstinting efforts of the Furniture Department," said Freddy sourly. "But the fact remains that if I hadn't persuaded Madame Valbonne to sell her Chagalls in June the Impressionist Department figures would be even more disastrous. And I don't need to tell you that the Impressionist market is crucial to any auction house's success. That's where the really big money can be made..."

"26.19% of turnover in the twelve month module to 31 December," added Ron informatively.

"Exactly; thank you, Ron. My feeling is that unless we take decisive steps to improve matters, it will be too late."

"What do you propose?" enquired Luce.

"Whatever we decide I urge that we bear in mind the necessity of the containment of costs within the wider parameters of a set profit: turnover ratio," volunteered Ron helpfully.

"It's all a question of getting out and meeting the right people in the right places," Freddy told them. "Owners of top Impressionist pictures do not, sadly, seem to be the sort of people who are our traditional clients, the chaps we know, our neighbours in the country, that sort of thing. No, the new clientele is rather more international. So I think, as I say, that I am going to have to get out and about a bit more. Spend two or three weeks in Gstaad in February, for instance: that's the time to catch Madame Valbonne again. Given a reasonable length of time with her, I think I can twist her arm to sell her two Mattisses. And then there's King Wattle. His collection would be the big one to land. I might be able to meet him in Paris or Zurich next month, otherwise it will be a question of my having to fly out to the Caribbean to have a chat with him."

The other two nodded, torn between appreciation of the desirability of the King C. Wattle Collection of Impressionist pictures, and annoyance at the thought of Freddy Fairbanks sunning himself in the West Indies or enjoying three weeks' skiing in Gstaad at the firm's expense.

"This is all very well, Freddy," said Luce carefully, "but can someone of your importance be spared from London for so long? We have to harness your business-getting talents to their most telling effect. Think of the opportunities you may be missing here while you're away."

"I agree with Endymion," said Ron. "I think we need to tackle the problem from a different angle. We can't expect Freddy to do the work of the Impressionist Department for them. We need a new man, a proper replacement for Denzil. We need to look for a high profile appointment, someone who will count for something in the Impressionist field and will hopefully reverse the recent trends."

"That's right," agreed Luce. He rarely agreed with Wheale about anything, but joint opposition to Freddy was one of the few conditions which could compel them into uneasy alliance. "If we could find someone of sufficient stature to go out and take on the Valbonnes and the Wattles of this world from a position of technical knowledge and strength, someone who's a respected authority in their field, it might just bring home the bacon. And that would free you, Freddy, a little more. I mean if you didn't have to make that aggravating and inconvenient trip to the Caribbean you could spend the time profitably securing and setting up that house sale on the premises in Wales. I can't help feeling that if you could manage a few days at Aberystwyth in November it might just swing the whole thing in our favour."

"Well, of course, if we could find the right man then that might alter the situation," admitted Freddy. "But a high-profile appointment? Someone of stature? People like that don't grow on trees, you know. They're bloody difficult to find."

"I don't think it should be impossible if we act with a little determination," persisted Luce. "Is there anyone in the trade who could be persuaded in to do the job?"

"No-one springs to mind. Most of them are bloody crooks, anyway. And anyone who's any good is going to ask for an outrageous salary."

"Salary" was one of those words which set off alarm bells in Ron's brain whenever he heard it. "Higher technical remuneration structures need constant monitoring," he warned.

"What about an academic, then?" suggested Luce.

"A pretty useless crew as far as I am concerned. Mostly pinko intellectuals who can't make up their minds whether it's Tuesday or Wednesday without requiring time for further research. Complete wankers."

"I'm not so sure. People like Wattle, for instance, are always rather impressed to be confronted by someone who's written a few books about his subject... I agree it's got to be someone who has some experience of the ways of the world, too."

"A pretty tall order if you ask me."

It was determination to prevent Freddy from carrying the day which galvanised Endymion into dredging in his memory for the name of someone whose identity had impinged briefly a week or two ago and lain submerged since. He was hopeful that this person might just fit the bill. Yes, now he remembered: it had been someone who had caught his attention in that month's 'Harpers and Queen' by virtue of having appeared twice, once as the author of an article on the big Neo-Impressionist exhibition at the Grand Palais, and the other time in his own right in the social pages, photographed at a reception at Grosvenor House with Lady Olga Maitland. It had not been possible to tell much from the postage stamp sized illustration, but as far as one could make out he looked presentable. "There's a man called Connard," he announced. "At least I think that's his name. He's at the Institute, I believe, and he's got a good reputation. He's seen about a bit, knows a few people."

Freddy shrugged. "I can't say I'm very optimistic, but if you think it's worth it let's get him for an interview. What do you think, Ron?"

Ron considered the matter. Certainly academics were less likely to ask for outrageous salaries than some other potential candidates. He gave qualified approval to the plan.

"Why don't you make contact with him, Endymion, as you know

about him?" suggested Freddy. "In fact you might try and get the letter off today. The less delay the better if we're to make an appointment in time for it to have any sort of an effect on the spring sales."

"Right you are," said Luce. "And now if you'll excuse me I really must dash. Urgent business, you know, an appointment I really can't postpone."

Two minutes later he burst into the office of his secretary. Miss Fyffe-Knightley jumped slightly at the suddenness of his irruption, coming as it did with frenetic instructions to take an extremely important letter quickly as he had a most pressing engagement at 4. This sort of urgent request would not normally have nonplussed her since she was used to the minor crises and unheralded panics which erupted continually in her boss's life. However, at the moment of his entrance she had been immersed in an article in a women's magazine, an article of more than usually horrific nature purporting to purvey the latest developments in the battle of Medical Science to contain the spread of sexually transmitted diseases. She found it hard to concentrate, even that her shorthand pencil was shaking in her hand as she wrote; but still she managed to capture the gist of what Endymion was saying.

"Got that, Mandy?"

"I think so, Mr Luce."

"Of course it's absolutely confidential, you understand. It's to go in the red file."

"Absolutely. Can I just check the spelling of the name again? Is it Connard with two n's?"

Luce looked up in exasperation. He had his coat on and his hand was on the door. "Christ, I don't know. I'm not even sure that was his name exactly, and I can't check now, I'm late already. Why don't you ring up the Institute discreetly and they can tell you."

"Leave it to me, Mr Luce."

He departed, and Mandy sat for a few moment trying to calm the turmoil within. Of course the Dettol precautions were all very well and a step in the right direction, but now she had just discovered that the Aids virus could survive on a toothbrush bristle in warm water for up to forty-eight hours. And last night, horrors, she had used her flatmate Fiona's toothbrush by mistake. You had to be on your guard the whole time, it seemed. Not that Fiona was necessarily a carrier, being of the dimensions and personality that did not immediately attract other members of the human race into sexual activity, but it was a risk undeniably. And another thing, what was this safe sex that everyone kept talking about? No, she must take a grip. Deep breaths, as her old gym mistress used to prescribe, then on with the matter in hand.

"Yes, dear," said the homely lady at the Institute, "I've got a list here. Whose name were you looking for?"

"I think it begins 'CON' something. The initial is E."

"Oh, yes, here we are, got it. Mr Evan Conrad, that'll be the one. He's a research student."

"Thank you so much."

It was five o'clock when Endymion Luce returned, his thinning locks coiffed and curled by the ministrations of André at the discreet salon just off Bond Street. What a nice boy André was, thought Endymion. Perhaps next time he might persuade him round to the flat to do the job in private. The very thought put him in a good mood as he strode up the steps into the front hall of Rokeby's and turned left to take the short cut to his office past the telephonists' room. This was where the central switchboard of the firm was situated, and Endymion was unwise enough to glance through the glass door as he passed. Here he caught sight of the leering countenance of Lance Peerman, and his good spirits evaporated instantly. To be reminded of the existence of Lance was to be reminded of an error of judgement which did not sit well on the shoulders of an aspirant Chairman of Rokeby's. Lance had been a dreadful mistake. Of course he had proved an amusing diversion for an evening or two, and when the little tart had asked him for a job it had seemed an amusing whim to get him one at Rokeby's. Too late he had realised the danger. Lance had rapidly turned into a horribly querulent little queen with a proclivity - hinted but not yet articulated - to blackmail. This meant that his removal could not be achieved without some considerable diplomacy. The whole aggravating problem of Lance was absorbing his mind as he sat down at his desk and Mandy put the letter to the man at the Institute in front of him for signing. He did so at once without reading it, and called sharply for a cup of coffee which tasted oddly of disinfectant.

THREE

"Is this a joke or something?"

It was the following night, and Renata waved the Rokeby's letter in the direction of Evan Conrad with a mixture of surprise, distaste and indignation. He had persuaded her round to his flat - mercifully bereft of Roger for the evening - on the promise that he had something pretty amazing to show her, and it had certainly absorbed her attention while she studied it. It read:

Private and Confidential
Dear Mr Conrad

I write to you after discussion with my co-senior directors on a matter of some sensitivity, which I naturally trust you will treat in the strictest confidence. We at Rokeby's have been searching for some time for ways of improving an already outstanding team of experts in our Impressionist Department. Your name has been suggested to us as someone of exceptional ability and proven standing in the field of Impressionist and Twentieth Century Art. We are also confident that you may be one of those fortunate few for whom the transition from academic life to the commercial art market may be accomplished with reasonable facility.

Naturally the salary we would be prepared to pay you should you choose to join us would be commensurate with your outstanding art historical achievements and with your envisaged high responsibility as a major business getter. An initial trial period with us could be expected to lead fairly shortly to a seat on the board.

I do hope that you will feel this letter is of interest and that you will excuse its presumption in view of the fact that we have not actually met. Please telephone me to arrange a time for further discussion.

Yours Sincerely,
Endymion Luce (Joint Deputy Chairman)

"I don't see why it should be a joke," said Evan a little peevishly. "It seems to me fairly self-explanatory. They need an expert in Impressionist pictures, so they turn to the leading art history institute in the country to find one."

"But why you?" demanded Renata with unforgiving persistence. Evan found her incredulity more than a little irksome.

"It's my field, I'm young, someone must have put in a good word for me. Why not? I think it's a great opportunity."

Renata considered the matter. "You'd be selling yourself to one of the most immoral engines of capitalist exploitation in society. There's very little to be said for the commercial art market, you know. It's not as if it actually does anything for those contemporary artists whose work really has relevance. And this board at Rokeby's: how many women are there on it? I think it stinks that women are given so little chance in that sort of male-orientated establishment. It's a top priority issue on a committee which I run, actually."

"Well, here's my chance to work from within the system to change it. Like I said, it's a fantastic opportunity."

"So you're determined to pursue this?" Evan sensed distant thunder, a warning of imminent storm, almost inevitable when he proposed a course of action inimical to Renata's principles. Moving an inch or two further away from her on the sofa to take cover from the outburst he felt sure would come he said:

"I'll go and talk to them, certainly."

But on this occasion he had misread the signals. Renata frowned and said mysteriously: "You might be right. There are times when the end justifies the means." Emboldened, Evan continued: "I certainly won't throw away all the effort I've put into Hartier, of course. I'll go on working on him in my spare time. In fact being at Rokeby's might even give me more opportunity for research."

"That irrelevant pillock," said Renata. "I wouldn't shed any tears over abandoning him. I've told you before, you're wasting your time there..."

Next morning Evan reflected that Renata's opposition to the new direction his career was taking had been by her standards insubstantial. Indeed it was possible to read into the fact that she had foregone an appointment with the Women Say Yes to Troops out of Ireland Committee in favour of spending the night with him a qualified seal of approval for the project. What an extraordinary turn events were taking. Twenty-four hours earlier he had been a struggling research student, diligently plying his trade in the calm obscurity of Academia. Now wonderful new vistas of wealth and success had opened up for him as a leading business-getter in the most glamorous department of the world's oldest auction house. Any doubts he might feel about his competence to cope in this new world were temporarily and euphorically allayed by the confidence expressed in Rokeby's letter that he was the sort of person to make the transition with facility. They should know, for heaven's sake. So he would shortly be entering the world of Rolex watches, beautiful women, and private jets. By joining Rokeby's he would certainly see an immediate improvement in his personal financial situation. It would be no cause for regret to move out of the basement flat, with its frayed carpet, its lumpy and misshapen sofas, its coffee table propped up by a pile of vilely stained Dental Journals interspersed with copies of Penthouse and Aussie Weekly. There would be little sorrow in bidding farewell to Roger and his prodigious nocturnal activity. No doubt there would be some unpleasantness about the settling of accounts and the repayment of deposit money, but it would be well worth it to be shot of the whole set-up once and for all. He finished his ablutions and wandered into the kitchen for a cup of coffee. Then he would telephone Endymion Luce for an appointment.

"Morning, cobber," said Roger cheerily as he came in. "You're looking pleased with yourself. And I think I know why."

"Do you?"

"Yup." Roger leered unpleasantly. "Glenda and me, we heard you at it last night, giving that little raver of yours a right going-over. Cripes! We thought we might have to call the fire brigade!"

Evan bridled at the coarseness of the accusation, and to his fury found himself blushing. It was pretty rich considering Evan had made love, he felt, with great discretion the night before, and had himself been put off by the pulverising action coming from Roger's room. But oddly, now he came to think of it, the lovemaking of Roger and Glenda, for which he had started to apologise to Renata, had actually had an unexpectedly stimulant effect on her, and yes, it was true, there had been a moment at which he had even had to ask her to quieten down. Hard to believe next morning as she had swathed her person in her sack-like Guatemalan peasant woman's poncho, affixed various politically correct badges to her clothing, and pecked him frigidly on the cheek before departing.

"I've had a bit of good news," confided Evan, attempting to deflect Roger from conversation about sex, a topic on which he could hold forth interminably. "I may be going to get a job at Rokeby's."

"At Rokeby's? What, selling million pound paintings? Sounds cushy, mate." Roger yawned and stretched. He was wearing a soiled-looking tee-shirt which rose to reveal an ample paunch, while simultaneously a bushy and foetid quantity of underarm hair emerged from his armpits. "Hell, hold on a minute, sport. Doesn't one of my patients work for Rokeby's?"

"Really?"

"Yeah. that's right. Pretty high-up sort of bloke. I think he said Rokeby's, but it was a bit difficult to tell as I'd just fitted him with a new set of dentures."

"Who was he?"

"Let me see now. High-powered, that's for sure: he kept fiddling about with his calculator as I was trying to clamp his jaw. Ronald Wheale, that's his name, said he was some kind of deputy chairman."

"Are you sure?"

"Certainly am. Very touchy about his teeth he was," Roger went on. "But do me a favour, cobber: don't spread it about. I don't think he wanted it generally known that he had a set of false gnashers. Some people are funny like that. He kept asking me how detectable they were, kind of pleading to be reassured." Roger picked up a not very clean looking shirt and pulled it over his filthy vest. "Well, I must love you and leave you. So long, sport."

Evan stood silently for a moment, thinking things over. There was something not quite proper about the exalted ranks of Rokeby's being intimately known to the likes of Roger. It almost devalued the offer made to him that an Australian philistine of Roger's proportions should have the run of the joint deputy chairman's mouth, should be privy to his oral secrets. But someone had to, he supposed, a bit like the Royal Gynaecologist. Better not to dwell on it.

Now: the moment was approaching. Where was the Rokeby's

telephone number? He must ring Endymion Luce at once.

He dialled, and a mincing male voice at the other end said: "Rokeby's, can I help you?"

"Can I have Endymion Luce, please?"

"Oh, I don't see why not, dear. Everyone else has. Just putting you through."

A little more than a week later, Ron Wheale climbed sprucely into his Ford Sierra and glanced at his watch. It was still dark, and the time was 6.45 am, rather later than he normally liked to make the start from Hemel Hempstead. Still, he should be in by 8. Whenever possible he made a point of being the first into the Rokeby's building of any of the managerial or technical staff, and he was generally the last to leave. It gave him a feeling of power, of control of the firm's affairs to arrive early and leave late. Also it meant the run to and from the leafy avenues of suburban Hertfordshire was that much easier, being conducted either before or after the rush hour. You wouldn't catch Freddy or Endymion in so early, nor on the premises as late as 7 pm, except in the direst emergencies. Yesterday afternoon, for example, Freddy had not been in at all, as he had important clients to visit in the country where there was also a day's shooting on offer. And Endymion had left on the dot of 5.30 for a bath and change of clothes at his flat in South Audley Street before going on to Covent Garden. Both his co-deputy chairmen's respective extra curricular activities caused Ron to muse as he joined a minor hold-up at Totteridge. He had been to an opera once a couple of years ago with Janet, a production of Carmen. Quite frankly, never again. Could there be anything more futile than grown men and women prancing about a stage declaiming emotions in song, and in words which were largely unintelligible? It was completely unreal, people just didn't behave like that. No, for his career's sake and by natural inclination he was much more intrigued by Freddy's line of leisure pursuit, shooting. It was much more the hobby of a man of action, and such, in his moments of private fantasy, Ron saw himself to be. His periodic sessions with the clay pigeons were definitely increasing his confidence in that direction. Naturally he realised there was a difference between an adequate success rate in the artificial surroundings of his present endeavours and actually potting live birds in the more pressurised social context of a real shoot. But it was a challenge he was determined to meet, and had already hinted to Freddy that he was a not unproficient marksman, paving the way perhaps to an invitation for a weekend's sport at Leatherby sometime in the future. In this respect he felt he had probably judged rightly the most effective way to ultimate advancement in the House of Rokeby. To be a decent shot, to know how to handle a gun, was more likely to count in your favour than to be seen every night of the year in a private box at Covent Garden; cynics might even argue that attendance at a few good shoots was from this point of view a more compelling plus-point than the possession of a History of Art degree, but Ron, as the herald of meritocracy in Rokeby's, did not hold with that sort of talk. However, if there was one aspect of shooting which did alarm him, it was the one which touched on his single weak point, his Achilles heel (to use an anatomically inexact metaphor), the one area where he was absurdly and irrationally vulnerable. When the gun kicked in recoil, he would involuntarily clench his teeth sharply, visiting on him the fear that his dentures would fracture, thus revealing the guilty secret which was known to no-one at Rokeby's, the fact that he wore the things. Such a revelation would do drastic damage to Ron's image of himself, the self-confidence on which he based his authority.

Away with such thoughts, he told himself as he crawled into heavy traffic outside Lord's. A more positive mental activity was to preview the events of the coming day. There was to be another executive board meeting, followed by the interview, conducted by the three of them, of Evan Conrad to see if he was the man to breathe life into the Impressionist department. Ron sensed that this was an issue on which he might well hold the casting vote: Freddy would oppose the appointment because Endymion had suggested the candidate; Endymion would fight to take the man on in order to do Freddy out of too much limelight and glamorous business travel. Of course Ron would rise above such absurd personality politics and cast his vote entirely on the objective merits of Evan Conrad, an individual about whom he had an entirely open mind. His one regret was that old Mr Terence Rokeby would not be present to witness how once again it would be only the cool Wheale level-headedness that piloted the good ship Rokeby through the troubled waters needlessly worked up by Messrs Fairbanks and Luce.

Three and a half hours later, in the familiar surroundings of the boardroom, Ron was reflecting once more on the manifest shortcomings of his two colleagues as displayed in the turbulent executive meeting which had just passed. Freddy had been as hopelessly off-beam as usual about anything to do with administration and yet as infuriatingly sure of himself in a general sort of way about all things to do with Rokeby's. Ron had completely floored Freddy by asking him for a cost analysis of some patently uneconomic scheme to hold picture sales in Gstaad, but Freddy had simply not registered the futility, the lack of viability of this project. It was on occasions like this that Ron could do with slightly more potent support from Endymion. Instead all he did was drum well-manicured fingers on the table and stare abstractedly out of the window. Not for the first time Ron was moved to question how a man bearing such a ridiculous Christian name could really be taken seriously. No, Endymion was not a genuine possibility as the next chairman of Rokeby's. For some unaccountable reason, the only occasion on which he had become animated during the morning's meeting was when he, Ron, had suggested a cost-cutting exercise incorporating selective pruning of non-technical staff numbers. When he had proposed a reduction of manning levels on the telephone exchange, Endymion had suddenly snapped at him quite offensively, "When will people like you learn that indiscriminate slashing of manpower is not the way to expand the business?", so much so that even Freddy had asked him what was so special about the telephone exchange. An odd and unsatisfactory altercation. But now the meeting was at a close and they must turn their attention to Evan Conrad. A faint and diffident knock on the door indicated that the candidate himself was about to make an entrance.

"Come in, come in," welcomed Freddy at his most dangerously charming. "How do you do, Mr Conrad?"

"How do you do, er - Mr Luce?"

"No, no," said Freddy, laughing with great suavity at the very idea he could be mistaken for someone so earthbound as Endymion. "I'm Freddy Fairbanks, and these are my two colleagues, Endymion Luce and Ronald Wheale." Everyone shook hands; the three Rokeby's men took their seats behind the boardroom table, while Evan was encouraged to draw up a chair facing them, isolated and exposed. Freddy went on: "Now then, tell us a little bit more about yourself. Where do you come from, where's home?"

Evan looked perplexed, and ventured blindly: "Earls Court... I share a sort of flat.."

"I mean, what part of the country do your parents live?"

"Oh. Well, Coventry in fact."

"Coventry?" Freddy looked genuinely mystified.

"Yes. That's to say... on the outskirts."

"Warwickshire," said Endymion helpfully, and Freddy, relieved, went on:

"Ah, Warwickshire. Then you must know the Benson-Truebloods."

"No ..."

"Then probably you know the Urquhart-Gowers at Ribley."

"No ... that's to say not well."

"Or the Renton-FitzMaurice-Sykes, Octavian and Clarissa?"

"I - I seem to know <u>of</u> them," replied Evan miserably and unconvincingly.

"Really, Freddy," interrupted Luce with asperity, "this is rather off the point. Mr Conrad is here to talk about Impressionist pictures, not for a ramble through Debretts. Mr Conrad, let me ask you, what are you working on at the moment?"

Thankfully Evan set off on surer ground. He held forth enthusiastically about Claude Hartier and his place in the Neo-Impressionist circle, waxed lyrical about the stature and importance of his new discovery, and indeed displayed an eloquence hitherto unsuspected, not just by his audience but to a certain extent by the speaker himself. When he came to a halt an expression of some satisfaction played about Endymion's features.

"Thank you, Mr Conrad. I think my colleagues will agree that was most interesting."

Freddy and Ron, for whom terms like Luminism and Divisionist Fracture held little meaning, looked bemused and not entirely unimpressed. Overall, Ron found it difficult to make up his mind about the young man who sat opposite them. Of course his academic record was undeniably impressive, what with a high position in the Institute and several books, apparently, under his belt, but he looked so extraordinarily young for one who had achieved so much. From one point of view this evident youthfulness was confirmation of his prodigious qualities, an explanation of why he was so highly regarded in his own field. But would it be an advantage when dealing with the sharks and piranhas known to infest the waters of the Impressionist picture market? And would he have the authority to run the department at Rokeby's? How were his man-management techniques? Would he prove an ally in Ron's lone and heroic mission to introduce total computer literacy throughout the firm?

"Mr Conrad, how do you see the role of the VDU in the running of the Impressionist department?" he enquired.

"I...er..." Evan looked miserable again. "I am not entirely sure that I understand what..."

Once again Endymion came to his rescue. "I don't think Mr Conrad should have to bother himself immediately with those minutiae of company practice. His role would be business-getting, backed up by his own enormous knowledge."

Ron was not convinced. He listened dubiously as Freddy returned to the fray with a series of questions about important private collections, the inquiries at times hardly more than a pretext for a display of Freddy's own glittering array of connections, a heady catalogue of names, a display of social pyrotechnics put on as much for the benefit of his two colleagues as the interviewee. Even so, this mode of approach was clearly unnerving Evan Conrad, who, feeling it incumbent upon himself to assert some sort of significant personal connection, identify someone who would establish a mutual relation with one of his three interlocutors, suddenly blurted out:

"I do share a flat in London with Roger Brady." He looked meaningfully at Ron.

"The Brady's... do they have pictures?" asked Freddy. "I don't think I know them."

"No, no. But I think he's an acquaintance of Mr Wheale's."

An appalling empty feeling afflicted the pit of Ron's stomach. A living nightmare was about to enact itself before him. How could it be that Conrad was threatening him with the name of his dentist? If he knew Roger Brady, then it was only a short step further forward for him to have been apprised of Ron's dental secrets. Or wasn't there, he speculated desperately, some sort of Hippocratic oath which would come into play here to protect him? But perhaps it didn't apply to dentists? Or not to Australian dentists? Whatever the answer to these questions, he must act quickly now in order to minimise potential damage.

"Oh, yes," said Ron firmly. "Roger Brady, yes indeed. Now, on to the question of salary. What sort of expectation do you have?"

Ten minutes later Evan Conrad withdrew, uncertain as to the impression he had made. The whole experience of the interview had been a curious one, unlike anything he had undergone in his life before. The three co-deputy chairmen were left alone to debate his candidature as head of the Modern Pictures Department.

"Frankly," said Freddy, "we don't know a thing about his people. One can't pretend he's wildly suitable from that point of view. Clients won't know him when he goes to see them."

"Come, come," said Endymion, "it's not as if he's joining the old master department. Most of the clients he'll be dealing with will be foreigners anyway. You're implying that he's going to eat peas off his knife, which he won't, but even if he did it wouldn't really matter as most foreigners don't know any better. And the point is he's not entirely socially negligible - there was a photograph of him in last month's Harpers and Queen at some reception."

Freddy shrugged, then added: "I am afraid I also feel he doesn't look old enough."

"I would have thought that this was the perfect opportunity for us to recruit some really dynamic young blood. He's a genuine authority on his subject, constantly in print. I realise that you're not a scholar, Freddy, but it could only be good for Rokeby's to have him on our side."

"I am not objecting to him because he's a scholar," scowled Freddy.

"Well, I am sorry, but I can't help feeling that there's some rather selfish ulterior motive in your opposition to his appointment."

Freddy looked up angrily. "And I can't help feeling that there's some rather sordid ulterior motive in your championing him. Could it be that he's rather your type?"

Endymion, with an enormous effort of self-control, said: "I'll disregard that last utterly puerile but sadly not untypical remark. Ron, what do you think about Conrad? Should we take him on?"

Ron was marshalling his thoughts on the matter. There was no question that Evan Conrad represented a threat to his own security and peace of mind with the knowledge that might or might not have come into his possession as a result of his friendship with the appallingly indiscreet dentist Roger Brady. It was a deplorable situation, but it had to be faced. If Evan was aware of Ron's secret, what use did he intend to make of it? Had there not been something more than a little minatory about the sudden way he had brought Brady's name into the interview? Assuming there had been a veiled threat of blackmail behind its unexpected introduction, what should Ron's attitude be? Placatory, surely; he must be as nice as possible to Evan Conrad and give him within reason what he wanted. And in this case what he wanted, surely, was the job on offer.

Having reached his decision, Ron took steps to present it in terms which would reflect best on Ronald Wheale. Portentously he addressed the other two: "You both seem to be having difficulty in resolving this one. It may help if I put things into perspective for you. Undoubtedly Mr Conrad is on the young side, but his qualifications are excellent. And I think you know me well enough to understand that I don't recruit people on the basis of their so-called social acceptability. I aim to build Rokeby's into a meritocracy in the best sense. Evan Conrad is the sort of young talent we need, and taking into account the fact that his salary expectation is within technical staff guideline parameters at 30K a year, I have no hesitation in saying that he's our man."

He was quite carried away with his own decisiveness, and the others accepted, with respective reluctance and enthusiasm, the inevitability of the majority decision. A triumph for his own strength of purpose and resolve, thought Ron, allowing himself to feel a measure of pity and disdain for the meek way his colleagues bowed to his will. The trouble with these public school prats, he thought candidly, is that they imagine they're born to lead but they've had it too soft too long and when the chips are down they lack the vision and grasp to make split second management decisions correctly. Toothless tigers, pronounced Ron, momentarily forgetful of his own embarrassing deficiency in that department.

FOUR

Three days before Evan Conrad's installation as head of the Modern Pictures Department at Rokeby's, Eric Steward finally cracked. By temperament a man who found decisions of any kind painfully difficult, running the multi-million pound operation which the Impressionist section of the auction house had become inevitably took its toll on him. He was tortured by uncertainty: should he have Madame Valbonne's Chagalls lightly cleaned before they went on view? Was it right to sign his secretary's petty cash form claiming for both fresh-ground coffee and Bath Olivers? Could Mr Katz raise the reserve on his Le Sidaner from $75,000 to $90,000? Would it be permissible to charge a parking ticket to the company when it had been incurred en route to a valuation but while he stopped off to buy a packet of cigarettes? Where were Mr Cohen's frames? Problems were endless, solutions elusive. The world turned in on him, and he panicked totally on the Friday afternoon when Ron Wheale's almost incomprehensible Departmental Budget Forecast Form arrived on his desk. It was the final straw. A gesture of rebellion, a cry for help, a gasping for air, call it what you will, but he responded by throwing his secretary's word processor out of her third floor office window then retreating behind a filing cabinet and attempting to cut his wrists with a paper clip. Later in the afternoon he was taken away discreetly in an unmarked ambulance and began a four month sabbatical in an expensive institution near Virginia Water.

So it was that Evan's only immediate colleague in the department turned out to be a pompous opinionated Frenchman called Jean-Pierre Grifon. He was in his mid thirties with huge pointed ears, a sallow complexion, lank black hair, and breath of an unimaginable awfulness, halitosis of Olympic standard, combining the odours of all the most cliched ingredients of the French kitchen. There was also a very tall and alarming Sloane Ranger secretary called Victoria Partridge-Pugh, whose father owned half of Herefordshire.

Ten days into his Rokeby's career, Evan sat in the office which he had been allocated and reflected that if it had been only a little bigger it would have made a useful stationery cupboard. He had chosen this alternative, however, in preference to the other option of sharing a larger office with Jean-Pierre the moment he had first been exhaled over by his new colleague. Now a knock came on the door and Grifon himself stood on the threshold.

"Zair is a man at ze reception 'oo says 'e 'as some peintures of Fantin-Latour. You wish I go to see 'im?

"No, no," said Evan, pretending to look very intently out of the tiny window at something which had caught his notice, in order to avoid a direct frontal whiff of the Grifon breath. "I'll go down and have a look at what he's got. What's his name?"

"It is Monsieur Dahlstrom of Stockholm. 'E come in quite regularly, and 'e bring mostly the crap."

"OK, thanks for the warning."

Evan made his way downstairs to the front reception area and was shown to a small consulting room where he found Mr Dahlstrom, a lugubrious bespectacled Swede of an intense seriousness.

"Good afternoon, sir," said Evan politely. "What have you brought to show me?"

"Dahlstrom is my name," said the other with great deliberation.

"How do you do, I'm Evan Conrad."

"I come from Stockholm, Sweden. Sweden is only a little country, but in this little country are many beautiful things and many fine collections."

"Yes, I am sure that's true."

"Many fine collections, many beautiful things." Dahlstrom spoke with that characteristically slow-moving Scandinavian lilt whose effect is at best soporific and to the less charitably disposed suggestive of a degree of mental subnormality. "Not as many fine collections as you are accustomed to seeing in your great British stately houses, but still for a small country many beautiful things."

"How wonderful."

"So. I show you first two pictures, which make together a pair. These pictures, they come from a very old, very fine Swedish collection. I regret I may not name this collection, but is a very old, very fine one." He fingered a large plastic bag apparently containing canvases.

"You have them in there?" enquired Evan encouragingly.

"I have them in here, that is correct. I can see you are impatient to see such very fine works from a Swedish collection. It is for me exciting also."

"Would you like to show them to me?"

Dahlstrom considered the question for a few moments, then, with an air of momentous decision, he proceeded to remove a pair of oil paintings from their wrapping. He set them on the table with great ceremony and turned to face Evan. "Here is the pair of pictures by Fantin - Latour," he announced. "Unsurpassed quality."

Evan surveyed them in silence. In this situation he dreaded the thought of a misjudgement, a genuine Monet being rejected as fake or, equally awful, a wrong one being greeted enthusiastically as a million-pound picture. However, to his relief there was no difficulty in reaching a confident verdict in this case. They were hideous flower pieces, bearing scarcely a hint of the style of Fantin - Latour, let alone anything approaching his quality or delicacy. But there remained the problem of how to communicate this opinion to Dahlstrom. He stood in front of them for some time frowning.

"I think you are admiring very much, no?" suggested Dahlstrom helpfully.

"Well..."

"Of course, Mr Conrad, I do not sell them."

"No?" asked Evan hopefully.

"You are disappointed, I can see it. I do not sell them but for a very good price."

"Oh. Could I ask how much that would be?"

"Two hundred and fifty thousand."

"Er - Swedish Kroner?"

"No, pounds. Each."

Evan clutched gratefully at the lifeline offered. He said: "I'm afraid I just don't think we could get that sort of price for you at this moment in time."

Dahlstrom nodded with great wisdom. "Of course I understand. New York is the better market."

Evan could have embraced him with gratitude. "Yes, yes. You might be right to try there."

"But wait, there is something more. I have also a turd."

"A turd?" Evan stepped back in horror as Dahlstrom dived again into his capacious plastic bag.

"Yes," said the Swede, pulling out his trophy. "I have already shown you two magnificent Fantin - Latour, now I show you the turd. It is number three from the same collection."

Intense relief that he was not literally dealing with a piece of excrement made the task of rejecting this final offering a lighter one than it might have been for Evan. Mr Dahlstrom was ushered from the small consulting room with his self-esteem reasonably intact, while Evan reflected on new lessons learned about this business. Mere technical expertise was not nearly enough to carry one through; a degree in psychology coupled with a diplomat's training would also be important aids to survival. He was just congratulating himself on a tricky situation tactfully handled when the front counter receptionist called his name and told him to go straight to Mr Fairbanks' office as the co-Deputy Chairman wished to see him urgently.

"Come in, sit down," said Freddy a moment later. "How's it all going?"

Evan began a faltering attempt at articulating his impressions of the art market after ten days' experience of it, but Freddy swept on with the authority of a man not accustomed to listening to replies.

"We've got to toss you in at the deep end, I'm afraid. Something's come up and it's something pretty big. I'm talking about the Wattle collection. I had him on the telephone over the weekend, and he wants a full current auction price valuation of his Impressionist pictures with a view to selling in the spring. We've got to move quickly. All our rivals will be in there too, of course, pitching to get the collection for sale, so we'll have to put together a pretty attractive package if we're to stand a chance. What I want you to do is to get out there and price the things, list the pictures and estimate what they'll sell for. But push the boat out a bit, we'll have to be competitive. There are only 15 or 20 of them, but I understand they're insured for something like 25 million."

"25 million?" repeated Evan feebly.

"That's it, pounds, not dollars. Do you think you can handle it?"

"I... I'll do my best."

"Wattle particularly requested the specialist," continued Freddy regretfully. "Said he wanted the man with the knowledge. He was pretty impressed when I told him you had written a few books on the subject. I had to lay it on pretty thick."

Evan tried to grin confidently, but was aware that his attempt lacked conviction. He had an uneasy feeling that Freddy was looking at him doubtfully as he continued: "You should manage. All we need at this stage is the list, with some pretty punchy estimated prices. I'll be talking to Wattle later about terms of business, all that side of things, so don't get drawn into that. And you'll have Gervase Hopkins going out with you to look at Wattle's old masters. He's an old hand, he'll show you the ropes. Good luck - you fly out the day after tomorrow."

So it was that two days later Evan found himself in a Business Class aircraft seat en route to Zurich. A general sense of disorientation troubled him, but there were two sharper and more specific anxieties on this his first mission to foreign parts for his new employers. The first was his suit. Had it been a mistake? He had bought it off the peg last week when the realisation had finally crystallised that he could not continue for the rest of his Rokeby's career with only one, and that one bearing all the marks of rigorous service throughout his university life. His new garment was advertised as being manufactured entirely of Flexilon, a washable, easy-care, man-made fabric, and at the time of purchase the convenience of the whole concept had appealed strongly. But when he wore it for the first time in daylight its coloration had changed alarmingly, assuming a luminous bottle-green hue, and it hung oddly from the shoulders. To be frank, through some vagary of the Taiwanese tailor, one shoulder was definitely cut larger than the other. Well, it would just have to do. But he wished he had something in which he felt a little more at ease to wear on this hideously challenging enterprise.

The second immediate cause for anxiety was the large, jaundiced, perspiring figure in the next seat to him. This was Gervase Hopkins, Rokeby's old master expert, heavily built, fifty-ish, veteran of many a three-hour lunch, and now just settling down to his second bottle of complimentary breakfast champagne. Up to this point in the journey he had been singularly taciturn, rebuffing Evan's nervous attempts at small talk with grunts or monosyllables, but this booster injection of alcohol seemed to be loosening the cogs of conviviality.

"First trip for you this, isn't it?"

"It is, yes."

"Ah, well, the optimism of youth; I hope you've got a bit of that?"

Evan agreed in much the same tone as he had employed when asked if he had remembered his passport.

"Yes, that's what you'll need," continued Hopkins, "a hell of a lot of optimism. Hard to muster at my age when you've been traipsing round in God-awful aeroplanes chasing dreadful pictures for nearly twenty years."

There was a pause in which Evan essayed a sympathetic noise, then Hopkins went on: "No, it's no bed of roses, you know. There you are with some bloody awful owner in front of their bloody awful picture with their bloody awful gin and tonic in your hand. No wonder you make mistakes."

"How do you mean?"

"The pressure - it's terrible." Gervase drew heavily on his champagne glass for consolation. "They want you to quote high, tell them their picture's worth more than it really is."

"But isn't it often important to give optimistic estimates in order to attract the business from owners?" queried Evan, who had absorbed some snippets of conventional auction practice in his thirteen days at Rokeby's.

"Well, it is and it isn't. Very often you find you've quoted too high on the second-rate thing and it ends up being bought in, that's to say not reaching its extravagant, gin and tonic-induced reserve price. And then on the really good stuff you haven't been optimistic enough and it goes to the bloody opposition and it makes a bloody fortune."

"But don't people sometimes want realistic estimates?"

"Don't you believe it, hardly at all. Everyone's fired up with the excitement of huge prices on the art market, and they want to be thrilled with pounds or dollar signs. Human greed, that's all we're catering for, that's the name of our game. Sheer human greed. You know, it never ceases to amaze me - excuse me, young lady, another bottle of this please - it never ceases to amaze me the way people decide which auction house to sell their collection at simply on the basis of the higher pre-sale estimate. Don't they realise that any irresponsible fool can quote high?"

"Still, at least you have the pleasure of working with old masters. That must be a particularly stimulating field."

Hopkins turned to inspect him, as if to check whether Evan was in fact a certified loony on a three-day pass. "Stimulating? Stimulating? You must be joking. You have got to realise that old master sales these days are composed of two sorts of pictures. One sort is the picture that looks like something good and turns out not to be; the other is the picture that looks like rubbish and turns out to be exactly that. They're either very dirty and when cleaned transpire to be old copies, or they're complete wrecks, largely the work of 20th century restorers."

"Won't there be something good for you to see in the Wattle collection?"

"No, this collection is a case in point. As an Impressionist collector, if you've got the money, you're much more likely to be able to acquire something near the top end of the quality scale in your field than if you're an old master collector. The great old masters just aren't available any more. So Wattle's Impressionists are reasonably good, but his old masters are pretty ordinary. He lost interest in that side of things pretty early on - or rather his advisers did - because there was nothing good around. It's all rubbish."

Evan ransacked his imagination desperately for some consolation to offer. Gervase provided it himself with a vigorous swig from his glass. He brightened considerably, and observed: "Still, let's not be too gloomy. You know what's a damned good alternative to Art? Just as good in many ways if you ask me?"

"No?"

"Alcohol, my friend, alcohol. Art and alcohol have essentially the same aims. They both stimulate you by enabling you to see life through distorted, enhanced, or romanticised eyes. They both aim to take you out of yourself. There's one difference between them, though: Art sometimes succeeds in its aim, but alcohol always does."

Evan could not accept such rank defeatism. "You must have seen one or two great pictures in your years at Rokeby's," he coaxed.

"I think I did see one in 1975," agreed Gervase thickly.

"What was that?"

There was no answer. Hopkins appeared to have fallen asleep.

As they commenced their descent, Evan's companion returned briefly to consciousness and leaned over to him once more. "There's something I should tell you about these trips abroad to see clients," he said urgently . "A bit of advice."

"Yes?" Evan sat up expectantly, awaiting the key to his future business strategy.

"Foreign women expect men to light their cigarettes for them. Bloody nonsense, but they like it. Don't forget now."

It was the first time Evan had been to Switzerland. Zurich was cold and grey on this chilly November morning. Driving through the city the only landmarks he noticed were banks. They seemed to proliferate in the way that Venice, for instance, is riddled with churches. There were big banks, small banks, private banks, foreign banks, bearing a variety of names, just as the churches of Venice are dedicated to a variety of saints, both local and foreign. Depression descended on him in the form of doubt that he could ever perform the task demanded of him today, that of valuing one of the most important Impressionist collections in the world. He was not happy, either, about his companion, now slumbering fitfully next to him in the taxi. What sort of support was it to have to work in tandem with a victim of terminal pessimism, embarked as they were on this trickiest of enterprises, to be yoked with a man who might well not be conscious by the time they arrived chez Wattle?

King C. Wattle III housed his picture collection in a suburban villa on the outskirts of the city, prettily sited overlooking the lake, and heavily guarded by security devices. As the taxi swung through the wrought-iron gates which opened as if by magic to admit them, Gervase Hopkins actually began to snore. The situation called for drastic action on Evan's part, and he rose heroically to the occasion, elbowing his colleague sharply but surreptitiously in the ribs. The effect was galvanic: Hopkins sat bolt upright and began lecturing in a loud and didactic voice about the School of Antwerp. At the steps to the front door Evan paid off the taxi from a healthy wad of Swiss bank notes which the Rokeby's cashier had thrust into his hands the day before, and the two of them, an unlikely looking couple with Evan striding anxiously forward and Gervase limping goutily behind, began the climb to the porch.

The servant who showed them in was clad in an ornate military-style tunic, heavily braided, which looked as though it was a rejected costume design for a 1950s remake of The Prisoner of Zenda. His white-gloved hands shook somewhat as he divested them of their coats and scarves. He smiled a sickly grin, which served only to increase the impression of deep personal unease which all his actions created.

"Ja. You follow me, please. That is good."

"That fellow's a pansy," observed Gervase in a loud voice.

They were ushered into an enormous white drawing room with views out over the lake. A fat sun-tanned man in late middle age rose from a sofa to greet them and in so doing upset a small side table. He was dressed in a loud shirt, open at the chest, and incongruously tight jeans. He moved towards them with a cumbersome enthusiasm suggestive of enormous clumsiness. "I'm King Wattle," he announced. "Mr Hopkins and Mr Conrad?"

They shook hands. Evan inspected his host with fascination. Here he was, face to face with one of the great collectors of his time.

"Meet my wife Thelma." An unsmiling heavily made up woman of unprepossessing aspect rose unsteadily from another sofa and more hand shaking followed. "Thelma and I celebrated our silver wedding last fall. We have been man and wife for twenty-five years and not a moment's regret. Ain't that so, honey?"

Mrs Wattle glowered at him in a way that suggested she might be inclined to dispute the assertion, but her husband was undeterred. "Oh, yes, she's a wonderful little lady, this one, and a great human being."

Hopkins' attention had been diverted. He had wandered over to the window to inspect the view, and from his direction emanated a loud and unmistakable hic-up. To cover the embarrassment, Evan found himself saying much too effusively, "Excellent, wonderful!" and grinning idiotically at Mrs Wattle.

Not a hint of an answering smile played about that lady's features. She merely inclined her head slowly towards him and raised a hand in a gesture of surly acknowledgement.

"So, Mr Conrad," continued her husband, "achievement-wise they tell me you're some high-flier in the academic game. Of course we're just simple folk from Detroit who happen to have made a bit of money and spent it on a few half-way decent pictures. But you ... you've written books, that kinda thing, and we would deem it a great honour to hear your comments on our paintings. I just hope you won't feel your visit has been wasted."

Mrs Wattle nodded again, and said "Sure" a little sourly. In a flash of revelation Evan was suddenly visited with the explanation for the way her skin seemed stretched so tautly over her jaw bones, like cling film wound round a chicken carcase. She had just had a face lift, and it had not been her first, either. Fascinated by his discovery he paused to savour it, congratulating himself on his powers of observation. It was like being able to recognise that a picture had been relined without having to recourse to inspecting its reverse.

Both Wattles were looking at him expectantly. "Oh yes, certainly. It's a great pleasure for me to see such a marvellous collection," he replied hastily.

"But where are our manners? I guess you Englishmen generally favour a glass of champagne at this hour." Before Evan could demur, King Wattle had clapped his hands and shouted loudly "Heinz!" and Hopkins had rejoined the group with extraordinary swiftness.

When their voluminous glasses were full to overflowing, Heinz, the same servant who had ushered them in, made to slink out of the room discreetly. But Wattle hissed him back. "You forgot something," he said in a loud and angry whisper. Shamefaced, Heinz edged over to a huge German baroque cupboard and opened it to reveal set within a large stereo system. Into this he carefully inserted a compact disc, shut the door solemnly, and disappeared with palpable relief. Moments later the quadraphonic stereo system was filling the room with an updated version of Ravel's Bolero, specially arranged for The Orchestra of a Thousand Strings.

"Thelma and I are devotees of all the Arts," explained Wattle, lurching forward and in so doing spilling a large quantity of champagne on the carpet.

Hopkins swayed out of the room clutching his glass and murmuring that he would start his list of old master paintings in the hall. Wattle, clearly moved by the music, announced in a tremulous voice:

"So, Mr Conrad, you see around you my Impressionist collection, eighteen masterworks gathered together in one commodious room viewed against the background of the highest strivings of the world's greatest composers." Excited by the vision of his enterprise, the magnificence of his achievement, Mr Wattle swung a heavily-ringed hand round in a broad and grandiloquent sweep, but in so doing caught his wife, who was standing on his blind side, a glancing but forceful blow on the side of her face, possibly on the join of her recent facelift. She tottered away speechless with pain, while King himself, oblivious to the havoc he had wrought, thundered on: "Yes sir, Chef Doovers of the truly great talents of the Impressionist circle, men who triumphed over prejudice and ignorance in their own time to emerge as justly acclaimed giants in their field: here hang three Monets, two Renoirs, a Sisley..."

Evan wondered desperately what he should do. Thelma was no longer visible: had she collapsed behind the sofa? What was good form in this situation? Should he interrupt his host? "Excuse me sir, but you have just knocked your wife unconscious". No, it didn't sound right, and Wattle was still rolling on: "A magnificent Cézanne, a pointillist masterpiece by Georges Seurat..." Without moving too conspicuously Evan edged over to peer behind the sofa and registered with relief that Thelma was not horizontal behind it; she must have made it to the door and staggered out to seek medical aid. That crisis weathered, he gave his attention back to Wattle: "...and here, Mr Conrad, is something which I venture to say is just a goddamn little bit special..."

He led the way to an alcove where a smaller pointillist work was hanging, withdrawn somewhat from the glittering array of masterpieces by more famous names. To Evan's mounting excitement, verging on incredulity, he saw it to be signed with the unmistakably familiar initials C.H. "Not so many folk have proved equal to the challenge of identifying this little baby," remarked Wattle playfully. "Any ideas, Mr Professor?"

Evan stood momentarily transfixed with delight at the appearance of his sixth Hartier. It was the most glorious coincidence that on the first serious valuation which had fallen to him as a Rokeby's expert he should be confronted with such a perfect opportunity, both to display his own knowledge and to expand his catalogue raisonné of the artist's work. He pulled himself together to announce with a carefully calculated blend of nonchalance and authority: "A very rare master. This is by Claude Hartier, of course."

"Gee, you're a wonder." King Wattle was genuinely impressed. "The guy from Christie's hadn't a clue, and the other fellow said Henri-Edmond Cross or some such name. You hit the bullseye."

Evan felt a surge of pride. "Could I ask the history of the picture?" he enquired.

"I bought that little beauty in Paris six months ago. Fellow called St Jacques in the Rue St Honoré sold it to me."

A new confidence bred of this breath-taking initial success now galvanised him. He felt ready to do battle with the remaining pictures in the room, to list them and give them estimates of auction value. What had he been so worried about? Even his suit seemed to be fitting better now. In fact if he dropped one shoulder a few centimetres, cultivating a not inappropriate scholarly shuffle, then the whole thing seemed to hang much more convincingly as he moved round the walls describing and pricing. He reached the end of his circuit and totted up the values he had given to the eighteen masterworks which comprised the Wattle collection. To his horror the total amounted to only a paltry 9.2 million pounds. He chewed his pencil for some minutes wondering how best to revise these figures, all of which had seemed dangerously generous at their time of computation. Stuff it, he said to himself finally and, swigging down the remainder of his glass of champagne, he multiplied every price he had on his page by a factor of three, thus ending up with the much more impressive looking aggregate of 27.6 million pounds. It was a strangely satisfying feeling to do this. He looked again at the pictures and yes, they seemed better for the higher values he had given them. He snapped closed his notebook and walked through to lunch. A good morning's work. If he could keep up the favourable impression his identification of the Hartier had created through the meal to come, then his Rokeby's career could genuinely be judged to have got off on the right foot.

There were just the four of them round the Wattle's dining table. Conversation was again uneasy as Gervase Hopkins had relapsed into surly taciturnity, showing enthusiasm only for his wineglass which was refilled frequently by the shadowy but assiduous Heinz. At least Thelma Wattle appeared to have recovered and she sat unsmiling but vertical at the head of the table, a small plaster on her jaw the only evidence of the earlier encounter with her husband. King Wattle made regular flattering references to her in his conversation, speaking of her disconcertingly in the third person, archly protracting the pretence that she could not hear him although he often raised his voice to attract her attention. "That little lady's been the power behind my throne for some twenty-five years now. Yes sir, she's been my prop and stay, and I'm proud of her. We built a mighty cosy little nest together over the years. You married yourself, Mr Hopkins?"

Twice divorced, Gervase turned glassy eyes to his host. "We're all queer in the art world," he announced.

King Wattle blinked, then burst into seismic laughter, contorting himself into such spasms that he beat his gold-chained wrist against the table-top in a mock gesture of submission. "Oh gee, that's very good, Mr Hopkins, very good. But you forget that in King C. Wattle you're dealing with an honorary Britisher. I understand your English sense of humour, and I adore it. You slay me, you slay me. Oh, yes, that's very good indeed!"

At this point Mrs Wattle turned to Evan. He was aware from her expression of profound seriousness that she had something of extreme importance to impart. She stared at him a little unnervingly for a moment, as if debating whether or not he was a suitable recipient for the momentous question which her mind was framing. At last she said:

"Mr Conrad, have you ever been to Lourdes?" She pronounced the name with reverent emphasis, sounding the final s.

"Lords?" He was on his toes, of course, prepared for anything, but Mrs Wattle's interest in cricket could not have been predicted. "No ... that's to say not for some time. I think I went once when I was at school, but I must confess I'm not a great devotee."

"I was myself privileged to visit the shrine this summer." An expression which could almost have been described as beatific, given the limitations of extensive cosmetic surgery, descended on Mrs Wattle's features.

"The shrine? Ah, of course." Her language was undoubtedly extravagant, but he did dimly recall once hearing the place described as the mecca of cricket-lovers.

"I found the experience very moving." she continued.

"Moving?" He paused again. "Really? But.... but did you understand what was going on?"

"Why should I not?"

"I mean it must be difficult for a..." - he had been going to say 'foreigner', but his burgeoning sensitivity to nuance restrained him - "...for someone not brought up to it."

"What makes you think I was not brought up to it?" Her tone was distinctly aggrieved. "Just because I happen to hail from Detroit..."

"I'm so sorry... I didn't mean..." Evan noticed Gervase Hopkins' head now inclined in their direction, and unwisely elected to bring his colleague into the conversation in order to distract from his own confusion. He said quickly: "We're talking about cricket. Mrs Wattle visited Lords this summer."

"Oh, Christ! Lords!" exclaimed Hopkins loudly. "I think I've been more bored in that place than anywhere else on God's earth."

"Bored?" Mrs Wattle could speak in scarcely more than an outraged whisper.

"Yes, bored. The whole procedure strikes me as an exercise in futility. It's absurd when you analyse it: I mean, all those men in white crouched about in positions of intense concentration - they almost look like they're praying, don't they? That tremendous sense of expectation: and what does it all amount to? More often than not, absolutely nothing. And then they all crouch down and prepare to do it all over again!" It was obviously a set-piece, this, one that had gone down well at dimly-remembered gatherings of like-minded spirits in Hopkins' past. He seemed oblivious to the effect of his words now, indeed was rather warming to his theme: "You know the only incident of any interest I can remember witnessing there was when one of the poor buggers got hit behind the ear and had to be carted off to hospital."

Mrs Wattle caught her breath; for a moment Evan feared she was going to weep. "Mr Hopkins, but that is terrible," she gasped.

"I'll tell you something else that was terrible, too: all those drunken louts at the Tavern. By six o'clock some of them were completely sozzled. They were shouting abuse and making the most appalling racket. I can't think that they contribute much to proceedings - I really don't know why the authorities allow it. I suppose they get a rake-off from the bar profits."

Mrs Wattle shook her head miserably. She was beyond words. As if to signal that the conversation should proceed no further, she turned away and fumbled for cigarettes in her bag.

Even in his bemused state, Evan's heart now beat faster. This was the moment he had been waiting for all day. In order to score socially in this sort of smart foreign circle, in order to make the right impression indelibly on your hosts and anyone else who might be watching, you could never let a lady light her own cigarette. This much had been made clear to him; it was the one practical tip he had received from Gervase. Although a non-smoker, Evan had taken the precaution of actually equipping himself at Zurich airport with a book of matches for just this very eventuality. He now snatched from his pocket this book, opened it feverishly, tore out a match, and struck it viciously as he leant towards his hostess. To his horror, the flaming head of the match broke off from the stem and fell unerringly on to his own trousered thigh. The material of which his machine-washable easy-care suit was made conflagrated easily, burning a gaping hole an inch square and scorching his leg severely in the split second before he doused it with a snatched napkin. He doubled up, biting his lip with pain but fortunately let no cry escape him. Tears welled in his eyes, but miraculously no-one seemed to have noticed; Mrs Wattle had lighted her cigarette with her own lighter and her husband and Gervase Hopkins were engaged in an exchange of views of unusual mutual absorption concerning Havana cigars.

But what was this? Just as Evan was feeling that the situation was approaching manageable proportions again, a new horror imposed itself. He could bear the pain, he could conceal the hole in his trouser leg, but now, wafting up from below, came evidence of the odorous chemical reaction inevitable when Flexilon conjoins with fire, a peculiarly pungent smell which Evan was powerless to control, contort himself though he might. It combined some of the pervasive stench of burning rubber with the sulphurous scent of smouldering shoelace. If he took no quick action they would all be overcome by fumes and need hospital treatment. He could see the headlines now: "Billionaire poisoned by Rokeby Expert's Trousers: Surrounding Homes evacuated..."

Relief was effected thanks to an unexpected diversion. Gervase Hopkins rose unsteadily and lurched towards the balcony which beckoned invitingly at the far end of the room, muttering something about taking a closer look at the spectacular view of the lake. Before anyone could stop him he encountered the plate glass, and the next ten minutes were spent in Gervase assuring anyone who enquired that no, he didn't think his nose was broken, and yes, a small brandy would help settle his nerves after the shock, and in Mrs Wattle summoning extensive domestic assistance to ensure that the blood spilt would not stain the carpet. In the disarray Evan was able to retreat discreetly to the lavatory, to soak his malodorous trouser leg in a large bottle of scent he found there. He noticed it was called 'Avant le Désir'.

As he emerged from his refuge he perceived a figure lurking in the passage outside. It was Heinz, fretfully shifting his weight from one foot to another.

"Herr Conrad!" he said in an urgent low voice.

"Er - yes?" said Evan, trying to look as natural as possible with a handkerchief draped idly over his scent-doused upper thigh.

"Herr Conrad, I must speak with you. You understand, this is not me."

"Not you?"

"To dress like this I do not enjoy."

"No, no, of course not."

"It is beneath my calling. I am an intellectual."

"Of course."

"I was top student at University of Zug. Intellectual."

Evan grinned weakly and tried to edge past back to the dining room. "What subject?" he enquired awkwardly.

"Theology. And Food Studies."

"Ah.

"It is better you should know, because you are intellectual also. We have the sympathies. Unfortunately it was necessary to take this employment through personal financial shortage."

"I am sorry to hear it. I must be getting back in."

"Ja. You return."

"Nice to have had this chat."

"Oh, Herr Conrad."

"Yes?"

"Your leg is wet."

Back in the dining room the revival of Gervase had been accomplished, and there remained little to be done except to take as dignified a leave as possible.

"I'll be in Paris next week staying in the Ritz," King C. Wattle told them as they bid farewell in the hall. "Bring me your proposals there. We're flying back to Detroit that weekend and I want to get this whole business sewn up before then. I'll make my decision in Paris."

Evan held his notebook over his upper trouser leg as they retreated down the steps to their waiting taxi. As they drove away their host was embracing his still unsmiling wife with great ostentation on the doorstep.

"They seem very fond of each other," observed Evan.

"Silly prats," said Gervase Hopkins.

FIVE

The following Tuesday evening four separate couples in four different locations of London and its suburbs were engaged in four conversations of varying degrees of rancour, jealousy, animosity and lust.

Freddy and Melissa Fairbanks sat at the elegant dining table in their flat in fashionable Ennismore Gardens, over some fairly ripe Brie and a bottle of Montrachet. Freddy had been acting upon an irresistible impulse to be nice to Melissa ever since he had returned home that evening. He had arrived with flowers ('because you're looking particularly lovely at the moment, darling'), told her that the new curtains in the drawing room were an unqualified success ('another tribute to your impeccable taste, my sweet') and promised her a weekend in Rome in the spring ('just as soon as the hideously busy time at Rokeby's is over'). There was nothing false about these compliments, nothing forced about these promises; it was simply that Freddy was obeying an almost Pavlovian response mechanism, the desire to please his wife following an infidelity on his part. This had occurred forty-eight hours before, when Freddy had returned from the country early on Sunday afternoon on the pretext of catching up on some work but had actually passed a couple of torrid hours in a hotel room with a French girl called Genevieve whom the Fairbanks family had employed as an au pair three years ago. Genevieve was now safely packed off back to Montpelier, and Freddy was restored to the bosom of his family being nice to his wife. He said:

"Darling, you know what we must do? We must decide who we're going to invite for that weekend shoot at Leatherby in January. The only people we've got coming at the moment are the White-Watneys, those Krauts the von Tortrops, and Cyrille de la Guerre. Who else would you like to ask, my love? I leave it absolutely up to you."

Melissa was no fool. She recognised that Freddy was in one of the generous moods which periodically descended on him for no very evident reason. She knew nothing specific about Freddy's marital infidelities, and more to the point she did not want to know. She sensed that his present pleasantness might well be motivated by a desire to compensate for some misdemeanour about which he felt guilty; but better to leave it at that and to accept that here was at least a situation to be exploited for her own benefit. Life married to Freddy was 'no bed of roses', as that appalling old soak Gervase Hopkins was wont to say, but it was marginally more stimulating than life without him. So she hung on. She was tough and resilient, and she was ambitious. She had borne him three children, three hooks of steel which linked him yet more firmly to her, emotionally and financially. And at 39 she was still an attractive woman, with the power, used sparingly, to make Freddy himself feel jealous of her.

"That's very sweet of you, darling," she replied. "Right, let's think. I'd very much like to see Peter and Jemima again. Shall we ask them?"

"What, the Claydons? Why not?" Freddy grinned amicably. Peter Claydon was an old beau of Melissa's, a frightful bore, but she must be allowed to choose freely.

"And then it's ages since I last saw Erica."

This time Freddy flinched. He only permitted Erica Mannering into his house under exceptional circumstances. She was a nightmare. The proposition was the ultimate yardstick by which to judge his own aberrations. Did he feel sufficiently contrite, was he visited by the requisite truly inordinate amount of guilt to countenance Erica for the weekend?

"That's fine, darling, if you'd like her to come."

"I would."

"And who else?"

"One or two youngish bachelors might help. Is there anyone at Rokeby's these days? I seem to remember you telling me you were looking for a little new blood."

Freddy thought for a moment. The only name that sprang to mind was, perversely, Evan Conrad. He'd spoken to King Wattle that day by telephone and it really did appear that Conrad had done rather well on his valuation there. He'd certainly made a favourable impression on Wattle. Perhaps, come to think of it, the time was coming when it would be no bad thing gently to usher the young man under his wing, and an invitation to Leatherby for the weekend should sufficiently sweep him off his feet to ensure that he became a Fairbanks ally for the future.

"There's a young fellow who's just joined the Impressionist

department," he suggested. "He's very brilliant - an academic, you know. I believe he's reasonably presentable. He might be amusing."

"He sounds very high-powered, why don't we give him a try? I'll drop him a line: what's his name?"

"Evan Conrad."

"Good, I'll write to him tomorrow at Rokeby's. Who else?"

Like a stag loose on Hyde Park Corner, outlandish yet suddenly not completely implausible, a strange wild thought careered across Freddy's mind. Why shouldn't he after all? The weekend promised to be pretty bloody anyway, what with those two old bores Jemima and Peter Claydon, the von Tortrops and de la Guerre (Rokeby's representatives in Germany and France respectively), that dreadful MP Bill White-Watney and his wife Antonia, the unspeakable Erica and now the unknown youth from the Institute. Why not put the cap on it, write it off completely with a sort of glorious abandon, by asking Ron Wheale and his dowdy wife? What was her name, Janice or something? Ron spent quite a lot of time dropping heavy and unsubtle hints about his shooting prowess, an unlikely enough boast, but why not put it to the test and have them for the weekend? Obliquely, Freddy could sense some advantage accruing to him in the race for the Chairmanship through such a manoeuvre. A weekend spent by Ron Wheale in the grandeur of Leatherby might convince him once and for all of the inappropriateness of his own feeble claim to the crown as against that of a natural leader of men like Freddy.

"We could ask the Wheales."

"The Wheales?"

"Yes, Ron Wheale."

"What, that awful little man who talks about computers all the time? I'm sure he doesn't shoot."

"He tells me he's rather a good shot."

"And his wife? She's probably a nightmare. Terribly nice and all that, no doubt, but she'd be like a fish out of water."

"Melissa, darling, the more I think about it the more it seems really rather a good idea. In the longer term, you know. It might just be helpful to my prospects of succeeding to the chairmanship."

"I don't quite see how, but if you say so."

"I do say so." For the first time that evening there was a note of irritation in Freddy's voice. "And anyway I haven't raised any objections to any of your choices."

Melissa saw the danger signals. Here was the time to stick with what she had got rather than twist for any more and run the risk of losing everything. "Right, darling, that's settled. I'll write to them all tomorrow."

In Manchester Square it was 11.45 pm and Ewan Connard was entertaining. That is to say he had persuaded the lady next to whom he had been sitting at a dinner party in Islington that (a) it would be no trouble to give her a lift home to Kensington and (b) a pause en route for a night-cap in Ewan Connard's flat would be a civilised way of extending the evening's festivities. There were two ulterior motives in this stratagem. The lady in question was the relatively youthful editress of the London Arts Digest, the august and highbrow art-historical journal for which Evan occasionally wrote, mindful of its small but influential readership on both sides of the Atlantic. From a professional point of view it would be no bad thing to have Dr Fabia Neate-Panker in his corner. A favourable mention of his name in an Editorial, perhaps suggesting him as an imaginative choice for the vacant directorship of the San Pietro Museum, would not come at all amiss. A friendship must be cemented, and Dr Neate-Panker must be left in absolutely no doubt of the excellent academic credentials of Ewan Connard. This was one objective of the present late-night encounter over cognac. The other aim was less rarefied, indeed related to a more basic physiological urge. The editress was a tall and striking woman in her mid-thirties, recently divorced, with long auburn hair and an overbearing style. It was her reputation for severity of manner, coupled with her palpable strength of will bordering on arrogance, which excited Connard horribly. She cried out to be conquered; and the higher she held herself, the harder she would fall. But how far would the pursuit of this second aim compromise his success in achieving the first? Evan was inclined to take the view that if the situation was properly handled the two targets could be gloriously complementary.

"Here, let me take your coat," he said affably as she came into the drawing room. He allowed his eyes to linger on the bare shoulders which were revealed, and then asked: "Brandy for you?"

"What an elegant room. Are those Steffano della Bella's? Yes, a small brandy would be nice."

"You know," he said, handing her a glass and sitting down next to her with his own cradled in his palms, "this is the first time I've entertained an editor of the London Arts Digest à deux so late at night. I'm rather enjoying the experience."

"I'm pleased to hear that." There was a certain frostiness in her tone, suggesting that you contemplated putting your hand up the skirt of a literary figure of her eminence at your peril. "Personally I find it important to keep in touch with contributors. I admired your last piece, that review of Professor Throg's Neo-Impressionist book."

"Thank you. I'm afraid I found the professor's style a little hard to take." Ewan smiled at her. Oh dear, she was not going to be easy. She was a classic example of a very distinctive species of womanhood, the pretty Oxbridge girl of some intellectual attainment who cannot work out what her attitude to her own good looks should be. At university she stands out as a beauty, and this has a head-turning effect. This sense of her own desirability intensifies her self-confidence, but is tempered by two uncertainties. One is the threat of the great metropolis, her future field of operations. In London disport any number of attractive women, some appreciably more attractive and glamorous than she is. Should she compete? Should she want to? For the second quandary concerns the question whether intellectually it is acceptable that such a chance and superficial phenomenon as pleasing looks should have any effect on personal behaviour anyway. They could even be a disadvantage, in view of the infuriating tendency of many men not to take seriously the mind of a beautiful woman. Hence this unresolved ambivalence in women like Fabia Neate-Panker, now sitting next to him on the sofa wearing a tight black shoulderless dress and fluttering her eyelashes provocatively, but simultaneously evincing a gritty determination to talk only of matters academic, intellectual or professional. The situation clearly needed careful handling, reflected Ewan, but when in doubt the direct approach often paid surprising dividends.

"You know, Fabia, I would estimate pretty confidently that you are the most ravishing editor of an art history journal anywhere in the world."

She coloured slightly, there could be no doubt about that, but she went on as if he had not spoken. "I must say I did enjoy the Neo-Impressionist show at the Grand Palais. There were moments when the approach was absurdly facile, of course, and I thought that the catalogue lacked perception, but a number of intriguing questions were thrown into higher relief, did you not feel?"

Ewan edged closer and said: "You really do have the most lovely hair." He liked the way it was drawn back from her forehead with classical severity, only to cascade down behind in luxuriant profusion over her bare shoulders. Was it an allegory of her nature, a facade of severity masking delicious abandon? He put out a hand, and with consummate casualness, began to stroke a few stray locks. She did not turn away, but continued resolutely:

"One of the most significant revelations was surely the Italian dimension. It is arguable at least that some of the innovatory achievement of Seurat and his circle has been eroded by this exhibition in the way it subtly points up the work of the Divisionists in Milan. Is there perhaps scope for..." She caught her breath as Ewan gently squeezed the lobe of her ear between his fingers, then resumed her track a little faster: "Is there perhaps scope for an article here, an objective analysis unbiased by any French or Italian parti-pris?"

Ewan eased his hand round to the nape of her neck and began a slow but sensuous massage. It was a well-worked ploy, seldom known to fail, and he was gratified to observe that her elegant shoulders began to rise and fall with perceptibly more animation, as her neck arched back a degree or two allowing fuller expression thereby to the magnificent sculpture of her breasts, encased within their increasingly irksome taffeta prison. Still her voice carried on as if her life depended on it: "I mean, the claim that Divisionism was a flowering of Pointillism in its own right, entirely separate from and uninfluenced by the French branch, cannot be dismissed out of hand. The evidence presented.... denying contact.... between Paris and Milan in the 1880s.... seemed to me.... undeniably compelling." Her mounting physical excitement precluded the expression of her viewpoint on these crucially important aspects of late 19th century European painting in anything other than brief phrases interspersed with gasps. Ewan, interpreting the signs as propitious, decided that a simultaneous advance on different fronts might now carry the day. In one superbly orchestrated and agilely executed manoeuvre he succeeded in locating with one hand the zip at the top of the back of her dress, easing it down swiftly an inordinate distance, and with the other grasping the freed left breast which burst joyfully from its constriction into his tender ministrations, and as a coup de grace he shot his tongue into the ear close up against which his mouth had been brought by his exertions.

She groaned with delight, and then, miraculously, her voice gasped out again: "The Italian manifestation's significance.... is that it presents a fascinating body.... of its own independent colour theory..." - She paused here as her busy fingers encountered a temporary recalcitrant button on Evan's own shirt - "and there is an extraordinary similarity... in the lines of research pursued.... mmmm.... pursued.... mmmm.... pursued by each group's theorists." Ewan's lips met hers to stifle the flow. Willing hands grappled mutually with the further restrictions of clothing, Ewan expertly combining an ornate rococo of caresses with the direct functionalism of the actions necessary for the removal of underwear. In the swirl of passion, Dr Neate-Panker was slewed across a low coffee-table, the black dress breached conclusively at top and bottom and bunched up heedlessly round her palpitating middle regions. Even now she continued to blurt out the exhibition review which was apparently the indispensable concomitant to her pleasure: "Markedly higher degree of social awareness with the Italians.... Divisionism as a root of Socialism.... avowedly working class choice of subject matter...."

Ewan felt the power of her finger-nails digging tremulously into his back, and eased himself into overdrive. His probing hand traced the graceful curve of her buttocks beneath him, while she, quivering at this revelation of her body's majestic geometry, continued her breathless yet implacable catalogue: "Major talent of Giovanni Segantini.... intellectual weight of Carlo de Grubicy.... social involvement of Angelo Morbelli...." The mounting crescendo of names hovered momentarily as she sought the elusive finale: "And Pelizza.... Pelizza.... Pelizza...."

"Pelizza.... da Volpeda?" offered Dr Connard through clenched teeth.

"Pelizza... da Volpeda!" shrieked Dr Neate-Panker in ecstatic agreement.

In a basement flat off the Fulham Road, Evan Conrad received Renata Crum for the first time since the joyous release from his uneasy menage with Roger Brady. There was a drawing room, a bedroom, a clean kitchen and bathroom complete with avocado suite; best of all, the tables stood up without the support of Dental Journal. An exhilarating sense of freedom and confidence permeated him as he showed her round. His new-found affluence excited him; he yearned for a reciprocal excitement from Renata, if possible mixed with a degree of admiration. However, the situation did not command her unstinting approval.

"I really can't accept it, you know," she announced.

"Can't accept what?"

"I really can't accept the way you have compromised so abjectly with the status quo, consented, tacitly perhaps, but consented nonetheless to the concept of male domination of all wealth producing engines in this country."

"But Renata, it's only a basement flat."

"I'm not just talking about that. I'm talking about your whole attitude to working at Rokeby's. As far as I can see you've just lain down without a fight, become one of them. I mean it was Zurich last week, now you tell me you're off to Paris next."

"What do you expect me to do?"

"I don't expect you to go joy-riding round Europe when there are clearly more important issues to be addressed back at head office."

"What do you mean?"

"I mean that you ought to be taking active steps to right the appalling imbalance between the sexes on the Rokeby's board. I've been reading through the list of directors, and I'm horrified to see there's only one woman as against seventeen men."

Evan shrugged. "Come on, Renata, what can I do? Be realistic..."

"Being realistic is just an excuse for meekly accepting grotesque abuses. We've got to get something done about it. As it happens, I've been discussing the situation with my co-members of WAMPRIC."

"WAMPRIC?" queried Evan nervously.

"Women Against Male Predominance In Commerce."

"And what do you advise?"

"The committee's feeling is that you should withhold your labour until measures are taken to rectify the situation."

"What, stop working at Rokeby's until they appoint a few more women on to the board?"

"I think that would be appropriate," mused Renata. "And if you took that sort of industrial action, if possible carrying some of the existing workforce with you, then my committee would be right behind you. We'd organise secondary picketing, benefit concerts, that sort of thing. Actually, we'd be prepared to make you our case of the month."

"I'm sorry, Renata, it's just not on. I'm in the middle of a very important deal, and the outcome could make or break my future."

"You are incredibly unaware. You could at least make a gesture."

"Like what?"

"Like refusing to go to Paris next week."

"I must go to Paris. Apart from seeing Mr Wattle, I'm also going to take the opportunity to look up Louis Ranchec and find out a little bit more about Hartier. Why should I give up going to Paris, anyway? What's so special about Paris?"

"Paris itself is not the point."

"Renata, are you jealous?"

"That's a ridiculously chauvinist question. You're turning into the most obscene sort of capitalist, and I refuse to stay here to be contaminated by you any longer." She stormed out, slamming the door, and Evan did not attempt to stop her. He had been intending to ask her to mend the hole in the upper trouser leg of his Flexilon suit, but judged that now would not have been the moment.

Endymion Luce was relishing the thought of an early night. Sometimes virtue gave him almost as much satisfaction as vice; now he was sitting alone in his flat in South Audley Street congratulating himself on his single-mindedness in resisting the temptation to nip down for a drink in that deliciously seedy club in Soho. Instead he had cooked himself a little light pasta, and was about to bend his attention to checking the proofs of the next furniture sale catalogue for an hour before retiring. It was with some annoyance, therefore, that he heard the telephone ring.

"Luce here."

"How are you, you cheeky beast?"

"Who's that?"

"It's Lance, your naughty telephone operator."

Luce's heart sank. If it wasn't bad enough having to cope with Lance's dangerously compromising intimate banter every time he lifted the telephone to call the exchange at Rokeby's, now here he was being bothered at home. Dear God, he was certainly being made to pay for that original thoughtless frolic of six months ago which had been the occasion of their first encounter. What can have possessed him to find Lance that job on his own doorstep? Some misguided sense of charity, he supposed. "What is it?" he said sharply. "I'm very busy."

"Oo! Hark at her! That's hardly the way to greet an intimate pal, now, is it?"

"Have you been drinking?"

"The odd one or two, dear, yes. And very well I feel on it. As I was feeling so well, I thought I'd give you a little tinkle for a chat, because the sort of chat I have in mind you just might not want to have at work."

"Now what's the problem, Lance?" Luce's tone was a shade more accommodating.

"I've been having some trouble recently, making ends meet (no, not in the way you're thinking, you filthy great fairy). I mean Rokeby's are hardly the most generous payers, are they? And I thought to myself, what can I do about it? I know, I'll go to my old playmate, the man at the top (not to mention the man on top), and see if he can help out."

"Now look here, you're being paid a perfectly reasonable rate for what you do, and you were lucky to get the job in the first place. I find your attitude most unreasonable."

"Oo! Most unreasonable, is it? Well, sweetie, I'm sorry you're taking this line. I've been doing a little checking up at Rokeby's, and I've found out that you could be next in line to be Big White Chief, couldn't you? But it's a tricky time for you till the spring when old Mr Rokeby makes up his mind. And he might not like to hear about the way you seduce innocent young telephone operators, force your evil attentions on them. No, he just might not like to hear too much about what an old pervert you are."

This reading of the situation was not inaccurate, reflected Endymion ruefully. While there was widespread awareness of his sexual preferences, so long as he was perceived in the higher echelons of the firm as discreet, this did his career prospects no very serious harm. But if Lance started trumpeting foul stories far and wide it would count most crucially against him at this very delicate stage. The whole situation was tiresome in the extreme. And Lance was a vile little jerk. So far as Endymion could see, however, there was nothing for it but to play him along for the next month or two, until the question of the succession was settled.

"OK, I'll have a word with Mr Wheale about it, and see if we can't do something about increasing your salary. But now leave me alone, I'm extremely busy."

"That's the spirit, ducky. We'll be in touch, as they say. And don't forget now. Cheery-bye."

SIX

For the trip to Paris, Evan invested in a briefcase. Its possession strengthened his sense of purpose and bolstered his self-confidence. As he travelled to Heathrow on the underground, he considered its contents, a reassuring inventory of items indicative of his new-found professional status and elevated life-style. There was, of course, the Wattle file containing all the correspondence and notes relevant to the collection; there was his own file of research on Claude Hartier; there was a sheet of paper given him the previous afternoon by Jean-Pierre Grifon listing Parisian restaurants of outstanding excellence personally recommended by the compiler; there was a copy of the latest edition of the London Art Digest, fresh from the press; and there was a letter from Mrs Freddy Fairbanks inviting him for the weekend to Leatherby, a communication so extraordinary, so daunting and yet so exciting that it would take considerable thought to frame a suitable reply. By comparison with his first trip abroad on Rokeby's business, the present one boasted several other advantages. From the point of view of romance and glamour it was infinitely preferable to be heading for Paris rather than Zurich. And on this occasion there was no Gervase Hopkins. Apparently the old masters in the Wattle collection had been of such inadequate quality that Hopkins had not deemed it worthwhile making the journey to Paris himself to discuss their sale.

"They'll be hard pressed to make £300,000 for the lot," he had told Evan. I'll just tack them on to the end of your list of Impressionist pictures, and you can discuss the whole deal with Wattle. What's £300,000 against the value of the Impressionists, anyway? £27 million, did you say? My lot's hardly worth mentioning."

Evan had assured Hopkins with as much conviction as he could muster that this was indeed the total of his estimates. The haphazard way in which he had reached this figure alarmed him when he thought about it, so he tried not to think about it. A discovery born of his brief experience to date was anyway dawning on him, that one could get away with a considerable amount when it came to giving estimates provided one said the figures with enough authority. Few people knew what things were worth, and most people wanted guidelines. "Ow much is zis worth, Evan?" Jean-Pierre had demanded the previous day, breathing garlic-ridden breath alternately over Conrad and a murky pencil drawing attributed to Rodin. "About 4 to 6?" Evan had suggested, and Jean-Pierre had nodded in sage agreement, although neither he nor Evan if pressed would have been able to state categorically whether this estimate meant 400 to 600 or 4,000 to 6,000 pounds. Freddy Fairbanks had also been impressed with Evan's performance to date:

"I must say, you seem to have done exceptionally well with Mr Wattle," he told him, continuing wistfully: "I suggested that I should come to Paris myself to present our proposals for the sale of his collection, but he insisted on seeing you. He liked the way you identified one particular picture, one which no-one else had been able to fathom apparently. He said it was a pleasure to be dealing with a young 'guy' who really knew his stuff. Well done."

Evan had looked appropriately modest at this accolade, blessing the day that he had decided to work on Hartier. Freddy had then become confiding in a man-to-man sort of way: "I don't mind telling you that I'm genuinely delighted to hear all this. What you have achieved so far has completely vindicated my idea of hiring you in the first place. I always felt that someone with a bit of academic pedigree was the answer for the Impressionist department, and although my colleagues tried to deter me I stood out for you. It's quite possible that Mr Terence himself may have a word with you if we bring this one off. Now if he does, I'm sure that you'll remember to mention my part in your appointment, and the dreadfully hostile attitude of Wheale and Luce to you at your interview."

Evan nodded seriously. There was no point in trying to understand everything that everyone told him in this hazardous but challenging new world.

"Now we're putting together some pretty attractive terms for Wattle, offering him just about everything he could want." Freddy had waved his arms extravagantly when delineating for Evan's benefit the extent of Rokeby's largesse. "No commission, we'll pay for the catalogue production and all the publicity, there'll be a special video. The main thing is to get the collection for sale. We need this business. And the Impressionist market is beginning to strengthen again. We've got to have something sensational to offer the punters - there's money waiting to be spent."

There could be no doubt that he was on a mission of supreme importance, and Evan did not intend to fail. He had made a promising start with Wattle, he told himself as he boarded the Paris plane, and there was no reason to fear the next round of negotiations. True, he had not succeeded in lighting Mrs Wattle's cigarette, but surely this could not be held significantly against him in the final account.

And there was a second purpose to Evan's visit to France. Once he had seen and dealt with King Wattle, he was going in pursuit of Louis Ranchec; and now Wattle himself had given him another lead in the shape of the dealer from whom he had bought his Hartier, M. St Jacques of the Rue St Honoré. A visit there was also called for. As the plane took off, Evan leafed once more through his notes on Hartier. So far he knew definitely of six works by the master. The first had appeared at auction two years ago, and had marked the beginning of the process of rediscovery of the artist. It had made $20,000, an inordinately large sum for a work by an unknown artist, but in the light of subsequent events this price now seemed relatively modest. Then had come Ewan Connard's article in the Burlington Magazine, illustrated by two further previously unpublished examples of Hartier's work, together with the famous letter from Seurat to Hartier. The two pictures illustrated in Connard's piece were both "in a private collection, Paris", and when Evan had asked Connard about their precise whereabouts, Connard had explained that the elusive Ranchec had shown them to him and provided the photographs, but he was not "in a position to reveal to whom they belonged". That question would have to be pursued with Ranchec once he had been tracked down.

The fourth Hartier had come up unexpectedly six months before in a sale in New York, and on the strength of the interest created by Connard's article had fetched 110,000 dollars. Evan was investigating the provenance of that one, but all he had found out from the auction house concerned was that it had come from a European private collection whose anonymity was to be preserved at all costs. Soon after, a fifth Hartier had been sold at auction in London. Its price had crept up to £80,000, but again its provenance had been unrevealing, emanating apparently from an unnamed continental collector. The final example was, of course, the coastal scene in the Wattle collection. Evan had chewed his biro for some considerable time in the voluminous drawing room in Zurich as he debated what this one would fetch at auction. At first he had written down £80,000 to £120,000, but with the prodigious revision necessitated shortly afterwards in order to bring the total up to scratch, this estimate now stood at £250,000 to £350,000. Still, that was no more drastic than a small Cézanne still life which had originally seemed about right at £250,000 to £350,000 and had now soared to £750,000 to £1 million. They had a certain unreal fascination, these estimates like telephone numbers. Evan had no personal experience of what it was like to handle sums of money of this magnitude, but as if engaged in some high-powered version of Monopoly, he relished manipulating and bandying about these figures.

Clad in his other suit and clutching his briefcase, Evan stepped confidently on to French soil. Suddenly there seemed nothing to fear. With ridiculous ease he hailed a taxi at Charles de Gaulle and administered in French directions as to his hotel which were understood and obeyed without demur. Two hours later he was debouching from another taxi at the foyer of the Ritz. Such was his euphoria that there was even the hint of a swagger as he made his way to the reception desk. King Wattle was in the palm of his hand, he told himself as he took the lift to the third floor having announced himself and been instructed to "come on up to the suite". The deal was as good as sealed; and what pleasure there was to savour in the thought of announcing its completion to his superiors at Rokeby's.

He walked into the palatial salon to find King Wattle slumped on a sofa, his head in his hands. Thelma Wattle, wearing an enormous hat, was supervising the removal of some luggage. She seemed to be on the point of departure.

"Gard! How I hate to see you go like this, honey," King was saying in heartbroken tones. "You know how I'll miss you, even for a couple of days." He became aware of Evan's presence in the room, and added in explanation: "My little baby has gotta go back to Detroit a coupla days early - her aunt's sick and she needs her."

Mrs Wattle nodded in taciturn confirmation. Recent cosmetic surgery still precluded the expression of anything very dramatic in the way of emotion.

"Mr Conrad, you know what gift I have acquired for my wife as consolation to her in her family difficulties? This morning I bought her an autobahn."

"An autobahn?" Wattle was rich, but this was extraordinary.

"Yeah, the guy who does birds. You know, makes the prints."

"Oh! Audubon!"

"Yeah, yeah, like I said."

A ghost of a smile played about Mrs Wattle's features. She was on her way.

"So long, honey." King embraced her. He seemed genuinely distraught with grief as he watched her go. The door shut, and Evan and he were alone. A silence, heavy with sadness, hung over them.

''Um.... Mr Wattle.... I've brought the estimates on your collection.... and everything. I don't know if you would like to see them...."

King seemed unable to concentrate. He picked up a framed photograph of his recently departed spouse and declared: "Poor baby! I just hope that darned Concorde flies safely. Great big iron bird carrying my precious bundle."

The decent thing, of course, was to distance yourself from a display of such profound emotion, but, after a lengthy period spent staring out of the window at the far end of the room further silence became unendurable for Evan. ''Mr Wattle, I wonder, are you ready to look at these? They're the estimates you asked for, and the terms."

Slowly, even leadenly, King dragged himself away from his wife's portrait, breaking a small glass vase on his path back to the sofa. Sitting down, he took the proffered papers, put on a pair of reading glasses, and began to peruse the documents.

"Yeah," he said after a few moments, "they're good, real good these estimates. Pretty favourable terms, too." He read on for a while, and then with a suddenness that made Evan jump, he slapped the papers down firmly on the glass table in front of them, laid his gold pen on top of the file, and removed his spectacles decisively and with an air of finality. He looked Evan straight in the eyes and announced: "Hey kid, I can't beat about the bush any longer, I gotta break it to you. I'm giving the collection to Sotheby's to sell."

"You're what?" Evan was subliminally aware of his lower jaw descending several centimetres precipitately and involuntarily. How could this be? The news came like a bucket of cold water being emptied over him. Everything had seemed to be going so well, the negotiations a formality, the collection all but in the proverbial bag, and his first venture for Rokeby's about to be crowned with sensational success. He could not believe this sudden appalling turn of events, he was not prepared for such immediate and total rejection.

"Sotheby's are selling the collection in the spring," continued Wattle. "They came up with a pretty good deal: hot-looking estimates, and they promised to exhibit the collection in Tokyo and New York prior to the auction. I guess they're just going to get the best results. I've always been the kinda guy who trusts to his instinct, and you know, Mr Conrad, that instinct of mine ain't let me down before. It tells me that the Sotheby's deal is the best one going. My mind's made up."

So that was bloody well that, reflected Evan an hour later, letting himself into the bedroom at his own distinctly more modest hotel. His first reaction had been to seize the heavy crystal ashtray from the coffee table and smash it into the face of the ridiculous Wattle as a token of his frustration. Fortunately he had restrained this initial urge, and gradually violence had given way to abject disappointment. Instead he had gathered together his files from the table, placed them with a silent dignity into his new briefcase, bid a curt farewell to his host, and walked into the drinks cupboard. Wattle's ill-concealed amusement as he extricated himself and found the correct door out had struck him as particularly assinine. But on the whole he felt he had behaved with commendable self-restraint although crippled with misery and impotent rage. What should he do now? Should he telephone back to Rokeby's with the news? Or should he go out and get blindingly drunk? He was inclined to favour the latter alternative. The unrewarding task of bearing tidings of his failure to the head office could be deferred till tomorrow. He had not felt so desolate, so utterly let down, since he failed his driving test that rainy autumn morning in Coventry.

With heavy heart he opened his briefcase again with the intention of looking over his Hartier files. At least he still had his scholarship. He would seek solace in it for an hour or so before going out to get a drink. An unfamiliar gold object caught his eye on the top of the Wattle file. Dear God, it was Wattle's pen: he must have picked it up by mistake in the storm of his departure. Now Wattle would find it missing and suspect him of stealing it in a fit of pique. This was dreadful: there would be telephone calls of complaint to Rokeby's, and on top of his failure to land the Wattle collection would be piled the opprobrium of an accusation of theft from a very important client. His days in his new career were definitely numbered unless he took immediate action. From being a man on the crest of the wave of art market success he had been overturned into a desperate struggler in imminent danger of drowning.

He realised that he was left with no alternative but to retrace his steps immediately to the Ritz, and restore this bloody object to its rightful owner before things got any worse. It was a bitter experience to follow the now familiar route once more, rather like a batsman just dismissed for a duck being forced to repeat his journey out to the wicket and back again to the pavilion without being permitted the chance of facing another ball. To recall the optimism with which he had paid off the taxi earlier that day and strode into the hotel was to turn the knife in a very recent wound. Then Paris had seemed thrilling, charged with a very special electricity on this blustery late November afternoon, full of possibilities and lovely women. Now it merely appeared cold and windy, not dissimilar to Coventry on a bad day.

It was pointless to announce himself yet once more to the reception so he took the lift once again to the third floor and trudged along the passage to the familiar number of the Wattle suite. He paused at the door, knocked, and received no reply. He knocked again without result, then, noticing that the door itself was on the latch, he pushed it open and walked into the drawing room. No-one was to be seen here, but his eye was drawn to a half-empty bottle of champagne and glasses standing on the same coffee table at which he had sat to receive the bitter news earlier that afternoon. Where was Wattle? Carefully avoiding the door to the drinks cupboard, Evan approached the only remaining one that he had not yet tried. He knocked, and received an immediate if muffled shout of instruction from within. At this moment a strange demon took possession of Evan Conrad's hearing equipment: his ears, normally amongst the most reliable of his organs, received the external stimulus of a voice demanding "Leave the smoked salmon on the table outside", but transmuted this instantaneously into a message to the brain which read "Don't stand on ceremony, come right in." He obeyed automatically.

His entry precipitated something akin to a volcanic eruption in the vast bed which dominated the room in which he found himself an unexpected visitor. The eruption was the result of King C. Wattle leaping apart from his companion with a strangled cry of "Holy Shit!" and carrying with him the sheet, which he clutched as some sort of protection against discovery. In so doing he removed the covering entirely from his partner who was thus revealed to be naked, female, in her early twenties, and possessed of an extremely voluptuous figure. The suddenness of her fully frontal exposure appeared to nonplus her not one bit. There was the hint of a characteristically Gallic shrug of the shoulders, a coquettish smile directed at Evan, and then a languidly graceful arm extended to claim a cigarette from the packet on the bedside table.

Unfortunately the same coolness in the face of the unexpected was not being displayed by King C. Wattle. Such had been the force of his reaction to Evan's entry that, entangled in his sheet, he fell heavily off the side of the bed on to the floor where he was now lying inert, like some upturned turtle caught in a snare. "Christ! My back!" he moaned. "It's gone again. I've lost all goddamn feeling in my toes." It was apparent that any movement was indeed agony for him, because the large gold medallion which habitually hung from his neck had slewed round in the violent action and now lay across one eye like an absurdly piratical patch, but the effort necessary to remove it was quite beyond him.

Evan's first instinct had been to turn and bolt. The whole scene was unutterably embarrassing, just the sort of compromising drama to avoid at all costs. But how could he in all conscience desert a fellow human being in as much physical distress as the unfortunate Wattle? It was a delicate situation, certainly, but not one to back away from if self-respect was to be preserved, rather like being first on the scene of a motor accident. "I say," he said approaching gingerly, "are you all right? I mean, can I help?"

Receiving no reply except a low moan, he bent to remove the impromptu eye patch. A further groan of desperation, pitiful to hear, escaped his erstwhile client's lips. "Oh, my God! This is just the most dreadful thing that ever happened. I'm a skunk, a low-down skunk, you know that, kid? Oh, my God!" His tone was almost delirious.

"Shall I - shall I ring for a doctor?" asked Evan uncertainly.

"Yeah, yeah, do that. I'm a skunk, you hear that, a skunk..." He sounded a broken man, physically and mentally. It was terrible to listen to his wailings of self-denigration, to witness his orgy of remorse. Had he been a mediaeval knight the flagellants would have had a field day in accommodating his urge for expiation. As it was, Evan tried merely to prise a pillow beneath his head before ringing through to reception. He was promised a doctor in fifteen minutes.

"Hey, meester. What about my two sousand francs?" Evan had momentarily forgotten the presence of a third person in the room. She was now sitting on the edge of the bed replacing her shoes, having correctly surmised that there was to be no more custom that day from King C. Wattle. Her question elicited another groan from the heap on the floor.

"Oh, Gaaard! Oh, Mr Conrad, I wonder, could you oblige?"

"What? Oh, of course." Evan reached for his wallet as if it was the most natural thing in the world to find himself settling accounts with prostitutes. Should he add a tip, he wondered. Why were these things always so difficult abroad...? Now, of course, his expenses were perilously low, and he knew the Rokeby's authorities always required a receipt for any expenditure. How could be ask her for one?

"Er, here you are, Mademoiselle...."

"Merci, Monsieur." The notes he preferred were swiftly claimed and slipped into the pocket of a rather tight skirt. She flashed Evan an enchantingly conspiratorial smile, put her blouse back on, and walked to the door from which she took her fur coat. "Au revoir," she said. "See you. And Keeng, baby, next time, take it easy, huh?" She giggled and was gone in a breath of expensive scent.

Evan sat down on the bed and stared after her. You just didn't get receipts from girls like that, he supposed. Under other circumstances he wouldn't have minded getting to know her a bit better. She could have accompanied him to the Musée d'Orsay, and he could have explained to her the finer points of Seurat's technique: doubtless beneath her excitingly brazen exterior lurked a heart of gold and a sensibility capable of fine tuning could one but find the right wavelength. It was an opportunity missed... His fantasies were interrupted by another tortured outburst from the floor, an anguished reminder that there were more pressing problems to be addressed:

"Oh, Thelma, my Thelma! May she never know what happened

here this afternoon! How could I have done this to her? I am not worthy of her, no, sir, I am not. What a brute I am, what a goddamn creep!"

Evan attempted some consoling noises.

"No, Mr Conrad, this is terrible, this is just the worst thing that ever happened. You have witnessed something vile, something truly shaming. How can I persuade you never to breathe a word of this to Thelma? It would break her heart."

Evan was about to assure him that such a course of action on his part was extremely unlikely. He could not imagine circumstances under which he would ever meet Mrs Wattle again, let alone impart such controversial and intimate intelligence to her. Really, he was about to say, Mr Wattle need have no fears on that score, he could set his mind at rest. And yet he hesitated, no more certain how to express himself at this juncture than he had been when requiring a receipt from a fille de joie. He opened his mouth and no words came.

"I know, I know," King went on when he heard no immediate reply. "I can't expect you to agree. I have to make it worth your while. Well, listen to this then: Rokeby's shall have the collection, you guys can sell it in the spring. I haven't signed any contract with Sotheby's yet, I'm not committed, I'll just tell them I changed my mind. You have it, you have it all, yes it's yours. But never, never speak of this afternoon to Thelma. Oh my God, no, it would be the end of everything. Say you agree, Mr Conrad, oh please, say you agree." The pleading was heartrending to hear, the desperation was pathetic. Evan could see that decisive action was demanded, and said firmly, "I agree." King C. Wattle began to weep softly.

"You're a good kid," he gasped between sobs. "You won't regret this."

Minutes later the doctor arrived, and Evan was able to leave Wattle in his care. He let himself out of the bedroom discreetly, and as he passed through the drawing room paused only to replace the gold pen on the glass table.

SEVEN

Ron Wheale pulled the Ford Sierra into a sharp right hand turn out of Cherry Tree Avenue and swept decisively into the forecourt of his family seat. It had a certain stature, this property: when they had moved in he had persuaded Janet that a change of name was in order, from the existing Beechcroft to the rather classier Sterlings. It had rung simultaneously of money and of power (Stirling Moss had been a childhood idol). A programme of improvements had been instituted to bring the house and grounds up to a standard commensurate with such grandeur. By redesigning the front garden, he had managed to create the impressive central feature round which he was at this moment transcribing a rather tight arc, the sweep-in drive. It was the envy of the neighbourhood; several nearby households had attempted the ultimate tribute of imitation, but none with the success of the Wheales. But then Ron had the feeling that the neighbourhood already looked up to them, although some of them might not openly admit it. He, after all, was joint deputy chairman of one of the most glamorous establishment institutions of the West End, an auction house whose name featured regularly in the media. He had flown so much higher than the surrounding bank managers and golf club members that they could only hazily glimpse him in the blue ether above them. He harboured a secret fantasy that many of them already looked on him and Janet as a sort of honorary Lord and Lady of the Manor of the locality, and that Sterlings was the natural focus of their social ambition. If, and when, he reached the heady heights of the actual chairmanship of Rokeby's, he could well envisage that Janet would be receiving invitations to perform traditional local duties such as opening the flower show or the Church bazaar. In this area one would have to be careful, of course, not to accept any requests which would be compromising to a certain level of dignity: he would make sure that Janet drew the line at opening supermarkets or DIY shops. But it all added up to the inescapable conclusion that the Wheales were people of substance, and it showed.

A minute later, having let himself in at the front door, he received further confirmation of their rising social stock in a manner which surpassed even his immediate fantasies. A white-faced Janet met him in the hall.

"Oh, Ron," she said, "look what's come."

She handed him a letter. From her anguished expression he supposed that it must be some unexpected bill, probably a final demand from those fools at the Electricity Board for the account which he had settled a month ago. Honestly, if he ran Rokeby's in the way these buffoons operated their accounts department, Rokeby's would pretty soon be out of business. He would write a letter to the top, complain as one deputy chairman to another... But on looking closer he saw at once that the envelope did not contain a bill. It was addressed to Mrs Ronald Wheale and postmarked London SW7. Impatiently he pulled out the letter. It read:

> Dear Janice
> Freddy and I would be very pleased if you could both join us for the weekend at Leatherby on 8th January. There is a shoot on the Saturday which Ronald may enjoy as Freddy tells me he has a fearsome reputation with a gun. We will expect you for dinner at 8.30 on the Friday evening when most of the party will be assembling. We do hope to see you then.
> Yours,
> Melissa Fairbanks

Ron blinked and turned in triumph to his wife. "I think you could safely say we have finally arrived," he announced. His one regret in this supreme moment was that the invitation had not been delivered in a form which could be displayed on the mantelpiece. Could it not be strategically folded and wedged legibly behind the carriage clock? He surreptitiously fiddled with it, but rapidly had to admit defeat.

"What I can't understand," said Janet nervously, "is why Mrs Fairbanks calls me Janice."

"Just a slip of Melissa's pen," said Ron. "It doesn't mean anything."

"Oh, Ron. I don't know if I'll be able to go through with it."

"Nonsense, of course you will. You'll have to get used to gatherings like this, you know. These people are my colleagues at work, and it's only natural that we should be drawn into their social set. This invitation proves it."

"Yes, but.... but Freddy and Melissa aren't really our sort, are they?"

"What do you mean, not really our sort? Talk like that is completely out of date. Class distinction has no part to play in an international business like Rokeby's, there's no room for it. Everyone in the firm is equal, and we're all where we are on our merits, and I like to think I'm largely responsible for that state of affairs. The moment I find anyone being given preferential treatment just because he's a lord, I stamp on it, I can tell you. People know that's my attitude and respect me for it."

"Yes, dear, I'm sure they do, but what about me on this weekend? There'll be all those people who I've never met before, and I won't know what to talk about. And what's all this about you shooting things? You haven't the first idea about it, you've never shot anything in your life."

"My dear, have no worries on that score." Ron permitted himself a quiet smile of satisfaction as he recalled the encouraging number of clay pigeons he had hit last weekend. "Look, let's discuss the whole thing over dinner. I think I might open a bottle of decent claret to wash it all down."

Janet looked at him oddly. For the first fifteen years of their married life to date, their evening meal when taken at home on their own had always been known at best as supper, and wine had been reserved for birthdays, anniversaries, and major festivals. She sensed a gear-change upwards in the way they lived, and she was not at all sure she was ready for it.

Having sat down to eat, Ron continued: "I feel I should tell you that I am no mean marksman. In fact I have been taking lessons, and have every confidence of bagging more than my fair share of brace of pheasant when I take my place in the line at Leatherby. No, you need have no worries on that score. Frankly, don't be surprised if you find yourself really rather proud of me."

Janet wondered if Ron was sickening for something. His whole manner of talking was different, quite unlike the way he's spoken when he got up that morning, before they had received this wretched invitation. Was it a symptom of stress or overwork? Did he understand exactly what a weekend at Leatherby would involve? She asked: "But what about all the equipment you'll need to do this shooting? Don't you need your own gun, and special clothes, and one of those caps? Won't it all be terribly dear?"

"That is all being taken care of. Of course the only thing I am short of is a good gun dog of my own. I suppose I'll have to do without that; pity, but it can't be helped."

Janet brightened slightly. "We could take Leila. She's a wonder at fetching things when they're thrown for her and she'd love a day in the country."

Ron closed his eyes. "No, dearest, what the situation does not call for is a French poodle."

"And another thing," added Janet a minute later, "what do they do in the evenings at those weekends in the country? I seem to have read somewhere that they play odd games, and they gamble a lot. You know how hopeless I am at cards - I can never remember the difference between hearts and spades - and I won't know how much money to spend on the betting. Then in some houses the men creep about the passage late at night and try to sleep with other people's wives, and that really is not nice at all."

Ron was momentarily undermined by this stream of insidious uncertainty. Would he be expected to part with large sums of money at cards or backgammon after dinner? Surely no male member of the house party would expect to sleep with Janet? What was he supposed to do if that happened? Go and find one of the women whose husband was elsewhere engaged? Would she realise that he wore a dental plate? No, this whole thing was absurd, a fantasy of women's fiction. He would not be party to any such funny business, anyway, and that would be an end of it. He told Janet so in terms which could not be misunderstood. But he did add as a safeguard: "You might look out that backgammon set Ron junior was given for Christmas. It wouldn't hurt for us to have a few practice games before we go, just as a precaution. There's no point in throwing good money down the drain. I mean, you know me, I play to win."

Janet tried to put the whole dreadful prospect of the Leatherby weekend out of her mind for the rest of the evening. She did not return to the topic until the two of them were preparing for bed. "And what do we wear? We're bound not to have the right things - you know, there are a lot of clothes you're only meant to wear in the country, not in the town. Oh, Ron we'll get it all wrong and people will laugh at us."

"Of course we won't. And no-one's going to laugh at us, they wouldn't dare. You just have to keep your clothes simple. I'll be in my shooting gear a lot of the time, of course, and we'll both just blend into the surroundings. I don't know why you're taking such a black view of all this, I really don't. Things are turning out very well, very well indeed."

"I know, Ron, I'm sorry. I'll try to look on the bright side."

"You should, after all, it's quite something to be invited to Leatherby."

"Yes, of course it is." Janet bit her lip and tried to see this latest development as just one more step up in the glorious rise to power of Ronald Wheale. "How are you getting on at Rokeby's now? Do you really think there's a chance you could be the next chairman?"

The answer that wafted back to her from the bathroom was unintelligible. Ron was engaged in removing his dentures for the night, an exercise which he preferred to keep as secret as possible even from his wife. But when he ambled back into the bedroom, a towel casually draped round his shoulders, it was clear from his demeanour that he felt considerable optimism about the future. He amplified his reply: "There's been an interesting development today. You know that lad I persuaded Freddy and Endymion to take on to run the Impressionist department, the art historian I was telling you about, the one from that college?"

"Yes," said Janet a little uncertainly, for she though she recalled Ron standing in the self-same attitude at the same hour of the night little more than six weeks ago warning her and the world in general that to appoint such a young and inexperienced operative into such a crucial area of the company's infrastructure was asking for trouble on the part of Freddy and Endymion. But perhaps she had got it wrong.

"Well," continued Ron, "the boy's gone straight out on his first job and landed the Wattle collection of Impressionist pictures for us. We heard this morning. That's 27 million pounds worth, apparently: it's amazing, and everyone's over the moon about it. It's certainly satisfying to have one's hunches vindicated in this way. He's a bit of a genius as far as I can see - he knows a lot about his subject, and he seems to have a knack of rubbing people up the right way. And he went to a grammar school - I was just leafing through his personal file again today. It just goes to prove what I was saying earlier this evening about Rokeby's being a true meritocracy. I don't mind admitting that a lot of it's down to my influence."

"Of course it is, dearest," said Janet, "of course it is."

She reached to switch off the light, but her mind was still in turmoil running through the preparations necessary for the coming ordeal at Leatherby. She had to learn backgammon, bone up something of shooting etiquette, recast her wardrobe without knowing what was required, send Ron junior and Andrew to her in-laws for the weekend, put Leila in the kennels, arrange for Mrs Slough to come in and water the Bizzy Lizzy, and still she was no closer to an answer to the question of why Mrs Fairbanks had called her Janice.

The room in which Renata Crum and her four companions sat was sparsely furnished. A simple electric bulb hung from the ceiling to illuminate them, a bulb whose shade had been hastily removed by Verna Grewcock, whose lodgings these were, minutes before the others' arrival for fear that such a decoration might be construed as too complacently bourgeois. Verna was Renata's contemporary at St Ethelreda's and lived in awe of her, striving to emulate her steadfastness in adhering to the feminist principles which ruled her life, following her footstep for footstep in the unceasing search for oppressed minorities in need of support. For Verna, then, it had been an honour to be asked by Renata to serve on this small committee, and to put at her disposal the front room of her Highbury digs for the purpose of this its first meeting. She was thrillingly conscious of being one of a pretty select group, a group chosen, Renata had informed them, because it comprised exclusively Women of Action, women who could be relied upon 'in the field'. Renata was proposing a project which demanded quick thinking and physical fitness, and she hoped the others would be with her when she told them what she planned.

Verna glanced round at the others. There was Mary O'Flaherty, the flame-haired girl from Dublin who was rumoured to have had a boyfriend high up in the I.R.A.. There was Sandra, who had recently been arrested, tried and fined for throwing a hot dog at the Prime Minister's car when he arrived to speak at the Small Businessman of the Year lunch at a Park Lane hotel. And there was Irma, a large, seemingly muscle-bound hulk of a woman much given to body-building, who had worked for a time on a building site in Birmingham. No doubt about it, they were all women of action. Thank God she had taken down that lampshade.

"What we will be up against," Renata was saying, "is one of the most extreme and unacceptable manifestations of male establishment barbarism that it's possible to imagine. They may call it by some other name, but the truth is it's just the systematic murder of a succession of defenceless targets. It must be stopped."

"Right on!" agreed Verna, raising herself slightly from he chair to lift a clenched fist in the direction of the ceiling.

"The time has come," continued Renata, "for us all to stop theorising and to stand up and be counted. We've got to get out there and do something positive. The way I see it, we can strike a blow simultaneously against both male privilege and male bloodlust, and we'll be seen to be taking direct action. I have been alerted to a suitable venue, and a suitable time early in the new year. So, Sandra, you'll look after the banners and placards, wordings to be agreed later. What else will we need, any suggestions?"

"Whistles, rattles, sirens?"

"Yes, noted."

"In the name of the holy saints, why don't we take guns?" asked Mary. "It would give them a taste of their own medicine. To be sure, I have a cousin who could bring them over the sea for us."

Renata paused for a moment. It went against the grain to have to adopt the voice of moderation, but there was a limit. "Look, I'm the last person to deny that any politically-motivated action must, in order to be valid, carry an implication of violence, and we should not shrink from it if necessary. But direct assassination of hostile elements might be counterproductive in the context of this operation."

Everyone nodded sagely. Renata turned to the solid mass occupying the armchair in the corner. "You haven't said much, Irma. How do you view the political implications of this action?"

"I'm looking forward to a bloody good ruck."

The elderly man sitting at the bar lit another cigarette and called for a cognac. There was an air of defeat about him, a sense of resignation to failure. He had been staying in this village for three weeks, but no-one had exchanged with him more than a few words. His desolation discouraged intimacy. He was certainly discussed behind his back: no French village community could sustain the incursion of a stranger, even such an uncommunicative stranger as this one, without speculating a little as to his status and origins.

"His clothes are good," said Maurice the barman, who noticed these things.

"But in a disgusting state. He takes no trouble any more. His cuffs, they are frayed, and his tie bears the record of many different meals."

"Still, he always wears a tie. He has known better times, I think."

If he was aware that he was discussed, it made little impact. He drained the last dregs of his cognac and pushed out of the door into the winter twilight. It had been a sunny day, but now at dusk the chill hit him hard. Up here in the hills the nights were very cold in December, a season for scarves and overcoats. But he refrained from turning right, back down the village street to his lodgings at the house of Madame Leclaire, and instead walked in the opposite direction. He wanted to postpone as long as possible the next encounter with his landlady, whose curiosity about him carried the constant threat of questions.

"From Paris, are you?" she had asked when he first arrived, directed to her door by Maurice who was some sort of distant cousin. "What line of business are you in, Monsieur?"

"I ... I am a schoolteacher."

"And what is your subject, Monsieur le Professeur?"

"I teach... history."

"History? Pah! I could never be bothered with it. Who wants to know what a lot of dead people did? You look like a man who lives too much in the past yourself. The present is the interesting time - you should get out and do things."

He had rapidly learned to take her advice in one respect, which was to spend as much time as possible out of the house. Even when Madame Leclaire was not dogging his footsteps, he was forever being accosted by her grandson Alain, a peculiarly aggravating child of seven who hung about the house awaiting his mother's return from work and pestering the lodger for sweets. So he would escape the boy's attentions by seeking refuge in the village bar, reflecting that at least the room he was renting was cheap. Sometimes he would sit and write at one of the tables, while on other occasions he would stare out across the famous view which promised on a clear day a glimpse of the distant Mediterranean. One day he had caught a bus which wound a ponderous route through numerous villages to Grasse, where he had sat at a bar for two hours before catching the same bus back.

Today he had finished the long letter he had been writing. He had put it in an envelope that afternoon, and it was now lying on the table in his bedroom, not yet addressed to anyone. Tomorrow he might decide to whom to send it, or he might not; in a sense its destination seemed less important than the fact that it had been written. It gave him a certain qualified satisfaction, the sort of satisfaction felt by the man with terminal gangrene who at long last succeeds in prising out the bullet from his original wound. It was too late for it to make any difference to his ultimate fate, but at least he had purged himself by laying bare the first cause.

He walked on past the church with the shuffling gait which gave onlookers the impression that he was ten years older than his true age. He came to a signpost which directed him to a point from which a particularly spectacular view was to be had, as far as Corsica on a clear day, or so the story went. Once again he followed the path round the churchyard and found himself, with a suddenness which never failed to surprise him, on a small parapet with a telescope, below which stretched out for many kilometres the foothills to the coastal plane, and then the distant sea. Far-off lights sparkled in the gathering gloom, but it was still possible to make out, as he leaned on the parapet wall, the sheer drop of fifty metres or so to the rocks below. A surge of vertigo swept over him in a sensation which was not altogether unpleasant. Perhaps the cognac helped. How simple to ease oneself a little further over the wall, to reach that point where gravity might take its natural cause, to find oneself falling, floating, free at last, the rushing air singing him into blessed oblivion.

EIGHT

Paris had stopped looking like Coventry to Evan Conrad. It was now a rapturous place, where it felt good to be alive, particularly when you had just secured the King C. Wattle III collection of Impressionist pictures for sale. He sat in the Boulevard St Germain at a cafe drinking a cup of coffee and feeling thoroughly at ease with his surroundings. It was a cold day, but he was warmed by the memory of the two telephone conversations he had had that morning. At 9.15 am King Wattle himself had been on the line, a pathetically contrite and ingratiating King Wattle calling from his nursing home bedroom. Yet once more Evan had had to reassure the snivelling voice at the other end that no, he would not be revealing to Thelma the true reason for her husband's hospitalisation, and yes, he was happy to have it confirmed that Rokeby's would be handling the sale. He had been informed, once more, that he was a good kid. Then had come the pleasurable task of relaying the news to Rokeby's. Freddy Fairbanks had requested that once the outcome was known he should ring through personally to his office rather than bother Messrs Wheale or Luce. The dreadful gay switchboard operator had fiddled around for an unconscionable length of time, but finally he had heard Freddy's voice at the other end. The delight of the joint deputy chairman had been gratifyingly perceptible even on the telephone. He announced that he himself would fly out to Paris with a contract for Wattle to sign, and that this fitted in rather well as he had an urgent business call to make in Montpelier. Evan was happy to leave these details in experienced hands; but he had requested permission to stay on himself till the end of the week in Paris in order to pursue his research on Hartier. Under the circumstances there was no objection, particularly as Hartier was one of the artists represented in the Wattle collection. So now here he was, free for two days, enjoying his well-earned cup of coffee and contemplating how best to set about the second stage of his mission to Paris.

For the moment his attention was diverted by the copy of the London Art Digest which he had brought with him from London but was only now finding time to peruse. It was essential to keep in touch with scholarly life, to prevent oneself from being totally carried away by the heady wine of success in the commercial sector. He opened the journal at its editorial and read:

The Directorship of the San Pietro Museum of Fine Arts is currently open for application, and various names have been mooted to fill the vacancy at this exceptionally well endowed foundation. Candidates have been proposed on both sides of the Atlantic. The trustees could do much worse than to direct their attention to Great Britain, where a vintage crop of young academics is now reaching maturity. Chauvinists of the 'Little England' variety may talk in alarmist fashion of a Brain Drain in this connection, but it remains the opinion of this journal that Scholarship should be international. Museums, and the exhibits and expertise of which they are the repositories, should know no geographical or political boundaries, should brook no limitation of their scope by considerations of narrow nationalism. The name which springs most readily to mind as an imaginative and stimulating choice for San Pietro is Dr Ewan Connard, the brilliant young lecturer at the London Institute. He has already written two innovative and challenging books on aspects of Post-Impressionism, and his views on a variety of subjects, from Steffano della Bella to Italian Divisionism, are pre-eminently worth hearing. The trustees may rightly judge that his hour has come. F. N.-P.

Evan sipped his coffee ruminatively. He was unaware that he had just read a love letter, or as close as the editress of the London Art Digest would ever get to writing one. But on the whole he was pleased that his former Director of Studies seemed so highly regarded and was being taken seriously as a candidate for such an exalted post.

To be reminded of Ewan Connard was to be reminded of Dr Louis Ranchec; through Connard he had learned of Ranchec and his crucial role in the rediscovery of Claude Hartier. Connard had even hinted that Ranchec might be in possession of documentary material relating to Hartier's life and work which was potentially as sensational as the letter from Seurat unearthed in the Bibliothèque Nationale. Evan's mouth watered at the thought of such a feast after the meagre crumbs with which he had had to content himself to date in his search for further information about his subject. What could this documentary material consist of? Birth and death certificates? More correspondence? A Liber Veritatis in the master's hand recording his entire oeuvre? Truly Ranchec held the key to Hartier, and he must be found at once. It had been frustrating, therefore, to telephone the man's number yet once more that morning, and succeed only in getting an engaged tone despite repeated further attempts. The time had come, resolved Evan, for positive action. Besides Ranchec's telephone number, he also had his address in the Rue des St. Pères, five minutes' walk from where he now sat. Why not go round and pay him an impromptu call? Admittedly his previous experience of impromptu calls on this trip had been somewhat explosive, but on this occasion he would definitely wait for the door to be opened to him before entering.

Evan called for the bill and paid it. Thank God he now had money in his pocket again, having replenished his resources with the aid of his American Express card, thoughtfully provided by Rokeby's. He was still a little uneasy about the lack of a receipt from Wattle's lady friend, but he supposed he could account for it under 'Client Entertainment - Miscellaneous' or, if pushed, 'Emergency Secretarial Fees'. He had an appointment at four at the Galerie St Jacques in the Rue St Honoré, but he had an hour and a half before that in which to visit Ranchec. He walked the hundred metres to the address, boarded a very rickety lift for the journey to the troisième étage, and emerged on the landing confronted by double doors with no name plate or other indication of who lived within. He paused for a moment, perhaps visited by a brief shaft of psychic prescience that he was on the verge of a transcendent encounter, then rang the bell.

When the door of the apartment opened, Evan recognised immediately that he was entering a new realm, landing on a continent about which he had only previously read. His perception of feminine beauty was circumscribed by the limitations common to many young men of his background and experience. In his mind's eye there was a hierarchy, at the top of which came the category of the beautiful women he had seen in films or on television, actresses and models in the pages of glossy magazines, goddesses, ideals, at several degrees removed from reality. He had also noticed women of serious attraction walking down the street, even talked to one or two at parties. His intimate personal contact, however, had been largely confined to girls in the plain to average category, although Renata, when she chose to take any care over her self-presentation, might legitimately be classed in a category several rungs above the rest. However, Evan knew now that new standards were being set, that the girl who stood before him was without doubt the most beautiful he had ever seen in close or even distant physical proximity. Effortlessly she sailed into the ideal class. She had long dark hair, flawless olive skin, large disconcertingly blue eyes, and a ravishing smile which betokened immediate and delicious complicity. She wore blue jeans and a loose pink shirt.

"Monsieur?" she enquired.

"I'm terribly sorry to bother you," gasped Evan. "I was looking for Dr Ranchec."

"Oh! So you are English!" she exclaimed with some pleasure. "That's nice. You know I had once an English boyfriend? No, Dr Ranchec lives no more here, I regret." She smiled at Evan in such a way as to make him wonder if he might shortly need medical help.

"Do you know where I might find him?"

"No, I do not know. And that is my problem also. Mais entrez un petit moment."

Evan needed a little encouragement to follow her into the apartment. Ranchec's whereabouts suddenly seemed rather less important than those of this breathtaking young lady. Her whole look, manner and scent were intoxicating. The hint of the coquette in her conversation was uncontrived and irresistible.

"I'm Sylvie," she said, holding out her hand, "Sylvie Legrand. Excuse the mess! I only just woke up. It was a late night last night."

"How - how do you do? I'm Evan Conrad." He took her hand. He had touched her.

"I do not know where is Dr Ranchec, but I seek him too," she continued, tossing her head and running her hand back through her hair. "This is my apartment, but I had to go away for a year and I - how do you say? - hired it to him. He was the friend of my friends, but I did not know him, I did not even meet him. My friends, they made all the arrangements. When I returned last month he was no longer here, he had gone, and he left no address, only many bills. All these I have to pay before I can use again the telephone and the electricity. I think he had behaved himself like a cochon to do this. But you.... you are perhaps an old friend of Dr Ranchec?"

"No, no, I've never met him." Evan hastened to disassociate himself from the agency of Sylvie's aggravation. "You see, I am an art historian, and I want to find him for professional reasons. He can help me a great deal with my research."

"Oh, you are art historian? That is wonderful. I once studied art - I love art, it is my passion. But sit down: you want coffee? I just made some." She swept back her lustrous hair again from her forehead in a movement which Evan already recognised as characteristic. He accepted her invitation with as much composure as he could muster, put his briefcase down and sank on to the sofa. Sylvie had disappeared for a moment into the kitchen which gave off the salon. Her voice carried back into the room, setting his adrenaline flowing again.

''What painting do you study? French painting, of course?''

Evan began to explain through the open door about his work on Hartier, his pursuit of pictures by the artist, and his newly acquired position of importance at Rokeby's.

"Mmm," exclaimed Sylvie, returning with the coffee, "so you work at the famous house of Rokeby. You must be very clever, very glamorous, n'est-ce pas?" Her smile was a mixture of teasing and admiration, and it inspired Evan with a sudden spurt of confidence. I am a glamorous young man having a cup of coffee with a beautiful woman, he told himself. I must be strong enough to take this proffered drink without rattling the cup in the saucer like a mountain goat's bell. By an enormous effort of will, he half succeeded.

"Eh, bien," she continued, "we both need to find Ranchec."

"We do, you are right. Are you absolutely sure he left no forwarding address?"

"No, he did not. I asked to the concierge. She said he left suddenly, some weeks before I returned."

"And he didn't tell her where he was going?"

"He only told her that he was going away, that he did not like the city in the autumn."

"And he took all his things?"

"Yes, he left nothing behind except the - how you say? - garbage, and a few papers, nothing important."

"What about the friends of his and yours, the ones who arranged for him to rent your apartment? Do they know anything?"

"Naturally I asked them, but they did not know. They were his pupils at the Beaux Arts Institute. He was professor there, I think."

Evan nodded: "That's right. But what do the Institute say about him? They must have some idea where he is, surely?"

"I even went there and asked to the authorities. They say Ranchec resigned at the summer. He reached sixty years, and he left. They have no more his address except my apartment. My friends, they did not see him since June either."

"This is absolutely extraordinary," said Evan. "A man cannot just vanish."

"I think that he can, you know. His friends have no idea where he is. I ask the Institute, has he family? and they tell me no-one, or no-one that is close. So I gave up to chase him. But you, perhaps you will have better fortune?"

"Well, I don't know. I mean, you seem to have followed up most of the possible lines of inquiry. I only heard of him through my director of studies in London, Ewan Connard. He told me he only actually met Ranchec once, in Germany about eighteen months ago, so that doesn't help much."

"Perhaps there is something in the papers which were left behind by him?" Sylvie had been sitting cross-legged on the floor. In one graceful movement she rose, and went to a desk. She extracted a file. "They mean nothing to me, but perhaps they will aid you."

Evan took them. For a moment he found it impossible to register anything of what he was reading, for Sylvie had sat down again next to him on the sofa and was peering intently at the file with him. Her closeness dominated his entire perception: he had no intelligence left to receive any other data.

"Here is nothing," Sylvie was observing as he turned blank pages mechanically. "Mais voilà! There is something."

Evan stopped turning and forced himself to look with more attention. There was a sheet on which was written two names and telephone numbers. The first was 'Gontier' and the second read 'St Jacques'. "Hold on a minute," he said, and reached for his own briefcase in order to consult his Hartier file. He survived a minor heart attack as his knee accidentally touched Sylvie's in the process. "Yes, look - St Jacques: that's the number of the Galerie St Jacques in the Rue St Honoré. He's on my list to consult in connection with my research. What a strange coincidence that Ranchec should have that number as well."

"And the other? The person that is called Gontier?"

"That means nothing to me. I'll just check the rest of this file." There were no more telephone numbers, but towards the end Evan made a further discovery. A number of closely-typed sheets were clipped together. They were entitled 'Claude Hartier, 1859-1902. Notes on life and work'. He was the prospector who had struck gold, albeit in a fairly moderate quantity, but there was no doubt this was a major find. He had stumbled across a significant helping of Ranchec's research to date.

"This is fantastic! Do you... do you mind if I borrow it? It would help me tremendously."

"No, take it all, all the file. It is to me no use. But what do you think to do?"

"Well, I'm going to study these notes in detail in due course. But I still badly need to find Ranchec. I've got an appointment to see St Jacques at 4 o'clock, so maybe he can shed some light on Ranchec's whereabouts, because they obviously know each other."

"Ah, that's good. It's exciting, this quest for Ranchec, n'est-ce pas?"

It was exciting. It was more than exciting. Through the agency of this divine girl he had stumbled upon these mouth-watering notes. And, even more thrilling, his destiny appeared to be entwined with hers in the search for Louis Ranchec, art historian and fugitive from debt. "I will not rest," declared Evan, "until I have found him. You shall have your telephone bill paid."

"But you are so gallant," giggled Sylvie huskily. "You sound like Superman."

The excitement of his recent discovery, the intimacy of Sylvie's manner, his own comparison to Superman, all combined to spur him on to further gallantry. He was just opening his mouth to give expression to it when the telephone rang and Sylvie rose swiftly to answer.

"Guy, c'est toi? Comment ça va, chéri?" She walked, cradling the telephone, into the kitchen so that Evan could hear no more detail of their conversation. He felt instantly cast down, suddenly sick with jealousy. The discovery that she could be on intimate terms with anyone else in the world struck him as indecent, almost obscene. And yet three quarters of an hour earlier he had not even been aware of her existence. This was absurd. He must think more sensibly, adopt a more positive attitude. If this goddess was indeed pursued by other men (a hardly surprising state of affairs), then he would fight them; there would be a succession of duels, he would kill for her. The Bois de Boulogne at 5 am: the scent of gunpowder and blood staining the snow crimson. The mysterious Guy would be the first to go, he decided bitterly. Why was she still in the kitchen talking to him?

He resolved to leave and rose from the sofa. He would find Ranchec: that would be his first mission of chivalry on her behalf. He would ensure that the money owing to her for the telephone and electricity would be forthcoming. And he would uncover Hartier. The typescript now nestling in his briefcase would be an important start, but Evan had no doubt that personal consultation with Ranchec was still essential to the project.

"Thank you so much for the coffee," he said as she re-emerged from the kitchen.

"Oh, you are going?"

"Yes, I must keep my appointment at the Galerie St Jacques. But don't worry, I'll let you know the news."

"Please, do that. You have my number of the telephone? Yes, of course. Au revoir, Evan."

Her voice framing the syllables of his name echoed in his ears all the way down in the lift. She pronounced it 'Ee-van', almost like a Russian name. He was a character from a Russian novel of the nineteenth century, heroic, impetuous, and above all strong. What would Vronsky do in a situation like this? He would certainly brook no prevarication from an insignificant academic like Ranchec. Once found, Ranchec was to be put through a severe grilling, and persuaded both to pay his debts and to cough up the full extent of his research on Hartier. Evan felt good in his new persona. If only his colleagues in the Institute could see him now: they would hardly recognise the old, diffident, infinitely placatory Evan Conrad. Nor would Renata Crum, he thought suddenly. Indeed it was the first time she had crossed his mind at all, really, since his arrival in Paris. She was not relevant here. Did she, in fact, fit in anywhere with his new mode of life? She belonged to another era, and it was not fair to pit her against the competition of an ideal being like Sylvie. If there was one thing that Sylvie did not do in the evenings, he speculated, it was attend meetings of Women Against Male Predominance in Commerce.

The interior decoration of the Galerie St Jacques followed an already familiar formula. There was the usual deep-pile carpet, the odd Boudin on the sparsely hung but richly upholstered walls, and the obligatory bored secretary cum receptionist lounging behind a desk at the far end. Evan strode in purposefully; what had Machiavelli said?

"It is better to be impetuous than cautious since fortune is a woman and it is necessary to master her by force."

"I've come to see M. St Jacques," announced the new blend of Vronsky and Superman.

"He's not in," said the blond girl and yawned.

"But I have an appointment for 4 o'clock."

She merely shrugged her shoulders and raised her eyebrows a fraction in a gesture of renunciation of all responsibility for such an arrangement. Then she returned her attention to a nail file. The impasse was resolved moments later when the door behind her desk opened and a sallow, weasle-faced man in his fifties emerged. He looked sharply at Evan, and then barked a noise of inquiry at his receptionist.

"He says he has an appointment with you, M. St Jacques?"

"And you are?"

"Evan Conrad, from the Impressionist department at Rokeby's in London."

"Ah! Mais oui!" The weasel's face smoothed itself into a sickeningly bland grin of welcome. "Monsieur Conrad, how do you do? Enter, enter through this door."

Evan was ushered through into St Jacques' elegant den and told to sit down. In a vinous moment on the plane back from Zurich, Gervase Hopkins had imparted to him his rule of life for avoiding trouble in the art world: beware of men who wear bow ties. Looking across, Evan was not altogether surprised to find that this was a conceit of dress affected by St. Jacques.

"Now, Monsieur Conrad, a cigarette? No? What is the matter I can aid you with? I always wish to help the great London auction houses, it is for me an honour."

"That is very kind of you. I have come for advice, really, and information. I'd like to ask about a picture by Claude Hartier which you sold to King Wattle earlier this year. I am very anxious to trace its previous history."

"Ah, yes, of course. That ravishing little river landscape, a gem, I recall it well. You wish to know where we acquired it before we sold it to Mr Wattle? May I ask why you have need of his information?" M. St Jacques was still grinning pleasantly.

"I need it for two reasons. First of all because we are selling the Wattle collection of Impressionist pictures at Rokeby's in March, and

I need details of the provenance of the Hartier for the catalogue entry; and the second because I am myself an art historian and I am researching Hartier, so every new work which comes to light is of the greatest interest to me."

"Admirable, admirable, Monsieur Conrad. Yes of course, I too am fascinated by Hartier. A major genius of the late 19th century, it seems to me, and I venture to say a seriously underrated one. But wait, and his day will come, oh yes, I am sure. And then the prices paid now for his work will seem - how you say? - like a joke." St Jacques managed a twisted little laugh to prove the point.

"And you can tell me where the Wattle picture was acquired?"

"Naturally, naturally. It came from a European private collection of the highest standing. Alas, I can say no more. It is required that the anonymity of his collection be preserved at all costs. You understand well the demands of security, no doubt."

"But.... but do they have any more works by the artist? Can you at least tell me that?"

"It is possible, but I regret I cannot confirm yes or no."

There was a pause. M. St Jacques continued to grin and Evan could think of no way forward in his investigation. Certainly no further information was to be volunteered from the present source. In fact he was no closer to tracing the provenance of this work by Hartier than he had been to tracing the previous history of any other of the artist's resurfaced pictures. It was tantalising and infuriating. He cut his losses and moved on to the next line of inquiry.

"Well then, perhaps you can help me in another matter which is connected. I am trying to trace a man who was largely responsible for the rediscovery of Hartier as an artist, Dr Louis Ranchec. Do you by any chance know where I can find him now?"

"Dr Ranchec? Yes, I have had contact with him in the past, a great scholar, I think. Malheureusement, I know him not well. His address you can find without a doubt in the telephone book, or from the Beaux Arts Institute. He teaches there, does he not?"

"He used to, but he retired in the summer and has not been seen since. I had hoped you might know something, because I found your number in his papers."

"Many people have my telephone number. I am not unknown in the art world." St Jacques added another of his strangled little laughs.

"Of course: I didn't mean to suggest..."

"But you speak of his papers. Tell me about these papers, Monsieur Conrad."

"Oh, just some things he left behind in the flat he had been renting. Odd scraps, nothing important."

"Was there anything related to Hartier, perhaps?"

"Oh, nothing much at all, really." Suddenly Evan felt uncomfortable now that St Jacques had become the interrogator.

"I should be interested to see them myself. Can I inspect them?"

Evan clutched his briefcase. "I'm sorry, I don't have them with me," he lied. "They're in the hotel."

"Another time, perhaps." St Jacques spoke amicably enough. "How long do you stay in Paris?"

"I have to go back to London early tomorrow morning."

Another pause. Progress had been thin, reflected Evan, frustratingly meagre in the quest for Ranchec, the one activity which bound him into that idyllic state, unification with Sylvie. He had nothing to report, and therefore no excuse for seeing her again, no pretext for coming back to her. It was ignominious failure, and his performance in her eyes would seem inadequate and inept. He cast about for some further avenue of inquiry, and suddenly remembered that there had been another name on Ranchec's list of telephone numbers in the file. It was worth a try. "Monsieur St Jacques, do you know someone called Gontier, also a friend of Ranchec's?"

"I never heard of this name. I regret not to be more help." St Jacques rose to indicate termination of the interview. "It was a pleasure to meet you. At what hotel do you stay in Paris?"

"A little place called the Hotel de Lyon, I'm afraid."

"Ah, yes, I think I know it. Well, Monsieur Conrad, may I congratulate you and the house of Rokeby? To have for sale the famous Wattle collection, that is quite a - how you say? - feather in the cap. I look forward to being in attendance."

"Oh, yes, indeed; thank you." Evan had forgotten his triumph of the day before. Even that had paled by comparison with the events of today; the continuing elusiveness of Hartier absorbed his intellect to the exclusion of all else, while his heart was full of his encounter with the incomparably lovely Sylvie. Sylvie. What was to be done about her? He vowed he would not telephone her until he had something more positive to report, something which would reflect better on him as a man of action. His resolve lasted until his return to the hotel forty minutes later. Then, with shaking hand and beating heart, he put through a call to her number. There was no reply.

In compensation he drew the file from his briefcase and settled down to read.

NINE

Claude Hartier, 1859-1901: Notes on his Life and Work

Claude Hartier was born on 20th May 1859 in the small town of Verrey in Normandy. He came of comfortable middle class stock: his father Guillaume Hartier was a respected local notary and his mother, born Celeste Barry, was the daughter of a doctor. Each of his parents had in their own way important formative influences on their only son's development (an earlier child, a daughter, had died in infancy). Apart from his legal interests, Guillaume Hartier was a keen amateur scientist in his spare time. He created a laboratory in the attic of their large village house and frequently spent his evenings engaged in research and experiment, a source of constant fascination to the young Claude and of fear and superstition to the servants who apparently saw him as some sort of dangerous alchemist. Nothing could have been further from the truth, for the master of the household was in fact an ardent believer in Positivism and viewed his work in the attic as a contribution to the task of the explanation of all worldly and human phenomena in strictly logical, scientific terms. It is no surprise that Claude on his visits to his father's laboratory developed a strong sympathy for many of his interests and concerns.

Celeste, on the other hand, was a talented painter, working in both water-colour and oil. She was fond of taking her son with her on sketching trips to the Normandy countryside, occasionally even as far afield as to the coast. It has not yet been possible to trace any examples of Claude Hartier's work from this his earliest phase of artistic development, but his aptitude was strikingly apparent to his mother. One must, of course, allow for the bias caused by maternal idolatry of an only child, but she gives an interesting account of his progress in her weekly letters to her sister Marie, and there may well have been some justification for her ecstatic tones:

> 20th June 1870. We reached Etaples by train and set up our easels overlooking the cliffs and sea. Claude painted some magnificent marine studies. His speed of execution is phenomenal, and I am lost in admiration (and envy) for the way he quickly grasps the overall impression of the scene he is depicting. His tonal sense is

also unerring. For an eleven year old he is undoubtedly exceptionally talented: his work will hang in the Salon some day, I am sure.

Five years later Celeste wrote to the same sister in a manner which suggests that while his youthful progress was maintained, yet there were now some reservations about aspects of his development:

> 12th May 1875: Claude and I painted again outside yesterday afternoon, and for once the sun shone on us after all the terrible rainstorms of the spring. I was pleased with my own effort, a corn field with trees beyond. Claude's picture, executed with his usual extraordinary speed, was very colourful. Set side by side with my work, it is hard to believe that we were confronting the same scene. I am even a little worried that his obsession with bright colour is now marring his progress as a painter. At times this obsession leads him into something worse than an exaggeration of nature, into a distortion of it. I also observe that the way he applies his brush to the canvas has taken on a strangely fragmentary and not altogether appealing character. It is as if he wants to break up his earlier smoothness and facility of style, as if he wants to do violence to it. What should I do, my dear Marie? I am much exercised by the question. I do not wish to criticise unnecessarily, to set him against me, but I have a horror that he will waste his talent. He says that the phenomenon of colour is much the most interesting element in Art. Is this not a little unbalanced? It seems to me that he needs better and stronger guidance than that which I can offer him. Perhaps if he decides that he wishes to pursue the calling of being an artist then he should enter the atelier of one of the great teachers in Paris, and that would serve to direct his ability aright. But it is by no means certain what career he will pursue. He continues to excel at school, and has specially favourable reports in science and in physics, aptitudes which naturally much please his father.

By the time Claude was eighteen it was clear that he could go on to university to study physics if he chose. But he opted for Paris and the life of an art student. That there was some parental division over his future at this stage was inevitable. Again the best evidence is provided by Celeste's continuing letters to her sister:

> 1st June 1877. It is finally decided, and the die is cast. Claude is to take lodgings in Paris in the autumn and is to inscribe himself in the atelier of M. J-L Gérôme for instruction in the fundamental principles of painting, a discipline from which I have no doubt he will derive benefit. Guillaume, Claude and I have burned the candle low on several nights in discussion of all this. Guillaume's preference for a career in physics was predictable, and he argued long and hard to persuade Claude that this was the right road forward. But in the end Claude's decision to embrace Art was accepted graciously by Guillaume, who seemed encouraged by Claude's assurance that he proposed not merely to study painting, but also to devote himself to a scientific study of the phenomenon of colour. This is something which Claude feels very strongly about, as he says no painter has yet attempted such a thing in a properly organised manner.

The artist whose studio had been chosen as a fit forcing house for the talent of the young Hartier, Jean-Léon Gérôme, was an academic painter par excellence, a pillar of the conservative establishment, a man built to straighten out any potential artistic deviance in a young pupil, such as unhealthy distortion of colour or stylisation of brush stroke. What the result of such an influence would have been must remain conjectural, however, for it appears that Hartier never actually entered the artist's atelier. His name appears on a preliminary hand-written list of prospective pupils for the autumn of 1877, but from the final list in the records for that year it is excluded. The explanation for this is provided in a letter from the young Hartier in Paris to his parents, dated 29th October:

> You have no idea how little sympathy I can muster for what goes on in the studio of that man (Gérôme). His methods and priorities are wholly antipathetic to me, and I realise that to place myself under his tuition would break my spirit. My concerns are quite different from the things he considers to be important. I have already made friends with other fellows, mostly young like myself, whose ideas about painting are much more stimulating to me. You must understand that the more I paint, and the more I test the

relationship between what I see (Nature) and what I use to reproduce it (colour) the more fascinating fields for experiment and research I find opening up for me. The friends which I have made here, other artists who have reached similar conclusions about the work we should be doing, agree that for us the conventional painting of the day is dead. M. Gérôme would have me sitting all day to copy antique statuary, would allow me only to compose pictures whose subjects are drawn from the most obscure historical and mythological sources. This empty rhetoric is meaningless to my studies and investigations. If I paint landscapes, he would prefer me to paint them like Poussin. And if finally as a supreme concession I were to be permitted to paint out of doors, en plein air, what exemplars am I told to follow? None other than the turgid masters of the Barbizon School, men determined to paint as if colour had never been invented. My friends at the Café Mark - a little place near to my lodgings where many of us take our meals - have a word for these painters. They are the Pluvialists, for it seems that they like nothing better than to wait till the skies cloud over before venturing forth to the woods to work in the rain, happy that the range of colour on their palettes may thereby be restricted to greys, greens and browns. What a depressing bunch, huddled together beneath their umbrellas! Their motto should be that no picture is good unless the artist caught pneumonia painting it.

Given the strength of feeling evinced in the above, it is hardly surprising that the young Hartier broke away from a conventional training before it had even begun. For the next few years he lived a Bohemian life in the avant garde of artistic Paris, a life largely centred on the Café Mark. The process of fragmentation of brush stroke remarked earlier by his mother now developed quickly into a full-blown pointillism. A series of river landscapes at Bougival on the Seine can be dated on the strength of circumstantial evidence to the early 1880s (nos. 3, 4 and 5). The artist is already handling paint in separate touches of strong primary colour. Hartier's development during this period is illuminated sporadically by a diary which he kept irregularly between 1879 and 1886.

26 July 1881. How do we see? How can we most closely

reproduce on canvas what we see? These questions absorb me to the exclusion of all else. I have been stimulated by my reading of a book which has recently come into my possession, an extremely interesting book by an Englishman named David Sutter on the phenomena of vision. I have myself begun to record notes towards a theory of colour in painting, based on my personal experience and practice. There is such a hunger within me to write, to record my instincts and my findings about these matters, that when Helène came knocking on my door last night I sent her away again. Her pride was hurt, no doubt, and perhaps I will not see her again. She is no better than a slut, anyway.

18 October 1882. I talked with Seurat again briefly at the Café Mark. He is sympathetic, intelligent and resourceful, and we see with the same vision on many matters. Our paths cross at many points. I recommended to him the scientific research of Charles Henry, work of which he knew but has not yet studied. I know he will find it as relevant as I have.

25 June 1884. Seurat, whom I had not seen for some time, finally took the opportunity to visit my studio last week. I think that he found the experience a revealing one, and he has written me a kind and generous letter expressing his admiration for what I have achieved. He said he had not realised what progress I had made, and he kept repeating that he had learned much as he left me. He particularly liked the two coastal landscapes rejected by the jury last year, and the river landscape with the distant windmill (no. 12?) which Durand-Ruel failed to sell. Failure and rejection have a cumulatively depressing effect; but words of praise from a critic as perceptive as Seurat compensate surely for a thousand rejections from short-sighted juries. Tomorrow I have promised to send Seurat a copy of my own notes on the theory of colour, including my attempt at a synthesis of the scientific and the aesthetic elements. Having listened to my brief resumé of my findings, he pleaded with me for the chance to read in detail of my conclusions and acknowledged that he had much to learn from me.

Hartier's written colour theory is a large subject and needs separate and detailed analysis. It exists in three hand-written volumes, whose editing and publication are of the highest priority. What seems likely to emerge from their close study is the extent, hitherto unsuspected, that they influenced Seurat's own colour theory. Hartier may speak modestly of paths crossing at many points, but there is reason to believe that Hartier's path was the first to be trodden. He brought a scientist's training to bear, and this qualification, coupled with his own considerable artistic talent and experience, lent him unique authority. He writes persuasively, lucidly and intelligently, and Seurat cannot have read what he wrote without, even subconsciously, absorbing many of his conclusions.

But other events, even more significant to the course of Hartier's life and work, were now taking place. Again his diary provides the most immediate record of developments:

> llth December 1884. At the Café Mark last night was Constance Lesrel, and I talked with her extensively for the first time. I knew some of the details of her past life already: that she was a widow, her husband having died two years ago. (He was the journalist Alphonse Lesrel who on one occasion mentioned my picture favourably in the short-lived Revue des Arts Modernes, and on others wrote kindly about Seurat). Madame Lesrel is certainly a women one does not forget. She holds strong views about painting and literature, and she is not afraid to give them expression. There is a fieriness about her and a passion which I find exciting, although Jacques finds her excessively dogmatic.
>
> 19 December 1884. Constance came to the studio yesterday. I found myself strangely nervous in anticipation of her arrival. But when she came she was more than flattering, indeed such was her praise and enthusiasm that I could be forgiven for holding rather a high opinion of myself today. It is comforting to gain a reaction like this from someone whose judgement I respect, after all the rejections of late, and the general criticism in the press of the aims of Pointillism, Tachism, or whatever -ism the ignorant journalists choose to stigmatise us with.
>
> 15 May 1885. A glorious early summer day. Constance and I caught the train to Bougival, she providing a hamper of the most delicious food and wine which we consumed in a field overlooking

> the river. Constance has convinced me that I should not submit any work to exhibitions this year. She says that if the contemporary public are so blind that they cannot appreciate the merit of what I am doing, if their credit and approbation are withheld, then that public should be denied the benefit of seeing my work at all for the time being. She is most vehement on this point, and no doubt she is right. I will therefore hold myself out of the public view, but continue privately to work as arduously as before on my painting and on my scientific research, and pray that the climate of ignorance changes.

> 17 August 1885. Constance and I were married today. our happiness is unclouded, except marginally by Mama's strange coldness.

More light is thrown on Celeste Hartier's 'strange coldness' towards her son and his newly-wed wife by the following letter from Celeste Hartier to her sister Marie:

> 22 August 1885. Well, it is done, and my little Claude has been taken from me, as I always knew he would. Yet I cannot find it within me to be entirely happy with his choice of bride. She is already nearly 40 (an exaggeration: she was 35 - Ed.), and that alone should surely have made them think twice before hastening into matrimony. She is strong-willed, opinionated, and I think a little unbalanced, but Claude follows her with a dog-like devotion. I cannot think that good will come of this union and I fear her influence on Claude's painting. She will turn him into something he was not intended to be. I am afraid for their future together, but of course I wish them happiness.

Within three years Claude and Constance Hartier had withdrawn from Paris. They settled in Provence in the house that was to be their home until their respective deaths, Claude in 1901 and Constance in 1933. Claude lapses into silence: his journal finishes in 1886 but, as if to compensate, Constance became the most assiduous diarist for the rest of her life. Was it in any sense an unwilling exile submitted to by Claude under the influence of the superior will of his wife? We cannot be sure, but Constance's account leaves the reader in no doubt that everything which took place was for Claude's own good. Again brief extracts will serve to outline the developments of the following years:

1 January 1888. We are happy here and can greet the new year with optimism. It is cold, but not so cold as it would be in Paris now. Claude's health is better: his bronchial complaint of last year has not repeated itself. And I have no doubt that when the summer comes and the sun shines the richer colours of the south will be an enormous stimulant to his work. It was right to remove ourselves from Paris, where what one may call the Art Establishment, that absurd group of men endowed with no artistic sensibility but connected by immense mutual vested interest, has never even tried to understand Claude's work. His hour will come. Meanwhile he can work and write in peace.

22 June 1890. My fortieth birthday. The question of having children was raised again yesterday, and I had to make the situation clear once more to Claude. Conception is not a possibility for me on medical grounds, and anyway children would be a distraction from the main business of our lives here, which is Claude's work.

11 September 1895. Claude returned this evening from his mother's funeral in a predictably melancholy mood. My absence was not, apparently, commented upon. It was better that I should not go, for the Hartier family have never really accepted me. The journey to Normandy took Claude through Paris for the first time for some years, and he stayed the night there last night. It was the first time he had been back since Georges (Seurat) died, and seeing his old haunts made him sad. Passing the Café Mark, he recognised no-one. Then this morning he called on Signac, but he was on the point of going out and they did not have much time to talk. I never liked Signac much. It makes my blood boil to think how the history of art of our time will be written in the future. No doubt Georges and Signac will have a long chapter devoted to them, but what of Claude? What injustice if he appears only as a footnote to the chapter on the other two! In the beginning they relied on him, were inspired by him even.

13 February 1901. The old trouble has returned and Claude's chest is worse than ever. He is too weak to get out of bed, and I must nurse him constantly, although Madame Lecartier calls sometimes to help. He always used to say in jest that the fact that I was nine years his senior would consign him to several years unloved and untended old age after my demise. How I wish I could be sure that this would be so. He is not well, and I fear for the future.

20 March 1901. Claude, my one and only love, died this morning at 6.30. Madame Lecartier was there, and Dr Goubie was summoned, but he came too late. No priests. My heart breaks, my life is at an end.

Despite Constance's protestation, her life continued for another 33 years, amply recorded in the pages of her journal. But at this point we should pause to ask, what was the nature of the last thirteen or fourteen years of Claude Hartier's life, the period of Provençal exile, or hermit-like seclusion? There is no evidence to suggest that he went to Paris more than three or four times throughout this period, and then only for brief, fleeting visits. He withdrew, and was to all intents and purposes forgotten by the time he was thirty. Did he ever actually sell a picture? Presumably one or two in the early Paris days, but after 1885 when Constance ordered him to cease exhibiting, to stop all contact with disturbing elements like juries, critics, art dealers and collectors there can have been little or no contact with prospective buyers. It seems that the work he did must have stayed with him in his studio, then come with him to exile in Provence. The four Provençal landscapes of which we know (nos. 19, 20, 21 and 22) presumably post-date 1888 and his withdrawal there. The vast majority of his life's oeuvre must, therefore, have been left in the studio when he died, an agglomeration of pictures which were latterly unstimulated by outside contact. We cannot yet know definitely, given the present lack of rediscovered examples, but it seems likely that the work of this last period grew somewhat repetitive and stale, while the innovative excellence of certain pictures dates them to the early phase of Hartier's working life.

The situation is undoubtedly complicated by the behaviour of Constance in the declining years of her widowhood. Again extracts from her journal provide the best evidence for her state of mind and her consequent actions:

> 15 September 1910. Xavier Vernon, our old friend from the Café Mark, appeared suddenly on the doorstep after all these years. He had driven here by motor car, the most extraordinary machine, all the way from Paris. He asked to see Claude's pictures, and I took him into the studio. He was appreciative and made many compliments, saying that he always felt sure Claude was one of the great innovators of the 1880s. Then he asked if he might buy one or two canvases. I refused, of course. I tried to explain that it would be wrong for me to release them now. The world is not yet ready to understand Claude's full achievement, and it would only do his reputation harm if a few of his pictures passed into general circulation at the present moment. People would be inclined to pass him off as a mere follower of Georges, which would be a travesty of the truth. As M. Vernon left he gave me his card asking me to let him know when he could buy one or two. He pointed to the general acclaim with which Georges' work is now greeted, bought by the national authorities and even American collectors. To protect Claude's memory, to ensure that his pictures make their full and proper impact when the right time comes, they must be held together and not dispersed. "Madame Hartier, you are a women with a mission," said M. Vernon. He is right.
>
> 8 April 1922. Madame Lecartier came to visit me again, and we had another fascinating conversation about the spirit world. She is an authority on the subject, having a natural sympathy. Those who have crossed over find her an excellent medium for communication, it seems. This is a marvellous gift.
>
> 3 May 1923. Another seance with Aimée (Lecartier). Claude spoke to me again, it is a miracle. I asked him if he was happy and he told me yes, except for one anxiety which exercises his mind and distracts him in the place to which he has gone. How I wish I could learn what this concern is. Whenever I ask him, something holds back the answer. Today the signals grew weaker and Aimée awoke suddenly and unexpectedly from her trance. It

is frustrating beyond words.

31 July 1923. At last Claude has spoken his heart to me. Our plan was successful: for three weeks we have forsworn all contact with the spirit world, in order that we might return to the quest refreshed and strengthened. He told me what it is that causes him anguish. He said it is his painting, that there are some canvases left in the studio which he wishes he had not executed because they do not do him justice. He broods on these, and has a horror of fretting about them eternally. The remedy is in my hands.

15 October 1923. Claude came to me again last night in my dreams. I no longer need the agency of Aimée in order to achieve contact with him. He told me of two more landscapes which he particularly regretted having painted. This morning I entered the studio and recognised immediately the ones he meant. It was not difficult to burn them, hateful objects. I trust Claude rests happier now.

14 December 1923. In the studio again this morning. Six more pictures came to hand, six more which Claude would never have wished to survive him. Thank God I have been granted this communication with him so that I now intuitively understand which work does him no justice for posterity. I burned them in the yard.

22 March 1924. Another bonfire. The flames clean and clarify. Every unworthy picture that I dispose of means that there is one less distraction to distort or impair Claude's achievement. Because of my purifying, Claude Hartier's light, hitherto hidden under a bushel, will at some future point shine forth with total clarity. A future generation will reap the benefit.

8 November 1926. To the studio again this afternoon. Claude was waiting for me, to congratulate me on the beautiful works I have chosen to preserve, pictures which crystallise his art. I sensed from his aura that he was pleased with me, that I had created a suitable monument for him with the pictures I have permitted to survive. Then he left, and I settled to the task of

adding his initials to the few remaining canvases not already signed. My work gives me satisfaction.

Constance Hartier died on 2nd February 1933, a rambling and incoherent old lady whose last years had been marked by increasing mental instability. She died intestate. The Hartier studio, such as it was after her depredations, was dispersed and split up between three distant cousins. Since that time a certain number of canvases have found their way, by various routes, into the hands of discerning collectors, and the process of Claude Hartier's reassessment, his long-awaited rediscovery as envisaged by Constance, has been set in motion. The recent appearance of portions of Hartier family correspondence and diaries will quicken and intensify research.

The 28 extant oil paintings identified by the present author represent only a small proportion of the artist's oeuvre. How many more remain to be rediscovered depends on the true extent of Constance's destructive urge. Her awful epitaph may well prove to be that in her anxiety to preserve her husband's artistic integrity, she succeeded in destroying all but the tip of the iceberg of his achievement, obscuring a full understanding of a very great painter.

TEN

The stewardess appeared from behind her alcove in the Business Class section of the Transatlantic Jumbo jet with a pre-selected, concretised grin of welcome set upon her face, a grin which represented not so much an expression of genuine emotion as a hefty tribute to American dentistry. She surveyed her cabin with a brisk and practised eye; Ewan Connard watched proceedings warily from his front row window seat, hiding himself as far as possible behind a copy of The Spectator. The aircraft began to taxi backwards off its stand in lengthy preparation for its ultimate take-off, and apparently taking this as a symbol of the cutting of ties with British culture, a signal to allow the American way of life to assert itself, the stewardess moved resolutely forward.

"Hi!" she exclaimed, accosting a front row passenger. "I'm Janie-Lou and it's my pleasure and privilege to be caring for you on your flight this afternoon. Whatever is your need, you have only to ask. What's your name?"

Ewan moved his journal into a yet firmer position of defence from these regrettable exchanges. Aggressive friendliness from stewardesses was an unavoidable hazard of travel on an American airline; but aggressive friendliness which demanded passenger response was transforming the exercise from mere error of taste into the realms of refined torture.

"Hi, Janie-Lou!" replied the passenger in delighted and strident mid-Western tones. He did not appear to share Connard's reservations. On the contrary, his burly frame was thrust forward towards her, restrained only by the constrictions of the seatbelt from offering actual physical embrace. Under the circumstances they had to satisfy each other merely with an orgy of handshaking, laughter and general bonhomie. "My name's Kent, Kent Peach from Columbus, Ohio. And I can see you're some little lady."

"Well, thank you Kent. And may I serve you with a cocktail just as soon as we are airborne? What would be your pleasure?"

Kent opted for a Scotch. Then, to Ewan's horror, the stewardess moved along the line to his own next-door neighbour. Surreptitiously eyeing her lithe form and well-groomed blond hair, part of Ewan's brain noted that at another time and in another place she would not have been at all unattractive; but her present manner and activity was utterly anaphrodisiac, rendering her to all intents and purposes devoid not only of sexuality but even of humanity. Could it be that this dreadful golden-locked automaton was going to subject every passenger in the cabin to the same deeply embarrassing catechism?

"Hi! I'm Janie-Lou. Your comfort will be my pleasure for the next eight hours. It's my aim to make your flight unforgettable. And what's your name?"

Connard's neighbour had already removed jacket, tie and cufflinks to reveal hairy forearms and a wealth of chunky male jewellery about his wrists. He too registered seemingly boundless satisfaction at the approach of Janie-Lou, greeting her as if she were his first human contact after three years on a desert island. "Well, hi there! I'm Morton, but you just go ahead and call me Mort."

"Welcome, Mort! That's mighty fine of you. I know we're going to get along real great. What cocktail would be your pleasure?"

Ewan took yet more resolute refuge behind his magazine, but its protection was pitifully inadequate. He peered desperately up to see if his seat was next to one of those exits from which one might quickly activate the emergency chute, but no such relief was offered. The concrete smile loomed over him.

"Hi! I'm Janie-Lou. My priority on this flight is your personal comfort. And who are you?" Ewan was uncomfortably aware of several heads turning enthusiastically in his direction the better to grasp this intelligence. He mumbled sullenly:

"Dr Connard."

"What's that? Pardon me, I didn't catch it."

"Dr Connard." He spoke louder, through clenched teeth.

"C'mon, doc, no need to stand on ceremony. Our airline aims to help you relax and have a fun flight. What's your first name?"

Ewan solemnly vowed never to patronise this airline again. If it were in his power, he would see it into bankruptcy, receivership, and extinction. He hoped all the chief executives would sustain massive coronaries. "Ewan," he admitted.

"Pardon me, that's a kinda funny name. Could you repeat it a little louder?"

"Ewan!" bellowed Connard, Fury suddenly outweighing Embarrassment.

"OK, Ian, no need to shout. We send the rowdies to the back of the craft. And what will be your pleasure drinkwise after take-off?"

For half an hour Connard was too angry to do anything but glower out of his window. However, calmed by three glasses of champagne, he gradually began to think more peaceable thoughts. He reflected on America and Americans. Despite Janie-Lou, there were many aspects of American life which appealed to him. He made a mental inventory of some of the advantages as he perceived them. He liked the comfort, the efficiency of things, the wealth, the fat fee checks for lectures, the adulation excited by his own suave brand of European scholarship, the climate, the drinks, and many of the tanned and healthy long-legged women. For these reasons his present enterprise stimulated him: he was embarking on a six-week lecture tour starting at the University of Chicago, taking in various other seats of learning, and finishing - climaxing, in fact - in a seminar at the Dwight Dobman Convention Hall, San Pietro, California, where he was booked to deliver a paper entitled 'New Light on Luminism: Divisionism Reappraised'. This would leave him handily placed for a few days' holiday before undertaking the round of interviews to which he had also consented, after which the Governors of the Museum of Fine Art would announce the name of the new director. He had every confidence that that name would be Ewan Connard. And from then on his Destiny would be closely tied to the Land of the Free. It was an exciting prospect, so long as he could minimise contact with manifestations of that strand in the American psyche which craved unbridled 'relating', particularly of air hostesses to passengers and vice versa, unfettered personal expression, the employment of shrinks, in short any aspect of the ceaseless quest for the Self which might become embarrassingly revelatory. He trusted that there would be a paucity of Janie-Lous, Kents and Morts, and a consequent disinclination to "let it all hang out", in the rather more rarefied circles in which he planned to move.

He pulled out his lecture notes and studied them. As always, to read what he had himself written gave him inordinate satisfaction. There could be no doubt that he was blessed with exceptional felicity of style combined with incisive clarity of thought, although he said it himself. Deeply involved in one passage of particular perspicacity and mellifluity, he failed to register the approach of Janie-Lou who bore down on him bearing a document. He started as she announced:

"Pardon me, Ian, but I wonder if I may trespass on your leisure to ask you to complete this questionnaire, which will help us to even further improve the service you enjoy when you next travel on our airline."

He looked up at the implacable whiteness of her teeth and decided immediately on the line of least resistance. "Of course," he said.

"That's mighty good of you, Ian. I'll be back later to collect it."

He contemplated the piece of paper she left with him. It demanded a variety of personal information about his background, business experience, and financial capability. Later, he noted with relish, there was a section in which you were allowed to offer your assessment of the quality of service received in the cabin, and after that to express your opinion of the airline in general. The best could be saved to last; he made a start on the first section. He dealt with Automobiles, number in household, regretfully confessed that his income was less than 150,000 dollars per annum, admitted that his main residence possessed neither a swimming pool nor a jacuzzi; then he paused over 'Commodity in which your business deals'. As a writer and art historian, he felt that the appropriate answer to his was 'Art and Letters', which he duly inscribed, smirking a little at the confusion this data would create in the Airline Consumer Department computer. At this point he was suddenly aware of Mort, leaning over the armrest to follow what he wrote with intensified interest.

"Hey! I caught a glimpse of what you put down there. You're from England, I guess?"

"I am," said Ewan shortly.

"Then I reckon we may be in the same line of business."

"Really?" This was too much: Mort, an art historian? Dear God, he was probably a colleague of Professor Throg at North Dakota.

"I'm also in medical supplies. Got my own distribution company out in Santa Barbara. Of course we deal in what you Brits call letters, too, but we call them Rubbers."

"Rubbers?"

"Yeah, rubbers, you know, condoms. Reckon we all hit the jackpot this past year or two. I guess you guys in Europe probably found the same. I mean the way I see it, this Aids thing was sent by God to punish the gays and make you and me a fortune."

"No, really, you don't understand..."

"Well, maybe I don't go big on all that liberal crap about the fairies, I admit it. You gotta realise, I'm a Christian, I don't care who knows it, and the Bible tells us that what those gays are doing ain't right. You stand up for them if you want to, but I say it's a punishment they called down on their own heads. And the good guys - that's us - finally get the chance to clean up. Take this line here: we just launched it, and it's going down a bomb, coast to coast. It's called Raunch. Here, I got a three-pack in my briefcase, take a look. Maybe you could market them in the UK? Try them out, take the sample, my compliments."

"No, honestly..."

"C'mon, c'mon! I tell you something, you know what? They're ribbed."

"Ribbed?"

"Yeah, ribbed for extra sensation. Some dames go mad for it that way. They're yours, take them."

Ewan smiled bleakly at the eager, perspiring figure next to him and then turned resolutely away, clamping his earphones over his head. It was the only escape. He stared out of the window with great concentration, and tried to think only of his Chicago lecture. 'New perspectives on the Neo-Impressionist Circle': he was incorporating his two Hartier slides, of course, they always went down well. And two rather pretty little early Signacs he had found in a French private collection. Yes, it would be a success. He felt calmer, now, if only... if only he could eradicate the insidiously insistent image of Dr Fabia Neate-Panker consumer-testing a three-pack of Raunch. His hand tightened over his free sample and he slipped it into his pocket for future reference.

The moment Evan let himself into his room at the Hotel de Lyon that evening, he sensed that something was not right. It being his last night in Paris, he had treated himself to half a bottle of vin rouge de la maison at the little bistro where he had dined alone, but that had not unbalanced his senses or distorted his memory unduly. No, someone had been in this room while he had been away, he was sure of it. His briefcase which he had left on the chair was now on the floor, for instance. Opening it, he found his papers disarranged, although nothing missing. In his cupboard his shirts (mostly dirty) had definitely been bundled into a different shelf from the one where he had left them that morning. With a mounting sense of panic, he turned to the place where he had secreted the most precious item in his possession, the Ranchec notes on Hartier. Feverishly he pulled open the drawer of his bedside table. It was empty.

The concierge was concerned but ultimately unhelpful. The manager, summoned on Evan's insistence, was sympathetic but unable to offer much practical consolation. "I call the police, naturally, but what can they do? They have no chance to catch the thief of some sheets of paper; they will not even try. They were not worth much, I think, these papers?"

"Well, maybe not financially, but in another way they were."

"Monsieur Conrad, I am deeply sorry that this should occur here. But I must point out that articles of value are not our responsibility if they are left unprotected in our guests' rooms. We state clearly that such articles should be handed to hotel staff for keeping in the safe."

"And no-one was seen going up to my room while I was out?"

"In a busy hotel it is not possible to follow every person's movements. I repeat, my deepest apologies. Please accept a glass of cognac from the house."

The documents which had been briefly in his hands before their cruel and untimely removal had thrown Evan into a turmoil of excitement and frustration. Here was the skeleton of Ranchec's research on Hartier, partially fleshed out with snippets of information of a tantalising suggestiveness, information which had obviously not been available to Ewan Connard when he had written the article in the Burlington Magazine. That article, apart from publishing the letter from Seurat to Hartier discovered in the Bibliothéque Nationale, had given few details of the artist's actual life, but had merely dwelt at some length on the works by him which had surfaced up to that point. Now here was a series of revelations about his career, writing, and personal life, revelations which implied that they were only the visible tips of vast icebergs of source material which were in existence; documentary proof of Hartier's birth and parentage, for instance, his mother's correspondence with her sister, his own letters home from Paris, his journal of the early 1880s, and Constance Hartier's voluminous diaries. Then there were the three volumes of Hartier's scientific work on the theory of colour, not to mention Ranchec's own attempt at a catalogue raisonné of the artist's extant pictures, numbering apparently at least twenty-eight.

It all spoke of a vast resource of original evidence unearthed by Dr Louis Ranchec, a series of seams of gold unsuspected in Evan's wildest dreams. Somewhere all these diaries, letters, and writings existed, awaiting the full rigours of scholarly analysis. But where? Had Ranchec got them all with him? Conceivably; certainly he would know their whereabouts, so locating Ranchec remained the top priority. Evan was in the curious and frustrating position of having acquired a significant amount of new information about Hartier, and yet being absolutely bereft of proof that this information was correct. These were not revelations which he could authoritatively share with the rest of the art world. The evidence for them was non-existent without Ranchec. And now that even the outline of Ranchec's research had been taken from him, he was reliant upon the few odd notes he had jotted down in the shell-shocked excitement of his first reading of the text.

Who had burgled his room? As he lay in bed that night, nursing the emotional tenderness of privacy invaded and thinking over the varied events of his stay, the realisation gradually dawned on him that this was no casual petty larceny, no sneak thief making the most of an unexpected opportunity. It had been an operation directed to one end only, that of acquiring the Ranchec notes on Hartier. And of course there was one obvious suspect: the rat-like features of St Jacques returned to him with shocking clarity. There was the man. But of course his guilt would be impossible to prove. What could Evan do? He might beard him in his gallery tomorrow, accuse him outright of the theft and demand the restitution of the notes. But he could imagine the outraged denial which would ensue, and worse the writs for libel. Yet who else but St Jacques even knew of the existence of these pages of Ranchec's research? Only Sylvie. Ah, Sylvie.

The next morning before he checked out, he telephoned her again. There was no reply.

ELEVEN

The journey from Hemel Hempstead to Leatherby House in Leicestershire was a reasonably direct one, straight up the A1, but for the Wheales on that momentous Friday evening it presented a number of aggravations. It had been a wet and miserable January day, most of which had been spent by Ron in grappling with the task of modernising the computer system at Rokeby's. The auction house, with its antique ways and built-in resistance to change, had never embraced computerisation with any enthusiasm. Ron had set himself both to streamline the equipment and to impose universal literacy in its language throughout the firm. It was a challenge which would have broken lesser men, but every setback only stiffened his resolve. And this afternoon he had encountered a series of more than usually frustrating obstacles, which had necessitated his leaving rather later than he had planned. The result was that he had been caught in the rush-hour traffic and his arrival at Sterlings to pick up Janet had been delayed forty-five minutes, a delay which had the apprehensive Janet hoping against hope that he might have sustained a minor motor accident, the sort that caused no lasting physical damage but was just serious enough to rule out their participation in the coming weekend. Cancellation, however, was very far from Ron's plans, and as they negotiated interminable contra-flow systems his mood alternated between suppressed excitement and frantic impatience.

"You realise, Janet, that we're on the verge of a major breakthrough, both socially and careerwise," he informed her, accelerating feverishly into the fast lane on a rare piece of clear road.

"Of course, dear." She paused uncertainly and added: "Ron?"

She could see his knuckles tighten in exasperation as he gripped the wheel through his Nigel Mansell "Grand Prix" simulated-leather driving gloves. "Yes?"

"There's something I've been wondering: will there be valets and chambermaids unpacking our things? And if there are, do we tip them? And if we do, how much do we tip them?"

"Don't worry about that. I'll deal with it."

"And Ron, all these foreigners who are going to be there - how well do you know them? I mean, are they quite... quite trustworthy?" In the back of Janet's mind still lurked uneasy memories of the Don

Juans and Casanovas who prowled at night about the corridors of country houses in the more lurid novels and memoirs she had read.

"The only foreigners who'll be staying there are the von Tortrops, Flipsi and Grizelda, and Cyrille de la Guerre. How could there be anything untrustworthy about Flipsi or Cyrille, they both work for Rokeby's. You're getting yourself into a state for no reason at all."

They left the A1 and took to the Leicestershire lanes. Much, much too soon for Janet's liking they found themselves passing through wrought iron gates and up the drive of Leatherby. As they pulled to a halt in front of the imposing 19th century Gothic facade of the house, she took a deep breath. The ordeal had begun.

There was a speedy unpacking of the car, Ron's precious gun being handled with particular care and reverence, and a dumping of luggage in their bedroom. Janet just had time to register with relief the absence of valets and ladies' maids, and to cast a swift last-minute glance at her W.H. Smith backgammon board, before hastening down for drinks before dinner in the drawing room. A large fire was burning and two Labradors slept in front of it with splendid abandon, impervious to the feet of the assembled guests as they shuffled around them. As they entered the room, Melissa Fairbanks came forward to meet them.

" Ron, how delightful to see you," she said coolly. With a well-judged degree of icy formality she pecked him on his cheek. "And this is Janice, of course."

"Janet," corrected Janet in a weak voice, but she was transfixed by the problem of whether or not to kiss Melissa in the manner of her husband's example. She lurched forward with her cheek extended, only to find her midriff encountering the iron impact of her hostess's outstretched hand. She recovered in time to clutch at this with her own, steadying herself in the process.

"Now, who don't you know?" continued Melissa, gliding smoothly over Janet's embarrassment. "Can I introduce you to Bill and Antonia White-Watney, and Peter and Jemima Claydon?" Bill was a heavily-built balding man who laughed loudly and heartily at the slightest provocation, while his wife was small and bird-like and greeted them with a long-suffering frostiness.

Jemima Claydon, on the other hand, brayed and drawled to such an extent in enunciating the four simple words 'How do you do?' that Janet wondered momentarily if she was perhaps an actress hired to play the role of an upper class lady on a weekend in the country, but rejected the idea on the grounds that no actress could get away with being quite as ham as this. Here was the real thing: truth was indeed stranger than fiction. Peter Claydon was slim, smooth and fair-haired, and looked rather younger than his wife. Ron greeted them all regardless with the greatest bonhomie: "Pleased to meet you, Bill and Antonia; how are you, Peter? Are you well, Jemima?"

Melissa ferried them on to the next group. "Of course, Ron, you know Flipsi and Grizelda, and Evan Conrad. This really is quite a little Rokeby's gathering, isn't it? And there's Cyrille over there, talking to Freddy in the corner. But can I introduce you both to Erica Mannering?"

More handshakes. Flipsi von Tortrop was head of Rokeby's Germany and was over from Munich. His looks suggested that he would have made an excellent Panzer Division Commander, although there was a certain fleshiness about the jaw and puffiness about the eye which told of several years' opulent entertaining on the Rokeby's expense account. He prided himself on his aptitude for idiomatic English but he still spoke with a strong accent. When in doubt in England it was his policy always to tell a joke about the war. He believed it broke the ice, softened any residual hard feelings. His wife wore an ostentatious amount of jewellery. Evan Conrad seemed to Janet the most sympathetic fellow guest, being at least quiet and unobtrusive. Erica Mannering, however, was a thoroughly alarming proposition. She clutched a cigarette and a large gin and tonic, undoubtedly not her first of the evening, and surveyed proceedings with bloodshot eyes. She had tired blond hair, wore a lot of make-up, and spoke in a loud, hectoring voice.

"Just back from the Caribbean," she announced. "Bloody airline was four hours late, of course, but at least the booze was free, that helped pass the time. Then a damned cheeky steward tried to pick me up."

Janet nodded sympathetically.

"You know the West Indies, then, Mrs Wheale?"

Janet was about to disclaim any experience of the area when she was astonished to hear her husband interrupting: "Not this year, sadly, Erica, but we generally try to fit in a couple of weeks there in February. That's when I find the batteries are most sorely in need of recharging, when one really appreciates a break in the sun."

"Ah so. But we have a preference for the skiing," declared von Tortrop. "You are perhaps skiers also, Ronald?"

"Most certainly," exclaimed Ron, flexing his knee joints in a grotesque motion intended to indicate his easy familiarity with countless black runs. "But this year, with all my extra responsibilities at Rokeby's, again it has not been possible. Verbier will just have to wait."

"Cyrille de la Guerre was telling me earlier that he skis a lot at Verbier," volunteered Evan.

Flipsi instantly assumed an expression of contemptuous amusement. "Monsieur de la Guerre is prone to exaggeration. His experience of skiing is on a lower level than my own. He is fundamentally what we should call a creature of the city." Von Tortrop directed his gaze disdainfully towards his colleague for a moment. Cyrille de la Guerre, unaware of the interest with which he was being inspected, continued to converse with Freddy in animated fashion. The Frenchman, it was true, was dressed in clothes altogether too English to be English. His tweed jacket was cut with a shade too much elegance, and his corduroys were ironed to an impeccable crease. Flipsi sniggered meaningfully to underline his point: to any right-thinking man Cyrille was something of a figure of fun.

"You know it's really been incredible," continued Ron, unabashed, "the volume of business this year. As I say, holidays will just have to wait. But I think the results so far have more than justified the effort put in." There was a pause, and Ron smiled disarmingly about him. "You know, you'll all have to bear with me as far as Rokeby's is concerned. I'm not ashamed to admit that I'm just a little bit proud of what we've achieved."

At this point Freddy and Cyrille joined them. "Now then, Ron," chided Freddy, "I heard your voice wafting over holding forth about Rokeby's. We have to listen to quite enough about that subject during the week. As you can imagine," he added playfully to the rest of the group, "Ron is an absolute slave-driver. But I understand he's no slouch with a gun, either, so we're all looking forward to seeing him in action tomorrow."

Ron made a modest gesture, as if to suggest concern only for the large number of birds destined to meet their maker through his agency on the morrow. But Erica was becoming fretful, and inquired aggressively of her host: "Where are the drinks, Freddy? No, don't you mix me another, you're so damned mean with the gin. I'll do it myself." She swayed off to accomplish her mission.

"Poor girl," observed Freddy. "Just been through her second divorce, a bloody messy business, so you have to make allowances. She's Melissa's oldest friend, absolutely devoted to her."

"Ja, divorce is always regrettable," said Grizelda von Tortrop. "In Munich we haff had staying viz us in our house for some weeks the Princess Heidelburg while she recovers from her separation from dear Prince Georg. They are both such old friends of ours, you know."

"Hoch!" Everyone turned in the direction of this Gallic exhalation, emanating from the lips of Cyrille de la Guerre. "That is nothing! The uncle of my mother, who before the war was on two separate occasions the foreign minister of Bulgaria, was divorced five times." He looked round in some triumph. He was a thin, fastidious, distinctly precious man in his late forties, animated by few things in life, but the opportunity to drop names was one of them. Clearly he felt that the Foreign Minister of a Balkan state to whom one could claim a relationship of blood outranked easily mere friendship with minor German royalty.

But von Tortrop himself was roused, and not in a mood to admit defeat. "It is interesting you speak of Bulgaria. My family once had vast estates there. In fact we were dining last month at the Wurtemburgs, and when the topic arose it transpired that my family had estates in more countries than any other family represented at that table. You will understand that this is no mean achievement when I tell you that also dining that evening were Hohenlohes, Schwarzenburgs...."

De la Guerre interrupted the flow of names with a renewed offensive of his own: "You are acquainted of course with the old Vicomtesse de St Antoine, who is related by marriage to three different Royal Families?"

Flipsi trod warily, sensing a trap. "I may have met her once at cocktails in Monte Carlo."

"My stepfather's sister," said Cyrille simply, executing the coup de grace.

Ron listened impatiently to these exchanges and now broke in: "I'm sorry, Freddy, but did you get time to look through the systems analyses I left on your desk at lunch time? They were particularly significant in relation to the specific demands of the valuations department." Freddy raised his eyes to the heavens in a gesture of mock despair at Ron's question, a gesture which nonetheless only thinly disguised his real annoyance. "My God, Ron, you know I'm never at my desk after lunch on a Friday. Be reasonable."

Ron continued jovially to the company at large: "You see what I'm up against! I'm trying to drag Freddy's working methods into the 20th century! I sometimes wonder if he knows a floppy disk from a .... a French letter!"

There was general polite or nervous laughter. Janet was slightly shocked by Ron. She could not accept that birth control accessories were a fit subject for the Fairbanks' drawing room. She would definitely have a word with him later. Evan too, for different reasons, felt distinctly ill at ease. It was impossible to relax being closeted with so many of his Rokeby's elders and betters on such unfamiliar territory. Still, he was determined not to be overawed. He sensed the annoyance of Freddy whose ban on talk about Rokeby's had just been flouted by Ron, so, casting about for any topic of mutual interest which was not concerned with the auction house, he turned to Janet and said:

"You know, Mrs. Wheale, by a strange coincidence I think your husband and I have a friend in common."

"Who's that?" asked Janet, happy to deflect the conversation away from her husband's smutty talk.

"His name's Roger Brady. He was my flatmate when I was studying at the Institute, and I think he's your husband's dentist."

"Oh, yes, that's right!" Janet beamed with recognition. "Ron went to him rather a lot last year." She turned to her husband. "Just talking about Roger Brady, dear, your dentist."

Ron paled. This was truly dangerous ground. On the innocent promptings of his wife, Evan Conrad was apparently about to reveal to the assembled company dental secrets of the most sensitive kind. The existence of his dental plate was information which must be suppressed at all costs. Its revelation would shame him beyond words, and he was bitterly and sharply aware of Evan Conrad's power to destroy him, a power with which Conrad might or might not now be taunting him. Taking no chances he said loudly to von Tortrop and de la Guerre: "Of course, you've heard the news of Evan's superb achievement in Paris in November? It's thanks to him that we have the

Wattle collection for sale. It should be a memorable occasion."

"Ja, Ja, it is very good," agreed Flipsi. "Fortunately I have personally many excellent connections with the newspapers and magazines in Bavaria, and I shall secure the widest publicity for this sale."

"And I," added de la Guerre, "have arranged a feature on ze sale for French television. I had dinner with the owner of the Fifth Channel last week."

The question of whether Flipsi or Cyrille presided over the more efficient publicity machine diverted everyone's attention from Roger Brady, and Ron relaxed again.

"You must tell us, Evan," Flipsi was saying, "which of the collection is the star piece?"

"Well, I suppose the most valuable could be the Cézanne still life," ventured Evan, flinching somewhat at the thought of the huge estimate he had put on it. "It's certainly a very beautiful example."

"Cézanne, did you say?" The name seemed to be causing Cyrille some excitement. "As it happens, I have the most ravishing Cézanne hanging in my own dining room. Many of my guests have been kind enough to say that it is the best they have ever seen in a private residence. Only last month when the Director of the Metropolitan Museum and the Marquis de Besançon were dining...."

"But don't talk to me about those things," cut in Flipsi abruptly. "You should have seen the magnificent Monets, two of them, which my father before the war bought in Paris." Cyrille looked as though nothing could have interested him less than the acquisitions of von Tortrop senior, but Freddy asked politely:

"What happened to them? I don't recall having ever seen them hanging in your house in Munich."

"Ve haff to compliment the RAF," replied Flipsi roguishly.

"Oh, I don't quite follow."

"Ja, ve haff to compliment them for their very accurate bombing. They managed to destroy both pictures in a raid in late 1944." He heaved with laughter at Bomber Command's recklessness.

"Shall we go through to dinner?" suggested Melissa diplomatically.

Later the men stayed at the table over brandy and cigars while the ladies withdrew. Evan's initial unease was being gently allayed by a steady intake of alcohol; he was prepared now even to savour the situation, to indulge in a little surreptitious self-congratulation. Gone were the bad old days of life as a penurious research student, gone were the days of Chinese takeaways, gone even was the Flexilon suit. He fingered for reassurance the rather better cut grey affair in which he was now clad. He was sitting at the dining table of the Hon. Freddy Fairbanks, on a shooting weekend at Leatherby, smoking his host's cigars. He had penetrated to the innermost core of the Establishment, and he relished the cosiness of it all. He filled his brandy glass again and silently toasted Rokeby's for making it all possible. There was a pleasant sense of being drawn into a club, whose members were all sustained by the same values and beliefs, partook of the same affluence, and supported each other instinctively in the confidence of their unspoken communality of interest.

"Stock market's been giving us some anxious moments recently, hasn't it?" declared Bill White-Watney to him in a man-to-man sort of way which presumed a sizeable investment on Evan's part and therefore common ground on which to commiserate.

"An unpredictable time," offered Evan knowledgeably.

"Still, the art market's holding up all right, isn't it?''

Evan agreed it was. In his present mood of mellowness he would have agreed to most propositions. Now his companion continued: "Bloody good racket you're in, I must say. I am a complete bloody philistine about works of art, that sort of thing, but I spent a bit of time in estate agency after I came out of the army, and I can see that 1.5% on a deal is nothing compared to the 25% you chaps are taking. Crafty buggers!"

Before Evan could comment, Ron Wheale had stepped in with the speed of an American press aide protecting a maladroit president of the United States. "Of course comparisons like that are in no sense fair," he declared importantly. "The mean commission take is in fact a little under 15.5%, and with costs rising at a steady 6.3%, turnover has to increase significantly on an annual basis if margins are not to be eroded." For a moment he appeared to be reaching for a calculator from his pocket, but he caught Freddy's eye and seemed to think better of it.

On Evan's other side sat Flipsi von Tortrop, who had reached the stage in the evening when Bavarians start to move in a mist of alcoholic sentimentality. The gathering was indeed gemütlich, the only conceivable fly in the ointment being the regrettable presence of the tight-lipped and old-maidish Cyrille de la Guerre. But so long as he did not actually have to exchange words with this irritating French pansy, Flipsi was happy, content in the companionship of his British friends and colleagues, secure in the brotherhood of Good Birth which transcends national boundaries. He drew on his cigar and cast rheumy eyes on Evan, this new young star in the Rokeby's firmament, doubtless the scion of some noble British family.

"Tonight we haff a good time, ja?"

"We do," agreed Evan.

"I must tell you that it is on nights like this I think often of my old father."

"Really?"

"Ja, my father, he loved a good time: parties, drinking, singing, dancing, always our house was, as you say, bursting at the seams with guests. In Munich my father was famous for his entertaining."

Evan nodded encouragingly.

"But I tell you something." Flipsi bent his head confidentially towards Evan while disconcertingly raising his voice so that others in the vicinity might also gain the benefit of the information. "My father, he was a man of true courage; after the war, many people told me, that man, he was a hero. A hero. " A pause ensued while Flipsi blew his nose emotionally into a large handkerchief. He continued: "Whenever I hear talk of the war, I remember my father and his heroism."

Evan had not so far that evening heard any talk of the war except from the lips of Rokeby's German representative, but this was no doubt a justifiable preamble to the revelation of the nature of his father's extraordinary courage. "What did he do?"

"Ah! What did he do? What did he do? Life was not easy for him after the July plot against Hitler in '44. He suffered terribly."

"He was involved in the plot, was he?"

"Certainly he was involved. A lynch-pin. But in secret, a closely-guarded secret: few people ever knew. It had to be that way. He was one of the prime movers, although you will not find his name in the history books. He was very discreet and very brave. The pressure he was under, it must have been appalling. It was the pressure which accounted for the later regrettable incident with the Chauffeur, of course. But no man should be judged on one lapse from the highest standards."

"No, of course not."

"None of our family were ever Nazis; it was the same with most of the aristocratic Bavarian families. Those who were well bred were too proud to submit to the will of a type of such low social origins as Hitler."

At this point another distinctively Gallic expression emanated from the lips of de la Guerre, a sharp exhalation of breath conveying a measure of disbelief. "Zis is so interesting, what you tell us now," he said with heavy irony. "But I still find one thing a little hard to grasp, a fact which - how shall I say? - caught my eye the other day when I had to study the personal files of the members of the Board of Rokeby's Europe. How comes it that you were actually christened as a second name 'Adolf'?"

Flipsi smiled with weary good humour at the sheer denseness of his colleague. "Ja, that is so; but I do not use the name now. It was necessary, of course, for my father to preserve cover. I was born in '44 and naturally he could not attract attention to himself at that delicate stage by failing to name me after the Fuhrer."

Meanwhile in the drawing room Janet wondered anxiously how much longer the evening had to run. It was marginally worse to be closeted solely with the four other females of the party than to be sitting at dinner with the entire group where there was more chance of losing oneself in the general hubbub. Now there was the pressure of constantly having to make conversation; and, although she was grateful she had not yet had to pit her wits to backgammon, nonetheless the situation was trying because the topics of conversation covered areas and experiences almost completely alien to her. Jemima Claydon had expatiated to her on the difficulties of getting a backward son into Eton, the relative merits of different Osborne and Little wallpapers, and asked her opinion on various incomprehensible equine problems which were afflicting the Claydon stables. Janet had tried to look intelligent and concerned where appropriate, but her contribution had been minimal. Then Antonia White-Watney had moved over to sit next to her on the sofa, and an even more unsettling conversation had ensued as she was put through a catechism of questions about various friends of Antonia's, and whether they were known to Janet. At each admission of non-acquaintance, Janet felt her already negligible social stature ebbing away still further, until she panicked and claimed close friendship with a hitherto unknown Beryl Danvers-Douglas.

"Tragic about the accident, wasn't it?" Antonia observed.

"Dreadful," agreed Janet nervously.

"I don't like to gossip, but do you think she will ever .... you know what again?"

"She.... she might."

"Do you really think so? But, my dear, how?"

Before she had to answer, an angel of mercy in the unlikely form of Erica Mannering came to Janet's rescue. Lurching towards them with a glass of Cointreau in her hand, Erica demanded:

"Now then, what are you two gossiping about? Out with it, I know it's scandal, and I'm sure it's pretty juicy."

"Nothing at all," said Antonia quickly, signalling frantically to Janet to reveal nothing of their recent speculations. "It's really not important."

"Balls," said Erica slumping down on the sofa between them. Antonia slid quietly and discreetly away, leaving Janet to fend for herself. Erica continued: "You were talking about men, weren't you? I can always tell."

"No, really. We were just ..."

"You know what I think about men?" interrupted Erica. "I think they're all shits. Take my first husband, he was a shit of the first water."

"Was he?" Janet braced herself. Bad language always unnerved her.

"You know what? I wouldn't be surprised if he hadn't turned queer by now. After three months of marriage he was completely inactive in the bedroom. Utterly useless, showed no interest. Can you beat it? But then men are such bastards, aren't they? Richard, my second, left me in July for his secretary. His secretary, I ask you. She was called Glynis, a really third rate little cow."

"I am sorry," said Janet inadequately. This sort of revelation embarrassed her acutely It was so completely beyond the range of her normal experience that she had no idea of the right form for coping with it. Such talk really wasn't nice at all, but there seemed no way of stemming the flow, and worse Erica was by no means finished.

"Yes, Richard was a real bastard. But I seem to pick 'em. Do you know - and I'm only telling you this because I'm a little tight - he had a real problem: he couldn't get it up unless he approached from behind."

What on earth was she talking about now? wondered Janet. Erica had genuinely lost her. The phrase she had just used to describe her ex-husband's difficulties made no sense, unless perhaps it was concerned with some particularly tricky motoring manoeuvre? Janet's edginess persuaded her to clutch at the first plausible explanation her fevered brain could provide. That was it, Erica must be referring to a problem encountered in putting the car away in the garage. Gratefully, she seized at the opportunity to steer the conversation into more conventional water, and she volunteered with some animation:

"I know, my Ron has that trouble sometimes. It's because it's on a strange angle after all the alterations he had carried out at the front. He's been known to scrape the side a bit when coming in, but it's fine if he's careful. And I must say, after all the work he had done, we are the envy of the neighbourhood..."

"Well," said Erica in a tone still largely dominated by disapproval of the ways of the male sex, but not entirely unmixed with admiration, "it certainly takes all sorts. Don't you have any objection?"

"Oh, no, not really. I'm generally prepared to put up with a little inconvenience if it gives Ron pleasure. And that's the way he seems to want it."

TWELVE

Saturday was a cold grey damp day. A freezing drizzle was falling as the shooting party set out from Leatherby House, the various guests nursing a mixture of emotions and a variety of hangovers. Squelching along the track which led to the wood where the first drive would take place, Ron strode out purposefully, his gun over his arm in approved fashion. On the whole things were going well: here he was on a shoot, hobnobbing with British and Continental aristocracy, and more than holding his own. He felt he was cutting a pretty stylish figure in his shooting jacket, boots and plus-fours, and although his equipment looked just a little bit newer than the others', nonetheless he was confident he blended in. The only thing which had given him pause when dressing that morning was the question of whether or not he should be wearing a tie, and having decided the answer was yes, what sort of tie it should be. In the end he had plumped for the Hemel Hempstead Golf Club, not that it really mattered. This was the life: he sensed the primeval joy of the hunter in pursuit of his prey, relished the prospect of reassuming the role for which Nature had prepared him as a Male. Now truly he was a man of action. He set his jaw firmly, partly to emphasise his image as a sportsman who would shoot with flair and distinction, and partly to check that his dental plate was securely in place.

Behind him walked four more males, Bill White-Watney and Peter Claydon separating Flipsi and Cyrille. The atmosphere of mutual hostility between the Frenchman and the German had not cleared. They exchanged desultory conversation with their English neighbours, but apart from a curt greeting first thing in the morning they were not speaking to each other. Some of their remarks now, however, were definitely intended to be overheard by the other, being made in louder tones. Thus Flipsi addressed Peter:

"I vell remember on a shoot in Bavaria, the old prince Max (I was like a son to him, you know) told me about an absurd Frenchman who was once shooting next to him. A bird was walking along the ground about ten metres away from them, and, to the horror of the Prince, the Frenchman took aim. The prince of course made it clear that to shoot a walking bird was appalling form, and the Frenchman replied: "Oh yes, I see. I do not shoot him walking. I wait till he stop!"

Flipsi wheezed with delight at the joke, and Peter laughed politely as if it was the first time he had heard it. The shaft found its mark, however, because Cyrille de la Guerre almost immediately began telling Bill an involved story about how the Duc de Besançon had banned a particularly ill-mannered German from his shoot after he had committed a variety of betises, from flagrant poaching of other guns' birds to peeing in the chapeau of the head beater.

Behind the men the women of the party followed obediently, camp followers clad in a uniform array of huskies, Hermès scarves and green gumboots. The only sartorial deviant was Janet, who varied the effect by wearing a see-through plastic mackintosh over the new Barbour with which Ron had kitted her out. The absentees were Erica and Melissa. The former had a hangover and was not venturing out early, while Melissa remained behind to keep her company and enjoy a really good gossip like the old days.

Freddy had gone on ahead to discuss final arrangements with the keeper. The weekend was turning out fractionally worse than he had feared, and his patience with a number of his guests was wearing thin. Erica was as dreadful as ever, of course, a harridan of a woman, about whom the mystery was not why she had twice been divorced but how she had twice persuaded men to marry her in the first place. Bill White-Watney was an empty-headed pompous ass, and the Claydons really were pretty dull, although one should not forget that she was the sole heiress to a magnificent collection of English sporting pictures. For a good Stubbs one was prepared to make allowances.

Then there were the foreign representatives of Rokeby's. He had not fully realised until this weekend the extent of their mutual antipathy. Cyrille was a ridiculously affected and precious old poof, with an unshakeably high opinion of himself, and not the least vestige of a sense of humour. Flipsi's phoney anglicisms and constant references to the war were equally wearing. And the snobbery of these foreigners! It had to be heard to be believed; and most of the families with whom they seemed so anxious to establish their closeness were pretty suspect anyway, being continentals. Freddy's attitude to people who felt the need to talk perpetually of their connections in some ways mirrored Janet's to those who talked openly about sex. Janet would have agreed that such behaviour was an error of taste, although she would have drawn the line at concluding, as Freddy did now, that it also betrayed an underlying inadequacy in the area of activity under discussion.

But enough of Gallic and Teutonic pretension. There was another angle to the Rokeby's interest of the weekend, represented by Evan Conrad and the Wheales. Evan, as the rising star of the firm, the man responsible for securing for sale the glamorous and publicity-creating Wattle collection, had to be allied as far as possible with the Fairbanks faction. Freddy was confident that this would be the effect of Evan's stay at Leatherby. Young and impressionable recipients of Fairbanks hospitality, overlaid with a healthy dose of Fairbanks charm, generally came away from the experience won over to the cause. The Wheales too, by their very presence here, by their absorption of the Leatherby ethos (as if imbibing insidious doses of some debilitating gas), would be put in their place, their aspirations undermined. They would look foolish, and Ron would be made to understand the fitness of his role as a lieutenant rather than as a leader.

But, God almighty, the women this weekend! There was not one to excite a flicker of desire. It was a serious piece of mismanagement to have arranged a party so utterly devoid of female glamour or attraction. Freddy preferred to be titillated on his shoots by the company of at least one pretty and if possible accessible woman. No-one remotely met requirements on this occasion. Possibly Erica was, if pressed, accessible, but the very thought turned the stomach. Freddy grew fretful as he contemplated the absence of any viable object of amatorial pursuit. Grizelda von Tortrop? No, thank you; it would be like making love to some overblown Viennese pastry. Jemima Claydon? You might as well go to bed with a horse. Antonia, or Janet Wheale? He would part with quite large sums of money in order not to have to touch them. It was an intolerable situation.

For Evan the morning passed slowly. He spent it watching the shoot with the women, having made it clear that he had no aspiration to participation. He had thought that it would be interesting to observe the ritual, but his attention wandered. He was tired and a little depressed. Sleep had come in slabs last night, ingrained with dreams of the most vivid and colourful character from which he awoke at intervals disturbed and in need of hydration. In one he found himself pursued across a rocky terrain by a detachment of storm troopers led by Obergruppenfuhrer Flipsi von Tortrop, accompanied on his flight by the mincing figure of Cyrille de la Guerre and the unlikely combination of Freddy Fairbanks being borne along on the shoulders of a perspiring Ronald Wheale. And in another he was tantalised by a vision of the celestial and infinitely lovely form of Sylvie Legrand, the goddess who still held absolute sway over his romantic imagination. She lay languorously in bed, her limbs stretched brown and abandoned across satin sheets, turning gracefully and breathing his name: "Eevan, at last .... you have been away so long."

This accusation was scarcely fair, for, although it was now eight weeks since that momentous afternoon when he had first encountered her, it was not for want of trying on his part that he had failed to make contact with her since. He had telephoned her nine times, but on each occasion had received no reply. He had resorted to postcards, every word mulled over and considered minutely as to its appositeness and effect, but these had elicited no response either. He had even telephoned Ewan Connard in the hope of help in pinning down the whereabouts of Louis Ranchec and thus having something positive to report to Sylvie, but Connard was apparently in America for an indefinite period. Evan had relived every detail of his first and only meeting with Mademoiselle Legrand, analysed minutely every word he could recall exchanging with her, savoured every movement she had made on the sofa next to him. But where was she now?

It was ironic that this period of enormous professional success, when the congratulations on his capture of the Wattle Collection had rained in on him incessantly, should coincide with a time of such frustration in three inter-related areas of personal interest. It was all very well for people to tell him how well he had done in persuading King Wattle to sell his collection at Rokeby's, and the acclaim was gratifying, but he could not be happy so long as his pursuit of Ranchec, Hartier, and above all Sylvie made so little concrete progress. The fact that he had been granted momentary illusions of proximity to each of these goals was all the more tantalising. He had had the bones of Ranchec's research in his hands, only for it to be snatched from him. Hartier, having drifted briefly into the most thrilling focus, had been reconsigned to the world of phantoms. And Sylvie had sat next to him on the sofa, had touched his thigh with hers, only to disappear completely from his view. Now that the glossily-packaged catalogue for the sale of the King Wattle Collection was complete and no longer demanded his attention, he resolved that he would return to Paris. If necessary, he would visit Hartier's birthplace near Rouen and start from scratch, retreading the track pioneered by Ranchec. But it would obviously be easier to find Ranchec, and thereby gain full and immediate access to the correspondence and the diaries which Ranchec had dangled so temptingly in front of him. And, as he told himself yet again, finding Ranchec would be a means to the end of capturing Sylvie. Had he not told her that she should have her telephone bill paid?

But in these enterprises he was uneasily conscious of the existence of rivals, any of which might be stealing a march on him so long as he was away from Paris. His suspicion that St Jacques was the instigator of the burglary of the Ranchec notes on Hartier had hardened into certainty. That being the case, St Jacques must also be pursuing Ranchec for the ultimate goal of complete knowledge of Hartier. Perhaps he had already found him? It was too galling to contemplate the juicy fruits of the Ranchec source material falling neatly into the lap of the rodent-like dealer. By the same token, what successes might not the dreadful Guy or others like him be enjoying in the favours of Sylvie so long as Evan was not on hand to press an alternative suit? The details did not bear thinking about.

It was towards the end of the last drive of the morning that Evan's thoughts were interrupted by a strange, almost macabre sequence of events. It all happened very quickly. First came a volley of shots as a squadron of birds flew overhead and the waiting guns let fire. Looking up, Evan saw several fall from the sky, and then, transferring his gaze to ground level, observed Ron Wheale momentarily punching the air with all the uncoiled delight of a Wembley goalscorer. A direct hit on one of the unfortunate targets was apparently a sufficiently rare event to demand celebration. If this physical expression of his joy unbalanced Ron slightly, it was the next, utterly unexpected, development which knocked him horizontal. Seemingly from nowhere, but presumably from a nearby clump of trees where they had secreted themselves, five or six unearthly figures dressed in a sort of combat uniform emerged screaming shrilly, waving placards, and turning football rattles. The heftiest figure in this team made an immediate beeline for Wheale, launched itself powerfully into a flying rugby tackle, and with a sickening crunch totally incapacitated its target, successfully effecting the complete collapse in the mud of the joint deputy chairman of Rokeby's.

The assembled company was momentarily transfixed by the sudden invasion, except for Bill White-Watney who, with considerable agility, threw himself behind a bush and clasped his hands over his head. Evan, horrified, strained to read the message on one of the placards and caught sight of the coarsely-daubed words "Women Against the Murder of Birds". It struck a dreadful chord of memory, resonating into a recognition which he strove instantly to suppress. It was too awful to contemplate: surely it could not be..... The protesters were still running around like whirling dervishes, but two of the guns recovered their wits sufficiently to take retributory action. It was Freddy who, with considerable athleticism, succeeded in collaring one figure and ensnaring its arms behind its body, while Flipsi stormed across towards the captive, pointing his gun menacingly.

"Schwein!" he shouted dramatically.

"Careful with that, Flipsi," said Freddy more peaceably. "Now what's all this nonsense? Who are you?" The small, balaclava-clad figure wriggled angrily but impotently in Freddy's firm grasp. Something about the way it tossed its head with annoyance betrayed femininity, and, to Evan, an even more disquieting familiarity. My God, it surely wasn't....

"My name is Renata X, front-line operational in the War against Blood Sports. I spit on you murderers!"

Evan groaned: here was the bad dream become reality. What would the affronted guns do now? Renata's companions, seeing that she had to all intents and purposes been taken hostage, whooped and circled with decreasing conviction until one by one they melted away into the woods. Even the belligerent figure responsible for the assault on Ron joined them finally in retreat, though not without one last blood-curdling war-cry accompanied by an obscene gesture. Attention now focused on Renata, and a little circle moved in round her, some to threaten, some to remonstrate, and some merely for a closer inspection.

"Look here," said Bill White-Watney pathetically, "you've frightened the birds."

"Good! It's a lot better than killing them, you capitalist assassin."

Cyrille was the next to offer an opinion. "But zis is meant to be a civilised country. Quelle horreur! It's an outrage!"

"You're an outrage to civilisation, you froggy ponce!" countered Renata, and a momentary smile of approval could be detected on

Flipsi's features. It was on Freddy, however, that her defiance had its strangest effect. He was noticeably excited by the act of holding her back, and as he restrained her with one arm he used the other to pull off the balaclava, revealing Renata's blond, close-cropped hair. For a moment her gamin attractiveness was distinctly perceptible, and Freddy clasped her a little closer.

"You're quite a little firebrand, aren't you?" he said admiringly. "So you're registering a protest against shooting?"

"Dead right we are. A protest against organised barbarism, and also against the rotten economic and class system which supports it."

"Listen, I've got a suggestion. If I release you, will you promise not to run away?"

Renata grunted assent and shook herself free. Unexpectedly her first action was to touch her hair into place.

"Now why don't we talk this out?" continued Freddy. "Let's try a little of what you like to call dialogue. I propose that you come in now with us all for luncheon, it's just about time anyway, and then we can discuss our differences over a glass of something."

"Vot is he saying?" exclaimed an outraged von Tortrop.

"English diplomacy, old chap," Peter Claydon assured him.

"She should be shot," asserted von Tortrop firmly and marched away in disgust.

It was only at this point that one of the beaters noticed the spread-eagled figure floundering in the mud some distance away, and, identifying him as one of Mr Freddy's guests, went to his assistance. Ron was still gasping for breath: he felt as if he had been run over by a lorry.

"All right, sir?" enquired the beater as he helped him to his feet and picked up his gun.

Rather to his amazement, Ron did not appear to have fractured any bones, and he pronounced himself capable of making his own way to the house. Janet ran anxiously over to take his arm.

"You poor pet," she said solicitously. "You need a nice hot bath."

Ron gave her a rugged smile to indicate that a man of action could take such physical assaults in his stride. He was therefore disconcerted at her reaction.

"Oh my God! What's happened to your tooth? There, the front one on the right - it's missing!"

Ron clasped a hand in horror over his mouth. It was true. In his fall he had sustained serious damage to his dental plate. One tooth was missing, and other felt distinctly loose. The gaping hole would undoubtedly be the source of embarrassing speculation amongst his fellow guests. By now they had caught up with the main party, and Ron clamped his mouth shut for the time being to prevent any chance of an untoward revelation. Fortunately attention was distracted from his plight by a further extraordinary altercation now taking place. Renata X had caught sight of Evan Conrad and raised her fist in his direction.

"Class traitor!" she declared loudly.

"I say, do you two know each other?" asked Freddy with some interest.

"Up to a point," admitted Evan. He turned to Renata and addressed her as discreetly as circumstances would allow: "For God's sake, you're making a complete fool of yourself. Get out of it, you shouldn't be here."

"Shouldn't be here?" shouted Renata furiously. "I've as much right as you have to be here."

"Renata, please....... Evan felt a dreadful responsibility for the situation, but his plea for Renata to remove herself had the reverse of the desired effect. Her resolve hardened almost visibly, and she turned to Freddy.

"I shall accept your invitation to lunch, and I welcome the opportunity to put over a few points about blood sports which may help you understand how you are victims of an outmoded set of political, economic and social attitudes."

"And I welcome the opportunity of entertaining an attractive girl to lunch," said Freddy roguishly. Evan flinched, anticipating the outburst which would surely be provoked by such a blatantly sexist and exploitative remark, but he was surprised to see that while Renata did not deign to reply the ghost of a blush played about her cheeks.

"I can't help feeling that Freddy's treating this morning's incident a trifle flippantly," confided Jemima Claydon to Bill White-Watney at lunch. "I mean, I'd have thought he would have been justified in prosecuting for trespass at least rather than inviting the chief culprit to lunch."

"That's Freddy for you," said White-Watney with a shrug. "I must say, the whole attack was dreadfully sudden. I'm alert to that sort of thing, of course - in my position you have to be, particularly after the threats I received as a result of my anti-IRA speech in the spring. But when they all suddenly appeared like that, I don't mind telling you, I thought for a moment My God, this is it, and began to wish I had opted for Special Branch protection when I was offered it. That was why I ducked down so quickly, you understand. No, even though they weren't armed, this lot certainly turned out to be violent."

"That poor chap Wheale rather bore the brunt of it, didn't he? He looks a bit off colour."

"And it's not very amusing for Melissa, either. I wonder what she makes of having this subversive little troublemaker as an extra luncheon guest."

Melissa was, as usual, taking the problem in her stride. On having Renata presented to her she had reacted with polite formality and seated her between Freddy and Erica. This was a relief to Evan, whose one desire was to give Renata as wide a berth as possible; he was pleased to find himself between Antonia White-Watney and Janet Wheale on the far side of the table. Events were taking a wild and disconcerting turn. Last night he had been congratulating himself on the facility with which he had come to terms with his new surroundings, the speed with which he had found his feet in Rokeby's circles, shedding his old uncertain student way of life like an old coat. Now suddenly the old coat, in the shape of Renata, had returned to haunt him, to embarrass him in his new situation. She was a grotesque intrusion here, absurdly out of place. Why hadn't she had the sense to realise it? And yet he had to admit that since she had arrived in the house she had made one or two not insignificant concessions: she had divested herself of the balaclava and khaki-coloured boiler suit in which she had been clad for the outdoor operation, and was now dressed in a reasonably presentable black jersey and unusually tight pair of jeans, a feature of her wardrobe unknown to Evan in the days when he had been privy to it. She had also dispensed with the name Renata X, and had given her full surname when introduced to Melissa. Now she looked flushed and animated: Freddy was filling her wine glass for the second time, and alcohol almost invariably went swiftly to her head.

For Janet, Renata's presence at the lunch table confirmed a suspicion which had lurked in her mind ever since the dramatic events of the morning. She had not liked to enquire the precise significance of the band of whooping ladies who had emerged so precipitately from the trees. Anything was possible; but on balance she had been inclined to believe that they had some prearranged and time-honoured role in the ritual of the shoot. Perhaps by turning their rattles and running hither and thither in such an unpredictable fashion they were in some way encouraging the birds to fly higher and thereby providing the "guns" with better "sport" (these were terms she had assimilated already). Quite why one of their number had found it necessary to launch herself into such a ferocious horizontal assault on her husband was, for the moment, beyond her, but doubtless even that would be made clear to her in the fullness of time. She liked to think it might be some arcane tribute to his shooting prowess. That the whole incident had been part of the normal pattern of things was anyway confirmed by the fact that the leader of the team was now lunching with them. For Ron, lunch was something of a torture, not least because he saw slipping from his grasp the opportunity to score a discreet point or two over his host. He could sense that several people present found Freddy's present conduct strange. How Ron yearned subtly to underline this strangeness by a well-judged remark, to emphasise the implicit instability of a man who could behave in this way. He could so well imagine leaning over to Cyrille or Flipsi and observing with quiet authority: "I'm sorry to have to say, it's not the first time I've witnessed Freddy going a little over the top; all very well socially, of course, but it can be dangerous in a business situation which calls for delicacy and tact." But sadly none of this was possible under the present circumstances. The impact of the flying form of protester Irma Budd, and the subsequent damage sustained as his gun shot upwards and caught him a glancing blow across the teeth, meant that speaking was now difficult, except out of the side of the mouth opposite to that in which his missing tooth left a gaping hole. It would be necessary to have the whole plate seen to first thing on Monday morning, but until then his conversation had to be largely monosyllabic. Fortunately his next-door neighbours, Jemima Claydon and Erica Mannering, showed no particular predisposition to talk to him.

Meanwhile the most animated intercourse of the lunch emanated from Freddy and Renata. Renata's voice could be heard at every corner of the table railing at the excesses of her host and his guests.

"I utterly refuse to accept that what you have been doing all morning is anything other than the flagrant butchery of innocent birds.

It's disgusting. And it's also a manifestation of a rather pathetic sort of masculine ego-tripping."

"Oh, I wouldn't say that," countered Freddy benignly.

"All this playing around with guns. Of course you realise what the gun is in this context?"

"No."

"It's a penis substitute."

Janet heard this declaration and paled. Jemima and Antonia pursed their lips and pretended to be immersed in their own conversations. Erica brightened somewhat and turned to follow more closely. Freddy, however, bent nearer to Renata to interpose his own less widely audible reply which caused her to pause, colour a yet deeper shade and then unexpectedly to giggle. She recovered herself with a swig from her wine glass and continued:

"I still maintain that you are indulging in an outmoded male ritual, flourishing because of a male domination of society which has got to be smashed. Quite apart from the sort of social privilege which supports this sort of set-up there is an even more disgusting male privilege. It hangs round here like a bad smell."

Erica could restrain herself no longer and joined in:

"You know, love, if you're trying to say what I think you're trying to say, that men are essentially shits, then I'm with you all the way."

"Right on!" exclaimed Renata. "Women should rise up and say no to a lot of the things men demand from them without having any right to. You may be interested to come to one of the meetings held by a group which I run in London. Here's an information pack."

Erica took the proffered cheaply-printed sheet which Renata had swiftly extracted from her pocket and looked at it dubiously. But after a moment's reflection, she slipped it decisively into her own bag and said: "You're absolutely bloody right. Both my husbands abused me appallingly, but I'm not going to take it any more. And of course I'm not alone in having suffered at the hands of men. Most of the women at this table have had to put up with the most degrading insults, though many of them would prefer not to rock the boat by admitting it. You should ask the gentleman on my left what strange practices he forces his wife to submit to on a nightly basis."

She gesticulated with her fork to Ron, who looked up with surprise and then horror as he realised he was being referred to.

Renata peered round with undisguised hostility at the alleged malefactor and said loudly: "You pig!". Ron's impotent outrage could find no expression because of his dental restrictions, but his anger was doubled at the sight of Freddy sniggering.

THIRTEEN

Jean-Pierre Grifon sat at his desk in Rokeby's Impressionist department, and contemplated the world as it appeared to him that morning. There was certainly a buzz of excitement in the air about the King Wattle sale, now only three weeks away. Since the catalogue had been printed and distributed world-wide there had been a tremendous surge of interest, and Lance Peerman and his colleagues on the Rokeby's switchboard had been inundated by calls of inquiry, from genuine potential buyers, happy mortals with a spare million or two to play around with, from the world's press, anxious to titillate its readership's vicarious greed with tales of pictures about to sell for prodigious sums of money, and from the merely curious public whose questions had wasted many hours of Jean-Pierre's working week. But he was usually happy to cope with these because he found his work stimulating. He enjoyed holding forth to the layman about his area of expertise. When he had first met Evan Conrad, he had been amazed at his youth, and inclined to take umbrage at Evan's appointment over his head. But he soon recognised that Evan was a prodigy, defying normal rules of conduct. Who but a genius could have captured so swiftly the entire Wattle Collection for sale, apparently single-handed? The news had, it was true, extended Eric Steward's nervous breakdown by a further three months, but that was hardly Evan's fault.

With the eyes of the art world about to be focused on Rokeby's, and the Impressionist Department in particular, Grifon decided the time had come to consult Evan about a personal matter. He briefly extracted from his top drawer a small mirror and contemplated his reflection, with particular reference to the lank black hair which hung down over his forehead. Then he gathered together the day's correspondence and walked through to the next door office in order to drink from the spring of wisdom which was the mind of Evan Conrad.

"Bonjour, Evan."

"Oh - good morning, Jean-Pierre. Yes, yes, take a seat."

"I 'ave 'ere the letters for your inspection. But first I wish your opinion on something else."

"What is that?" The office was small; the window was shut. Jean-Pierre had apparently eaten large quantities of gaspacho for breakfast.

"The English girls - I think they like blond men?"

"Er - up to a point." Evan buried his nose in a handkerchief.

Jean-Pierre smiled wisely. "Yes. That is what I thought." There was a pause.

"And the letters?" Evan's patience was thin this morning.

The correspondence which had arrived that day for Rokeby's Impressionist Department contained its normal proportion of communications from the nakedly greedy, the terminally optimistic, and the blatantly imbecile. A woman from Leamington Spa was writing for the second time. In her first letter she had inquired about selling a Forain drawing; now, in reply to Rokeby's request that she submit a photograph of her property, she had sent a snap of her four-bedroomed Victorian villa. A man from Switzerland offered a photograph of a picture purporting to be a genuine Manet. It was clearly an inept student's copy of the Déjeuner sur l'Herbe, but undaunted the owner was urging its claims to be the original, relegating the Musée d'Orsay's version to the status of replica. In support of this theory he advanced the evidence of the "suspicious" behaviour of the Museum, who had refused to follow his suggestion that their picture undergo scientific testing, "sure proof that they have something to hide". A third letter originated from Tucson, Arizona. It contained a transparency of a most implausible-looking "Degas" pastel, "valued by a local appraiser at 16 million dollars". Under the circumstances, reflected Evan, it was generous of the writer to suggest that Rokeby's might be interested in offering it in an Impressionist sale with a reserve of only 8 million.

As he wrestled with suitable replies to these inquiries, carefully positioning himself throughout so as to avoid being caught downwind of Grifon, the telephone rang. Jean-Pierre took it upon himself to answer.

"Evan, I 'ave a lady on the phone who wishes she speak with you."

"Is it about the sale? Can't you or Victoria deal with it?"

"But she say she know you."

"What's her name?" Evan really could not face any more lunatic time-wasters at this moment.

"It is Mademoiselle Legrand from Paris."

Mademoiselle Legrand? It took a few seconds for him to register that the unthinkable was happening, the long yearned-for but all but despaired-of event was taking place: he was about to speak to Sylvie again.

"Put her through." His heart was beating faster and his throat was dry. He croaked: "Sylvie, is that you?"

"Eevan, yes, it is me."

"Where have you been? I tried to telephone you many times."

"Oh, it was necessary to travel for my work. But now I am just returned, and I call you because there have been the things not very pleasant here."

"What's happened?"

"It's Ranchec, the man you were seeking."

"Has he turned up at last?"

"No, no, not exactly. The gendarmes, they came yesterday to the apartment here. They wanted to search it."

"Why? Has he been arrested or something?"

"I regret, no. It is worse - they found him, in a little village in the south. He was dead, he had fallen down a cliff in an accident. So the gendarmes, they came in and searched the apartment for information about him."

"My God! How dreadful!"

"I did not like that the gendarmes came. It made me a little... frightened." Her voice quavered momentarily, triggering protective masculine responses in Evan that he did not know he possessed.

"Listen, Sylvie, I'm coming to Paris, and I'd like to see you. Perhaps I can help."

"When do you come?"

"Tomorrow. I'll come to see you in the Rue des St Pères."

"OK, that would be nice. What time?"

"I'd like to take you out to dinner. Shall I pick you up at eight?"

After a moment's hesitation, Sylvie said, "Oh, why not? Eight o'clock."

"And Sylvie, don't worry, will you?"

As he replaced the receiver, something snapped and he found himself shaking. Had it really been his voice saying all those things, making plans so authoritatively, proclaiming the hitherto unformulated intention to visit Paris tomorrow, steamrollering the girl into accepting his dinner invitation? Now the thought of the enterprise filled him with trepidation, and he marvelled at the way he had handled the situation on the telephone. Well, for better or worse he was now embarked on potentially the most exciting evening of his life tomorrow, so he had better pull himself together.

Then, with a shock, he thought of Ranchec. Ranchec was dead. After all that, he would never actually meet the man. This was a bitter disappointment, for it was a serious setback in Evan's pursuit of Hartier. Unless the final fruits of Ranchec's research were available, perhaps, amongst his effects? Who were his heirs? Evan vowed to find out, to approach them, to secure, if humanly possible, the source material about the artist on which Ranchec had surely been working. All was not lost. Here was a secondary task to accomplish on his visit to France. He lifted the telephone to call Rokeby's travel department for a flight booking for tomorrow.

At seven o'clock that evening Endymion Luce found himself drinking a glass of dry sherry in a distinctly second-rate Mayfair public house. It was not that Endymion scorned out and out seediness. Indeed he genuinely relished and would eagerly seek out the sort of really sordid dive which promised flagrant degradation. But this was irremediably mediocre, the after-work haunt of sweating estate agents and unappetising computer programmers with unbuttoned collars and loosened ties, types which Endymion normally went to great lengths to avoid. This evening, however, he was here because he had arranged to meet Lance and it had seemed a suitably anonymous venue in which to have it out once and for all. He had determined to take a strong line with the errant telephonist. Now was the time to grasp the nettle: March had almost come, and big decisions were about to be made by Terence Rokeby in the matter of the succession. Endymion felt confident that his own stock had never stood higher in relation to Messrs Fairbanks and Wheale. If the problem of Lance could be disposed of for good, the one potential minefield in his approach to the victor's crown would be swept from his route. As to his two rivals, Endymion was inclined to dismiss Ron's candidacy for the chairmanship as ultimately untenable on grounds of social unacceptability, and to find encouragement in the increasingly unbalanced way in which Freddy was conducting his private life. Freddy's philandering was notorious, and rumours abounded concerning a recent escapade of more than usual irresponsibility to which even the long-suffering Melissa had apparently refused to turn a blind eye. Unbridled heterosexual activity was of course relatively more acceptable than Endymion's flings, but if Lance could be effectively suppressed and Freddy's excesses subtly underlined then the Luce cause would surely benefit.

Lance's arrival was heralded by a kerfuffle in the doorway as the mincing little figure collided with a rugby-playing estate agent and succeeded in spilling a large quantity of the latter's beer down his trousers. Heated words were exchanged, and Lance proceeded in stately fashion to Endymion's table followed by a volley of abuse which left no-one in any doubt as to the estate agent's reading of Lance's sexual orientation, nor as to his opinion of such proclivities.

"Really!" exclaimed Lance loudly. "I don't know what's got on his wick. Ill-mannered brute!"

"Stop faffing around and sit down," barked Endymion who hated flamboyant public scenes. "Pay no attention. What do you want to drink?"

"Vodka and tonic. Make it a large one, dear, my nerves need calming." When Endymion fetched it for him, Lance sat back and stretched. "So what's on your mind?"

Endymion drew himself up into as stern an attitude as the compressed dimensions of the discreet alcove in which they were seated would permit. "I'm afraid I have to give you bad news, Lance. I have decided that this absurd charade of your being employed at Rokeby's cannot continue. It was only out of the kindness of my heart that I got you a job in the first place. There is a limit to the length of time Charity can continue, particularly when it is so blatantly abused. The time has come for you to move on." He paused, awaiting some reaction, but Lance merely sipped his drink in apparent reflection. Encouraged, Endymion went on: "Normally you would only be entitled to two weeks' notice, but as a gesture to you I have decided to allow you four weeks. You'll also be provided with decent references. I think you'll agree that's more than generous in view of the way you have fooled around while in the firm's employment."

"Fooled around?" Lance looked up.

"Yes, fooled around." Endymion was confident enough to play his trump card. "I've had our telephone records monitored, and I'm in a position to prove that you have made a series of expensive private telephone calls to places like New Zealand and Los Angeles in the firm's time when your contract of employment expressly forbids them. It's tantamount to putting your hand in the till, you know, and there might even be a case for criminal prosecution against you, but I'm not necessarily going to take it that far. Four weeks' notice will do if you react sensibly."

Lance contemplated him in silence for a few moments. Endymion fancied a look of contrition was detectable in his eyes, and settled back to receive his resignation and apologies magnanimously. He only hoped there wouldn't be tears. It was remarkable what a strong line could achieve, how the exercise of natural authority could bring to book the most recalcitrant subject. He was just congratulating himself on a tricky negotiation skilfully handled when he felt something cold and wet dripping through his thinning locks. He looked up to see Lance pouring the remains of his vodka and tonic very deliberately over his head, and declaring: "Bitch! OK, throw me out, but you'll regret it!" The whole incident was most unseemly. Several computer operators and a couple of exceedingly vulgar secretaries giggled as Lance flounced out and Endymion repaired to the Gentlemen's lavatory to clean himself up. But he clung to the consolation that Lance appeared at least to have accepted the inevitability of departure; that, after all, had been the object of the exercise, and a drenching in alcohol and an empty threat were a small price to pay.

It was unwontedly late for Freddy to be sitting at his desk at Rokeby's. Even Ron had departed, and the executive floor of offices was strangely silent. Freddy needed time to think, to gather his resolve to terminate an absurd situation, a state of affairs which had got ridiculously out of hand. Even he, for most of his life blithely unaware of gossip or speculation about himself, now had an uneasy sense that people were talking. No, it had to stop. And yet even as these thoroughly sensible conclusions were being reached, he had his hand on the telephone, and before he knew it he had dialled the number of his own flat and Melissa was answering.

"Hello, it's me."

"Oh," said Melissa coldly.

"Look, I'm so sorry. Something's come up. I'm going to have to miss dinner this evening. Some problems with this house sale in Wales, I've got to get down there unexpectedly."

"So what do you want me to do?"

"Apologise to the guests, that sort of thing. They'll understand, you're so good at coping, and they know I'm a busy man."

There was an ominous silence. "Right, Freddy, I'll cope."

"Wonderful, darling," said Freddy optimistically.

"No, not wonderful. Not wonderful at all. In fact I think you'd better not come back to this flat again, do you hear me?"

"What do you mean?"

"You know perfectly well what I mean, just don't come back, not tomorrow, not the next day, not until you're behaving like an intelligent adult again. Got that? You're not welcome here, do you understand?"

Freddy shook his head. He picked up the flowers and left the office thoughtfully. A minute or two later he was pointing his car in an unfamiliarly northern direction. He noticed that his hand was shaking a little with excitement and anticipation.

The door of the dilapidated flat in Kilburn was festooned with two legends, "Property is Theft" and "Women Say No to Male Violence". He knocked, and a moment later there before him stood Renata Crum.

"Renata, my love. I brought you these."

"Flowers?" Renata scowled. "You'd better come in but look, next time don't bother with this stuff, OK?"

"Just a small tribute to your beauty."

"I happen to feel very strongly that this habit of plucking living things just because they're attractive is ecologically irresponsible. It can lead on to all sorts of atrocities, like seal culling."

"If you were a flower, I'd have to pluck you, you know."

"Try and be relevant." But Renata accepted his kiss and took his coat from him. When he put his arms round her she shivered a little in his embrace. He had never previously met anyone quite like her in thirty years' catholic pursuit of the female sex, and he savoured her extraordinary novelty. There was a glorious rawness to her, an abrasiveness that made him ache with lust.

"I don't understand it," she breathed a little later. "How is it that simply by wanting me so much you can make me feel so randy?"

"It's called passion."

"You understand that just because I make love to you it doesn't mean I approve of your politics."

"I don't think of love as a political act."

"The rich are constantly screwing the working class," she

whispered.

"Constantly? What, more than once a night?"

She tensed in a final moment of defiance, then relaxed. "I hope so," she confessed.

FOURTEEN

"When the gendarmes came, it was a shock you know. They beat very loud on the door very early in the morning, when I still sleep. They make me feel like the criminal." Sylvie ran her hand through her long dark hair to sweep it up and away from her forehead. She wore a loose jersey which fell away to reveal a bare shoulder, and in the candlelight of the restaurant she was mesmerically beautiful.

"How awful for you. And what did they say?"

"They ask me when I had last seen Dr Ranchec. I tell them I met him only once, when he came to receive the keys to the apartment just before I departed. Then they wanted to know if there were any things belonging to Ranchec left behind when I returned. I could show them nothing, naturally. All that there was I gave to you."

"Did you tell them about those papers?"

"No, it did not seem worth to mention. And I did not wish to make for you trouble."

Evan looked up from the book of matches he was abstractedly tearing into small strips to see that she was smiling at him with some amusement. "You were protecting me?" he ventured.

"No, I am teasing you," she laughed. "You look so serious sometimes."

"But it is a serious matter, all this." Evan reflected that the papers would not have been available for the police anyway, having been stolen from his room in the Hotel de Lyon.

"You are right, it is serious. But those papers, they would not have helped the police very much. They are trying to find the nearest relations of Dr Ranchec and the things like that."

"I suppose so. But did they find nothing helpful amongst his belongings in - where was he staying?"

"I think it is a little village in the hills near Grasse. I do not know what they found, but it seems not much. All I know is they found him. 'E fell down the cliff, they said, and they think he probably threw himself."

"It's terrible to think about. He must have been very unhappy about something. It's very difficult to imagine the state of mind which persuades someone to take their own life."

"You say that? Did you never think to do it yourself, when you were in love perhaps? And I thought you were - how you say - a romantic." The light of mockery lit up Sylvie's dark eyes, teasing but deliciously intimate.

"Why did you think I was a romantic?"

"I read your postcards when I got back. They were a little bit .... a little bit poetic."

Evan blushed. To cover his embarrassment he filled their wine glasses again, then he said: "I often thought about you since I saw you, you know. And I often wondered where you had gone when I got no reply from you. Where were you?"

"Oh, I was travelling for my work."

"What exactly is your work?"

"In films. I am assistant to the producer. Often we have to be away for many months when we are shooting. Often it is too long."

"Where were you?"

"I was in Africa, Gabon. It was not a good climate, too hot and humid. I was happy to come back."

"I was happy you came back, too. I suppose you travel all over the world?"

"To many places, yes. Last year, when Ranchec had my apartment, I was in America. I have been also in the Far East. I loved that."

"Me too." Evan drank again from his glass and relaxed a little more. "At least I love the East in theory, but I've never really been there. I have this fantasy about going to Bali, the pictures of it look so wonderful."

"Ah, Eevan! Bali!" The place seemed to excite Sylvie similarly. "You know, I have been there, but for two days only. You are right, it is a - how you say? - a paradise. You go there to forget the rest of the world. One day I go back, I promise myself."

"I'll take you," said Evan decisively. The wine was doing its work. His fantasy about Bali had been part of the furniture of his imagination for some time, but the introduction of Sylvie as an actress in this fantasy now gave it an irresistible life of its own.

"You think I could go alone with you, you think you are to be trusted?"

"I can't think of anything more wonderful," said Evan fervently.

"You are very sweet, you know that? I love that English what you call? - reserve, that blush when you say something un peu intime. It is not natural for you to flirt, is it?"

A cloud crossed Evan's firmament. Where had Sylvie received her data to make such generalisations about the English? Had she not confessed at the moment of their first meeting that she had once had an English boyfriend? His heart spilled over with jealousy. Who was the beast? He said uncertainly: "That's not always true."

"But you prefer to be formal. You do not like to speak your heart, that embarrasses you, no?"

"Sometimes it's not so difficult."

"Tell me what you are really thinking, then," she teased. She was playing with him. It was unsettling, but not altogether unpleasurable.

"Well, I'll tell you what I am wondering. I am wondering who was your English boyfriend?"

"My English boyfriend? Did I tell you of him? It was not important. He was funny, but it was long ago."

"You speak as if you are ancient."

"That's not very gallant."

"No, I mean, you are young and very beautiful. Nothing that has happened to you can have happened very long ago."

"You, chéri, are the one who is young. But you are a bit of a flirt, I think, maybe I was wrong."

"You asked me to tell you what I was really thinking, so I did," said Evan. He felt delightfully light-headed, exhilarated by the sensation that suddenly anything was possible. "I have so many questions to ask you, you know. I want to hear everything about you."

"You must not," said Sylvie seriously. "You should not want to know everything about people. Knowing everything destroys everything. You must tell to me things, not ask them to me. So we shall be friends for a long time." She looked at him full in the eyes, and Evan felt a surge of many emotions, a breathless combination of desire, elation, and panic. An irrational but strengthening conviction hit him that he was going to sleep with her. He called for two cognacs and lifted his glass to her.

"To Bali," he toasted.

"To Bali," she laughed.

When they left the restaurant and stood for a moment on the pavement, the cold February wind blew and Sylvie rested her head on his shoulder. "Mmm, I've had so much to drink," she said contentedly. "That happiness of alcohol, it is special, no?"

"I think you're special," said Evan. "What shall we do? Shall we go back to your flat for a moment?"

"Oh, so many questions, always questions."

"Let's go back to your flat."

Miraculously a taxi drew up. Evan gave the address in the Rue des St Pères and followed Sylvie into the back seat. She was only half way across, so when he sat down she was terribly close to him, and before he had time to think she was in his arms. One moment his face was in the fur of her coat collar, the next it was buried in her hair, and then he was right up against the softness of the skin of her cheek. A sequence of actions stretched ahead of him irresistibly. They did not speak in the lift, and like sleepwalkers they negotiated the doors to the flat and into the bedroom. For Evan the physical closeness of this beautiful girl was intoxicating, although subconsciously he also registered pleasure at the deeper intimacy implied by her yielding to him. Up till now every girl he had ever made love to had reminded him in some way of the lovemaking of a predecessor, administering piquant shocks of recognition of the physical details of coition. But Sylvie was unprecedented. There was a unique grace in the movement of her body, the vocabulary of her passion was that of a new and lovely language; and Evan, while he did not immediately grasp the full subtlety of its syntactical idioms, nonetheless proved more than adequate to the simple conjugation of its verbs.

Whenever people in the art world met together and the name of Terence Rokeby came up he was uniformly referred to as "one of the old school". Foreigners sometimes went so far as to classify him as "the perfect English gentleman", a description which had it reached his ears would have embarrassed him horribly. There was, however, general consent that he represented a type which was fast disappearing. Certainly he suffered from that peculiarly English reluctance, characteristic of many of his generation and background, ever to pass judgement on anything which belonged to someone else, be it his wine, his pictures, his wife, or his style of dress. To do so would have been considered very bad manners, an error of taste, a regrettable intrusion into the privacy of another. Some critics might have questioned whether this reluctance to offer any sort of opinion on other people's possessions was an ideal attribute in one setting out to be a Fine Art Auctioneer. But the truth was that the brand of pained inarticulacy evinced by Rokeby whenever he was confronted with a situation demanding anything so compromising as an expression of personal opinion struck a deep chord of sympathy in many of his older English clients. If pressed, they - and Rokeby - would have had to agree that ultimately there was something just a little bit unhealthy about Art itself. It was not a subject to admit to too close a personal intimacy with. Now Golf, Cricket, or Shooting, they were a different matter: all were perfectly respectable areas of interest, even of expertise. But Art; well, if you were somebody like Rokeby, involved in a business which had unavoidably some tangential connection with the subject, it was more reassuring to clients to offer an attitude of happy-go-lucky amateurism to it, to admit certainly to the existence within the firm of Rokeby's of specialists with a necessary job to do, but not to dwell too knowledgeably on their activities.

"Want to sell those spoons, old boy? Of course, delighted to help. Got some chap down in the vaults who's a genius at identifying the damn things. Reads the marks, or something. But don't ask me how!" Or then again: "Want us to flog your Rubens? But of course we'll take it off your hands. I quite agree: all that flabby female flesh about the place, it's enough to put a fellow off his food. Send it down and our chap will have a look at it for you. Don't be put off if he writes a damn ten-page essay for the catalogue entry. The buyers seem to like that sort of thing." Thus sellers' nerves were soothed: they were dealing with one of their own.

Terence Rokeby now sat is his office in contemplative mood. His day was nearly done, both literally and metaphorically. It was half past three, and he was 71. And the business was changing, sad to say. Sellers were less and less the sort of people one had been at school with, and the buyers were even worse. Of course the latter were predominantly dealers, which had always been an uneasy state of affairs, but now there were foreigners galore, Americans, Germans, Scandinavians, even a bunch of Japanese. In many ways his retirement which was due next month could not come too soon, and all that remained to be settled was the question of his successor as chairman of Rokeby's. He hated change, but it had to come. Effectively he had passed over control of the firm's day-to-day activities to his three deputy chairmen. He felt increasingly out of touch and depressingly certain that if he knew more of what was going on he would be increasingly unhappy. But a decision was imminently going to have to be made about which of them was to be given the reins of power. He was no closer to a decision than he had been six months ago; all he really knew was that each of three candidates was flawed and created in him serious reservations.

Freddy was made of the right stuff, no doubt about that, and the boy was his godson. His father, with whom he had been at school, had been a model of rectitude and dependability, virtues which his son had unfortunately not inherited to the same degree. The blighter seemed to have difficulty in keeping his flies buttoned up, if rumour was to be believed. Surprising, because he had a perfectly attractive looking wife. His unpredictability and his wildness made one question whether he was really stable enough to run Rokeby's. Some chap in White's at lunch had told him that Freddy had actually set up house with some feminist left-wing intellectual. What was he playing at? When sexual licence was conjoined with political unsoundness, then alarm bells rang, then it really did not augur too well for the future. No doubt he would in due course see sense and extricate himself from his present highly unsuitable liaison, but the fact that it had happened at all undermined one's confidence in him.

Then there was Luce. It had to be faced, the fellow was mighty odd. Perfectly able, certainly; but his preference was, well, for his own sex. That sort of thing always sent a bit of a shiver down the old spine, one could never really accept it. Yes, there certainly were a fair number of them in the art trade, and one couldn't ignore them. At times it seemed as though they represented a sort of Mafia, so to that extent it was good to have one of them in your ranks. He could talk the same language to the others, make sure that Rokeby's didn't miss out from that point of view. But it wasn't something to be encouraged, surely? It couldn't be right to have too many of them in the firm, and what would there be to stop Luce surrounding himself with queers if he took control? It was an awful possibility, but one which could not be discounted. Like attracts like and all that: the whole image of Rokeby's could be changed overnight. Rokeby shuddered at the idea of his firm manned (if that was the appropriate word) entirely by pansies, flouncing and mincing about the hallowed rooms.

If it wasn't Freddy or Luce, what then? Ronald Wheale? Oh dear,

Ronald Wheale. Now he came to think of it, hadn't Wheale fixed an appointment to come and see him about now? That was probably him knocking on the door at this very moment.

"Come in," said Rokeby.

Ronald Wheale strode purposefully into the room. His features were composed into a grin which combined obsequiousness with a steely determination to let no man pull the wool over his eyes.

"Good afternoon, Mr Terence." Wheale persisted in the traditional nomenclature for the Chairman, a throwback to the days when Terence's own father Major Cedric still strode the corridors of Rokeby's and a distinction had to be made.

"All well?" inquired Rokeby tentatively.

"Indeed it is," declared Wheale thrusting a lengthy document on to the desk. "I've just had this computerised print-out of market share predictions for next month, and I'm bringing it to you at once. Assuming only a mean yield estimate from the Wattle sale we should be seeing an 8.27 per cent swing in our favour, compared with a 3.16 per cent loss in share for the equivalent month last year, seasonally adjusted, of course, and reflecting a currency exchange vacillation factor."

"Most interesting," said Rokeby, playing for time. The man was talking gibberish, of course, but with a bit of luck he would not stay too long.

"I'd also like to take this opportunity of bringing you up to date with recent developments on the computer front," continued Wheale, flashing a smile of awesome sickliness in his chairman's direction. "The new Apple system should be in place and operational next month. You are probably aware that it incorporates some fantastically powerful new chips."

Apple system? New chips? Presumably this was something to do with the staff canteen, speculated Rokeby. A lot of nonsense, the whole idea. Wheale was looking at him expectantly, so he said: "In my day the clerks brought their own sandwiches and ate them at their desks, and on sale days if things had gone well they'd be given some extra beer money. I'd have thought what was good enough for them should be good enough for the present lot."

Wheale did not appear to hear. He was not to be deflected from his catalogue of exciting new developments: "Then there's the question of software. I'd like to know your views."

Software? What was he blithering about now? Clothing, perhaps? Some bloody awful newly-designed uniform for the porters? They ought to stop tampering with things that had been perfectly functional for fifty years. Or was it something to do with the Porcelain Department? Some branch of Gossware, or whatever that unpleasant stuff was called? He tried to look intelligent, and resorted to a ploy which had stood him in good stead for fifty years. He said: "Could you be more specific?"

Ron was galvanised by the question. "I'm so sorry, I'm not making myself clear. Let's get back to the basic concept. You were probably as worried as I was by the excessive glitch incidence in our former system, leading to an unacceptably high hanging frequency. At first this was analysed as a simple matter of inadequate gender benders, but I realised almost immediately that only a completely new system could significantly increase our Mips and Megaflops, which is after all the bottom line. Naturally I also wanted to ensure that the whole arrangement would be as far as possible hacker-resistant, and to that end I have incorporated a pretty exceptional dongle. You know, I've noticed that hardly anyone gives enough in-depth consideration to the implications of the input:output interface. After all, how many times have we seen that a system is only as good as its peripherals?"

Rokeby noticed an interesting thing. It was apparent from the way this fellow's jaw moved that he had a mouthful of false teeth. Significant, surely, of something. Neglect in childhood? Cowardice in the face of the dentist's chair? It was all right to be toothless at 74, as Rokeby knew from his own experience, but to be lacking a sizeable number at 44? It was one more reason, if reason was required, for viewing Wheale's candidature for the Chairmanship only with serious misgivings. The flow of words had broken over him, almost engulfing him in a sea of incomprehensibility. Now he said: "I've no doubt, Ronald, that you have the whole problem entirely in hand."

Ron bowed his head in silent acknowledgement that this was indeed the case. The interview was going well, he told himself: clearly Rokeby liked him and was impressed by his grasp, while the Chairman surely appreciated these periodic visits made to keep him up to date. Did Freddy or Endymion trouble to do such a thing, he wondered? Most unlikely; poor old Mr Terence. It was touching, really, he probably looked on Ron just a little wistfully, seeing him momentarily as the son he never had. No doubt about it, the Wheale star was firmly in the ascendant now that he had put once and for all behind him the Leatherby débâcle, and had succeeded finally in getting the damaged dental plate fixed. It had taken three highly secretive visits to that extraordinarily incompetent Australian dentist to achieve this. Twice he had to return because of faulty workmanship, and indeed the man had seemed more interested in giggling behind a screen with his female assistant than in giving his full attention to the matter in hand. It would be the last time he patronised him, that was for sure, but the need for swift repairs had necessitated returning to the man who had made the thing in the first place. Now it was done, and Ron was able to concentrate whole-heartedly on Rokeby's and improving his chances in the succession. He was certainly being helped by Freddy's current and much talked-of infatuation with that deplorable lesbian terrorist. It occurred to him that it could do no harm just to touch on the matter now.

"By the way, Melissa Fairbanks was in this morning."

"Good, good."

"A difficult time for her, of course."

"Er..... not easy, no."

"Naturally, I am one of Freddy's most enthusiastic admirers," continued Ron. "No-one appreciates his talents more than I do. But as one of his colleagues, and close friends, I feel that perhaps I should have a word with him about this strange lapse. Would you advise it?"

Terence Rokeby was acutely embarrassed. This was just the sort of personal conversation, touching on details of an intimate nature, which he detested having, particularly with a man like Wheale.

"I.... er...." he stuttered miserably.

"You've heard about it, of course? I mean the way he's left Melissa and set up with this Marxist terrorist?"

"Better left to sort it out themselves," mumbled Rokeby.

"I mean it's not as if we're not old friends," Ron assured him. "We're always staying at Leatherby, and Melissa and Janet get on so well."

By a huge effort of will Rokeby roused himself to deviate the course of this conversation. He said: "The Wattle sale next week seems to be generating a lot of interest."

"Very satisfactory," agreed Ron with enthusiasm. "You know, it's successes like this which I can't help finding very personally gratifying. It entirely vindicates my championing of young Conrad. I thank God I was able to pick him out, then give him the support he needed in order to secure that collection."

"Good show."

"I am afraid that Messrs Fairbanks and Luce were less than encouraging about his potential at the time of his appointment, but I suppose everyone has their blind spots. I'm pleased I was able to persuade them to take him on. It was quite a battle."

"Very commendable, splendid."

"Anyway, I mustn't take up any more of your precious time. I very much value our little chats. I can't help feeling they'll stand me in excellent stead in the years to come. Thank you again."

"Not at all."

"I'll keep in touch."

"Yes, do." Rokeby slumped down in his chair with relief as the door closed behind his colleague. Thank God that was over, and the intolerable little man was gone. Now at least he could relax. He felt he deserved a little reward for the ordeal he had just undergone, and reached for the decanter of whisky. Then he flicked on the button of the remote control of the little television. He was just in time for the last race from Catterick. Here was blessed release from present problems, and Rokeby gave his full attention to the horses in the paddock. The Turf was his passion, and while not given much to metaphysical speculation he was inclined to see in Racing analogies for Life. Three runners caught his eye out of the field of four. On form, each had a credible chance of success. He watched intently as they made their way to the starting line. Suddenly it came to him in a flash of revelation. The first of his choices was called Thruster, at 100-30. That was surely Freddy Fairbanks. The second rejoiced in the name of Dancing Fairy, at 5-1. No doubt he symbolised Endymion Luce. And the third runner, a relative outsider at 9-1, raced under the name of The Upstart, which it was surely forgivable to see as not entirely inappropriate for Ron Wheale.

Rokeby drained his glass and gripped the side of his chair. He would let the outcome of this race decide the Rokeby's succession. Whichever of the three was first past the post would, in their Rokeby's persona, become chairman. Endowed with this symbolic significance, the race became of consuming fascination, and he bent forward intently as they got away. At the first bend the field was tightly bunched.

FIFTEEN

Evan sat is his hotel room and pondered his situation. It was now midday, and the weather outside was bleak and cold. He felt depressed. A man who wakes up in the arms of Sylvie Legrand can hardly expect the rest of his morning to be anything other than an anti-climax, of course, a downhill run. But there was something particularly empty about his present solitude. She had awaken gorgeous, tousled, and a little abstracted. She had made coffee, but had broken away from his embrace protesting that it was late and she had to go.

"When will I see you?"

"I am not sure. I have to go away for a while, it is my work. I'll call you soon."

"But where are you going? Where can I get you?"

"Questions, always questions - remember what I told you, that makes me unsettled. You can't reach me, but I'll call you. Here, take this key and lock the door when you leave. Au revoir, chéri." She blew him a kiss and ran downstairs without waiting for the lift. Evan had followed her progress into the street from a window, seen her hail a taxi, drag a large bag into the back seat with her and disappear into the traffic. The melancholy had set in then.

Where had she gone? How could she call him when she didn't even know what hotel he was staying at? The only number she had was that of Rokeby's London, and today being Friday that meant there could be no contact between them till Monday at the earliest. The impossible chasm of the weekend stretched miserably before him. She could be heading anywhere, from Africa to California. This strong grain of independence in her, this determination to keep large areas of her life private from him was all very mature, but he wasn't sure he could cope with it. Rather than this very adult distance, he would have preferred a brief dose of good old-fashioned adolescent clinging.

He needed some distraction from brooding alone on the mysteries and wonder of Mademoiselle Legrand. The quest for Hartier, via Ranchec, must provide it. Now was his chance to pursue the matter, to go in search of Ranchec's source material, that tantalising body of documents which shed so much light on Hartier the artist, the theorist, the son, the husband. How best to proceed? He extracted from his file the page on which Ranchec had written two telephone numbers, one of St Jacques and the other of the shadowy figure called Gontier. Calling St Jacques again would only anger and frustrate him; dealing with the man who, he felt sure, had stolen Ranchec's notes from him would produce nothing. Should he try this Gontier man? No, he preferred to defer that option, to keep it in reserve. Instead he opened a detailed map of the south of France, located Grasse and then found the small village which had been Ranchec's final resting place. Estimating that it should be within an hour and a half's drive of the nearest airport, Nice, he lifted the telephone and shortly afterwards had obtained a booking on the 4 o'clock flight. He felt a little better. There was no substitute for direct action: a personal visit to the place where the old art historian had had his last abode would enable him to rummage around until he came up with some lead as to the whereabouts of the precious research. It got him away from Paris, where the memory of the elusive Sylvie was painfully fresh; and it gave him a purpose. As to the expense, Rokeby's American Express Card could cover it. He reckoned he was owed a little something in return for all the success and publicity he had brought the firm by securing the Wattle Collection.

Wattle. Suddenly the vision of Wattle upturned on the hotel bedroom floor, the stranded turtle ensnared, returned vividly to him. He shuddered, and reflected on the slender thread by which had hung his own success. Supposing he had not returned to his suite and walked into his bedroom that day: Rokeby's would not have the Wattle Collection, he would not have stayed on the extra time in Paris and so met Sylvie, nor would he have gained the staggering insight into Hartier which he had been temporarily vouchsafed. He thought of that other bedroom, the one where he had passed last night. That could never be taken from him.

As the taxi drove him to the airport, he considered what his strategy should be once he reached the village where Ranchec had met his end. Ideally, he supposed, he would come upon Ranchec's last known place of abode, lodgings, hotel room or whatever, and gain permission discreetly to sift through his belongings. No doubt the police had already done this, but they would have been looking for something rather different, evidence of his next of kin and other such personal details. What Evan hoped to find, unconsidered and untouched, were the mouth-watering volumes containing the journals kept by Claude Hartier in the 1880s, his correspondence with his parents, and the diaries of Constance. The more he thought about it, the more he reckoned it was likely that the purpose of Ranchec's exile in the south had been to free himself from the distractions of Paris in order to knuckle down to the absorbing task of making sense of all this material, with a view ultimately to writing the definitive monograph. Now, without being too vulture-like about the operation, Evan envisaged himself descending on the place, bearing off this priceless source material, and continuing the good work himself. Of course full acknowledgement would be paid to Dr Ranchec when the Conrad tome finally saw the light of day (pygmy standing on giant's shoulders seeing further than the giant, etc. etc.); but then again he could not in all conscience permit the actual dedication to be reserved for Ranchec, as that honour would necessarily go to Sylvie. Moving off at a tangent, Evan took inordinate pleasure in composing a sufficiently heart-felt inscription: "To Sylvie, My Eternal Muse"; no, no, not right at all, far too 1890ish and aesthetic. "To Sylvie, without whom this book would never have been written"; too prosaic and obvious. What about something appositely French: "A Sylvie, ma vie, mon amour"? Yes, he liked that. It had grandeur, simplicity and feeling. Now all he had to do was write the book.

At Nice airport it was as cold as Paris. But perhaps February was not the most welcoming month in which to pay one's first visit to the Côte d'Azure. It was also dark, but Evan resolutely went through the formalities of hiring a car, and navigated himself with some trepidation up to Grasse. After two involuntary circuits of the town's one-way system he extricated himself and found a hotel where he stayed the night. His last action before retiring was to put through a call to Sylvie's Paris number. It was a pointless gesture of devotion, but obliquely he felt it brought her closer to him. There was, of course, no reply.

"Bien sur, I knew well the man you ask about," declared the barman in answer to Evan's enquiry the next morning. He was clearly not averse to holding forth with authority about recent events. "Monsieur Ranchec, the poor fellow who was killed last week, he was a school teacher from Paris, recently retired I think. He came many times to this bar."

"A very sad business," said Evan. "Do you know where he was staying? Was it near here?"

"Yes, he took lodgings with Madame Leclaire at number 7, a hundred metres down the road. It was a great shock to us all, you know. Of course, we know he threw himself. Or he was pushed. It is not possible to fall there by accident, there are many precautions against such a thing."

"You think so?"

"Oh, but there is no doubt. Still, it is a matter for the police. And you, you are his friend, an American perhaps?"

"I am English, actually. I was a sort of colleague."

"Ah, a school teacher also."

"Yes, I suppose, a sort of school teacher," agreed Evan uncertainly, finishing his cup of coffee and preparing to move on.

"It's funny, you know." Maurice polished a glass ruminatively. "You are not the first stranger to come asking questions about Monsieur Ranchec."

"Not the first? Who else has been?"

"There were the gendarmes, of course, after the body was found. We all told them what we knew, but it was not much. Monsieur Ranchec, he was the sort of man who does not speak easily to others. But then came on Tuesday a man from Paris."

"What did the man from Paris want?"

"He asked the same question as you about where had been M. Ranchec's lodging. I sent him on to the house of Madame Leclaire."

"Who was this man? Do you know his name?"

"I don't know. He told me nothing about himself. But you must ask Madame Leclaire."

Evan's suspicions were not allayed. He bade farewell and thanks to Maurice and hurried out in the direction of number 7. Had he been preempted, had his nameless rival reached the holy grail before him?

Madame Leclaire ushered him into her small parlour, which was dominated by a very large television, and told him what a shock the whole business had been, what a respectable if unforthcoming lodger Ranchec had seemed, and how inconsiderate he had proved to have taken his own life when a week's rent was owing. She didn't mind telling Evan, her nerves were in a state. She was an overweight woman in her fifties, a chain-smoker with inquisitive eyes. Before Evan could broach the matter himself, she inquired of him:

"Are you also a relation of M. Ranchec, like M. Alexandre?"

"No, no, I'm a former colleague. Was it M. Alexandre who came here on Tuesday?"

"Yes, that's right. A most disagreeable man, with no manners. He was disgustingly rude to me, but as he said he was M. Ranchec's cousin, I had to show him M. Ranchec's things."

"He went through M. Ranchec's belongings?" asked Evan in alarm.

"He went through them like a madman. But he did not seem happy at the end. It was as if he was looking for something which he could not find. Probably the will, heh?" Madame Leclaire broke into a wheezy laugh at this image of human greed frustrated. "I asked him if he would be taking away the property of his cousin as I do not want it getting in the way here. He was very rude and told me he would be making arrangements later. Then he left."

Evan nodded as sympathetically as possible. "Would you be very kind and let me have a quick look at his things? I am just looking for two or three books, nothing valuable, but they would help me enormously with my research. I'm terribly sorry to bother you like this, particularly after the.... the outrageous behaviour of M. Alexandre, but I would be most grateful."

"Outrageous," repeated Madame Leclaire with some satisfaction. She obviously approved of Evan's choice of epithet. "Very well, follow me."

She led him stertorously up the stairs to the small bedroom in the attic. Evan suddenly did not relish the prospect of rifling through a dead man's clothes and belongings, but having got this far it was difficult to turn back. Once inside, he set to the job methodically. There were a few books on the window sill, but strangely they were all novels by Victor Hugo. There were some writing materials, but nothing of any significance. He opened every drawer he could find, looked in the empty suitcase in the cupboard, even knelt down to search under the bed. There was nothing. No stacks of unsorted correspondence, no leather-bound volumes of diaries in clear copper-plate hand. And of course he had been foolish to expect there would be. His fantasies had unbalanced his judgement, and he had been on the original wild goose chase.

"I beg your pardon for wasting your time," he said as he came out of the door on to the landing. Madame Leclaire shrugged indifferently. He was making his way downstairs again when he became aware of a small figure on their heels. Looking up, Evan saw a young boy of seven or eight who had presumably emerged stealthily from the second attic bedroom. Now it seemed the lad was trying to give him something.

"But what are you doing?" scolded Madame Leclaire, explaining to Evan: "Excuse him, he is my young grandson Alain."

The boy gabbled something largely unintelligible to his grandmother, who turned to Evan again: "He says that if you are a friend of M. Ranchec he wants to give you something. He likes you, you see, but he took exception to M. Alexandre."

"That's very kind," said Evan, taking the proffered gift. It was a thick brown envelope apparently containing several sheets of paper. "What is it exactly?"

The boy now whispered into Madame Leclaire's ear. Again she interpreted for Evan: "I fear little Alain has done something wrong. But he's not a bad boy, he means well. He says that he picked this letter up from M. Ranchec's room some time ago and hid it. He does these things sometimes, I don't know why, but he means well. Now he thinks you should have it as you were M. Ranchec's friend."

Alain seemed pleased when Evan took the letter. They continued on down to the hall where Evan bade farewell and shook the grandmother and grandson by the hand. Alain immediately ran back upstairs with considerable abruptness.

"He means well," Madame Leclaire repeated, lighting another cigarette.

Evan put the anonymous brown envelope into his breast pocket and walked off down the main street of the village towards his parked car. Whatever it contained was not bulky enough to constitute the yearned-for Hartier material. He would examine it later: it was probably nothing more than Ranchec's laundry list.

The man who emerged unexpectedly through the door into the library was disturbingly familiar, but Ewan Connard was momentarily unable to put a name to his face. As he rose to greet him, Ewan noted that he was absurdly tall and walked in a curiously maladroit manner, suggestive of profound embarrassment at his own thinness and height. It was as if he were constantly trying to distract attention from these physical attributes by a sequence of unpredictable shoulder movements. None of his clothes seemed to fit, and even the spectacles on his nose perched in a precariously lopsided position. He blinked at the shaft of unremitting Californian sunshine which flooded in through the window and advanced towards Connard with hand outstretched, a grin lurching uncertainly across his features before disappearing abruptly and disconcertingly from his face. He was one of those people programmed to smile as they speak to or greet others, but whose facial muscles have gone out of synchronisation with their brain; as a result the smile fades before the action or sentence which it is meant to accompany has finished, thus fatally undermining its conviction and validity. Now he announced:

"Er.... I'm Vern Throg. Dr Connard?"

"Oh, how do you do?" Ewan shook his hand. That was it, of course. He had half recognised him from his photograph on the dust jacket of Towards Opticality. Now the question was, did Throg realise that he was the man responsible for the destruction of that ridiculous tome in the review which had appeared in the London Arts Digest? Could he anticipate aggression as a result?

"I guess.... I guess that you and I could be accounted.... er.... competitively juxtaposed in the.... er.... present concatenation of circumstance," suggested Throg.

It was incredible: the man's speech mirrored his literary style. He was a walking thicket of verbal over-elaboration. But what he seemed to be saying, that they were rivals, was apparently true. The room in which they found themselves was a small library in the San Pietro Museum of Fine Arts. Ewan had been bidden here on the understanding that the candidates for the Directorship had been reduced to a shortlist of two, and his presence was required for a final round of decisive interviews. In the room beyond sat the band of moon-faced men and face-lifted women, a strange mixture of earnestness and vulgarity, who made up the Board of Governors. In their hands lay the ultimate choice. And the man with whom he had just shaken hands was apparently the second member of the shortlist.

"Well, it certainly looks that way," agreed Ewan.

Throg contemplated the situation for a moment. "So - you too are emigrant from Academia, purposing re-orientation career-wise?"

"Yes," said Ewan shortly. He could not bring himself to entertain too lengthy a conversation with this monument to verbosity.

After another pause, Professor Throg shifted tack: "Dr Connard, I am cognisant of a fact about you, my knowledge of which may promote surprise."

Oh no, here it comes, thought Ewan. The old bat's going to get at me about my review of his book. Well, it was a very bad book and I had to say so. But I refuse to be embarrassed by him.

"Look, Professor Throg, I'm really not prepared..."

"It concerns your neckware."

"My neckware?"

"Am I not correct in observing that the colorific and designatory significance of your necktie is status-indicative of your alumni-ship of Eton College?"

"Oh: yes, that's true actually." Connard very rarely wore his Old Etonian tie, but some atavistic trust in its efficacy occasionally persuaded him to bring it out for interviews.

"That item excites my covetousness in no small measure."

"What, you want my tie?"

"If I may adopt an explanatory mode: my private hobby, an area in which I aim to encyclopaedicise my knowledge, is your British Public School system. In North Dakota opportunities to further that knowledge contain a limitation factor conditioned by dearth of geographical proximity. However, on my travels I have acquired the Old Boys' ties of several notable foundations including those of Rugby School, Giggleswick, and Worksop College. The flower of my collection would be the equivalent article of your alma mater." The smile which had sedulously accompanied this declaration disappeared abruptly just before its close, leaving Professor Throg looking merely worried.

Ewan was relieved of the necessity of reply by the opening of the door to the Governors' room.

"Professor Throg, would you step inside? Thank you."

The angular figure loped off obediently. Ewan noticed distastefully that one Throg trouser leg hung so low about his ankle that it actually caught beneath the heel of his shoe as he walked. At least Connard would present a more satisfactory sartorial image to the Board of Governors. To be honest, there were few areas where he feared Throg as a rival at all. Surely the Governors would not be taken in by the painfully fraught verbosity of the man. And, while scholarship was clearly important in the Director of a museum of the stature of San Pietro, the ability to deal personably and effectively with a wide range of rich patrons was also crucial. Here Ewan was almost embarrassed to contemplate Throg's deficiencies, so palpable were they. No, unless something completely unforeseen cropped up, his appointment was surely in the bag.

Really the American trip could be accounted a success. His lectures, from Chicago onwards, had been uniformly well received; and the paper he had delivered in San Pietro, New Light on Luminism, had been regarded as one of the highlights of the Convention. Then had come the first round of interviews at the Museum, followed by a few days' vacation in the warm Californian sun. Into this brief respite had been incorporated a short dalliance with a well-built research student named Barbara Bouch, encountered as an eager acolyte at a drinks party after his masterly performance in the Dwight Dobman Convention Hall. Miss Bouch had now returned home to somewhere - could it have been Idaho? - to pursue her studies, and Ewan was on the last leg of his tour, the final round of interviews.

He rose and smoothed the creases from his well-cut lightweight suit. From the next room the low drone of voices was vaguely audible as Throg gave the Governors the benefit of his thoughts on various issues. What a waste of time this was, reflected Connard, to make him wait outside like some errant schoolboy while his opponent went through his paces. All he could do was kick his heels. Out of boredom he approached a little closer to the door. He found that if he actually put his ear to it he could make out much of what was being said. It was scarcely to be described as eavesdropping - in many ways he could not be less interested in what Throg had to say for himself - but it passed the time just to listen to a snatch of what was going on. Throg's voice was speaking:

".... nodal energies.... coloristic capabilities.... Seurat's vibrancy metaphorically moded.... prismatic conceptions concretised in my recent book " The snoring from his interlocutors was almost audible.

A male voice, belonging to a Governor who had obviously been doing a bit of homework, now interpolated: "In relation to our museum, Professor Throg, where would you stand acquisition-wise? Would you be going after works by recently rediscovered masters of the Impressionist circle, the new boys like Claude Hartier, for example?"

"It is my contention," replied Throg's voice, "that the built-in error potential in the acquisition of such works is congenital to the unproved status of Hartier.... derivatory modes .... muted ability to vibrantise opticalism.... secondary synurgic drive...."

"Are you saying, Professor, that you feel Hartier would not be a good buy?"

"In view of his output shortfall and deficient originality quotient, our descendants could view present acquisition of his work not without mirthful hindsight."

Not without mirthful hindsight. What rubbish the fellow was talking. Connard retreated from his listening post with disgust. Throg was shamelessly bad-mouthing an accomplished artist like Hartier just because Hartier had been discovered by his rival. It was grotesquely unprofessional and unethical, a travesty of the facts. The only consolation was that Throg's mode of delivery was such that the content of what he was saying was largely unintelligible to any but the most assiduous listener. One thing that Throg would certainly not now be getting was Ewan's Old Etonian tie. When he had first heard of the American's strange passion, Connard had toyed with the idea of sending it to him as a sort of consolation prize once his own San Pietro appointment had been confirmed. But now not even that gesture was worth making or even called for. Throg had put himself quite beyond the pale by the expression of his absurd reservations about the status of Hartier.

Half an hour later Connard was sitting poised and relaxed before the Governors. They bore the look of a band of shipwrecked sailors, grateful for their recent rescue from the sea of insistently meaningless verbiage in which they had been deluged by Throg, but not yet recovered from their ordeal.

"Dr Connard, would you favour us with a brief characterisation of your personal art-historical style and achievement?"

Ewan smiled urbanely about him and began smoothly: "My approach has always been direct and practical. Art history should be about painters painting pictures, and one should not lose sight of that simple truth even when dealing with movements such as Neo-Impressionism which feature a certain amount of theoretical and scientific content. It's too easy to get side-tracked into a lot of technical mumbo-jumbo which only muddies the waters." He paused, momentarily to savour the heart-felt nods of agreement emanating from his interviewers, and then went on: "No, I like to stick to practicalities, and I like to think that my methods have earned their measure of success. While others have become a trifle bogged down in the scientific theory of the movement, I've gone out and actually discovered a new pointillist artist, one of major importance: I refer of course to Claude Hartier. You probably saw my article in the Burlington, the result of some pretty elaborate research in Paris. Most of the informed art world now seems to be appreciating the significance of this painter, which is immensely gratifying." The reception of this speech only just fell short of spontaneous applause. The Board of Governors were rapturous, he could tell. Throg's goose was cooked; and what would undoubtedly be referred to by future historians of taste as "the Connard years" were about to begin at San Pietro.

SIXTEEN

It was not until the evening, when Evan returned to the hotel in Grasse, that he investigated the contents of the envelope thrust into his hand by Alain Leclaire earlier that day. He was at least sitting down when he opened the explosive document which fell into his lap, but he could hardly have been fully prepared for its shattering impact. In retrospect he could almost divide his professional life about the twenty minutes of its reading; looking back he could say yes, such and such an event happened before I had read it, before I knew, whereas another event definitely occurred after I learned its contents, when the world was different, changed irrevocably. Nothing could be the same once he had assimilated the knowledge contained within the innocuous-looking packaging. He took up the sheets of closely-written script and read:

This document is my confession. It is not the full apology for the life of Louis Ranchec: that would be a lengthy and deeply complicated exercise of interest only to the most morbid student of human frailty and inadequacy. No, this is intended as a candid explanation of certain actions on my part only, an account of how the events took place and circumstances arose which persuaded me into error, led me to bring shame on myself, dishonour to my profession, and so to blight my life to the point where it no longer has meaning for me. It is my hope that in writing down the full story of this sorry escapade I will achieve some sort of expiation of my guilt; at the same time I may also identify other guilty parties - one perhaps even guiltier than I - who are responsible for the crimes of greed and jealousy which have been committed. I have resolved to write only the truth, to be mercilessly honest as never before, withholding nothing, totally unsparing of my own shame. There is no point in hiding anything now, the time for deception is past. So I must go back some years in search of the root of the affair. The way I was then is the key to the way matters developed later.

I taught at the Paris Institute for twenty-three years up till this summer. I was a reasonably successful art historian specialising in French painting of the late 19th century. As a younger man I was stimulated by my subject and enjoyed my work, but I grew increasingly frustrated by my lack of progress. I am still convinced that my way forward was being obstructed by an obstinate clique antipathetic to me and my political views, which had at a period in the past been a little left of centre. There were two or three particular adversaries, pretentious, pompous figures, pillars of the establishment devoid of imagination, men who were determined that I, who challenged their whole approach and undermined their confidence, should not advance further in my career. I continued to teach and lecture, to write articles, even two books. But the books were not warmly received, thanks to the machinations of my enemies. I became bitter and disenchanted, a victim of a pervading cynicism. I think subconsciously I resolved that at some time in the future if the opportunity arose I would avenge myself and expose the humbug and sterility of the minds of the dominant forces in French Art History.

Meanwhile my personal life had begun to disintegrate. My wife Louise left me finally ten years ago; I had become difficult to live with, I admit, and perhaps if we had had children it would have been different. Then Louise died three years later. Despite the armour of cynicism which I wore, I suffered from loneliness. I had been drinking too much for some time and now the problem worsened. I sought refuge also in drugs, an expensive and ultimately illusory solace. On top of that there was my passion for gambling, an affliction which had always been with me, but one which now offered an alternative release from my other troubles. I lost a lot of money, a great deal of money at this time, and there came a point nearly four years ago when I was all but bankrupt. This was my secret life, unknown to my colleagues at the Institute or to my pupils. They may have guessed that all was not well, but they had no idea how bad the situation really was. So there it is: I do not offer this background as an excuse, but it is perhaps part of the explanation why my life has taken the regrettable course it has followed over the past two years. I was jealous of my colleagues' undeserved professional success, resentful of the way my career had been unfairly stunted, and ready to take some drastic action in order to relieve my feelings; I was also sorely in need of money and prepared to consider any means of making some. I was desperate, and I was bitter.

It was in this mood that I became friendly with Raoul St Jacques. He held an exhibition of Barbizon School paintings in his gallery, and he offered me a fee for writing the catalogue. An innocent enough beginning, I suppose, but it was my first step into the labyrinth of intrigue and deception from which I ultimately found it was impossible to extricate myself. I gradually became his tame academic, called in to produce scholarly notes for the pictures he was selling, to blind the public with science. At this stage I was not actually telling untruths, but I found myself writing more and more as a salesman, couching my sales-pitch in the vocabulary of art history. I discovered in myself a certain aptitude for this work, and I became a not inconsiderable asset to St Jacques. More important, the fees he paid me gradually began to ease my financial problems. Then one day he telephoned me unexpectedly and invited me to a private meeting with him as he had an urgent matter to discuss.

I was ushered into him in his office with elaborate secrecy. I remember that when we were alone he actually went to the door and locked it, which struck me as excessively theatrical. He was in a state of some excitement. He asked me if I would like the opportunity of making a sizeable amount of money rather than the relatively paltry fees I had earned hitherto. I expressed interest. He then explained that he had a proposition to make, a very daring plan for exploiting the art market in which he would need my help; in fact he went so far as to say that it was a scheme which would be impracticable without my participation. It might, he suggested, appeal to me as a huge and memorable practical joke aimed against the pretension of the Establishment. At the same time if it worked it would net a large financial return. I had no idea what he was leading up to, but my curiosity was aroused. I asked him to be more specific. In answer he drew from behind a curtain a pointillist-style landscape, painted on canvas, about 60 by 80 centimetres in size. It was superficially light and attractive, though not of outstanding quality. He asked me what I thought of it, and I gave this verdict as my opinion.

He agreed that the picture was not at all in the top class, but that it had a degree of commercial appeal. It was signed with the initials C.H., initials which were unidentifiable by me at that stage. St Jacques asked me for my views as to its age. I estimated that it could have been painted between 1900 and 1920, and he said yes, he supposed so; but if it had been painted twenty or so years earlier, say between 1880 and 1890, it would have been a vastly different proposition, both commercially and art historically, did I not agree? Of course that was true, but it was hypothetical and irrelevant: it had not been painted then. If it had, it must have been by someone immediately recognisable closely involved in the circle of Seurat. As no-one of these initials was known in that circle, the picture's chances of being accepted as dating from this time would be negligible. St Jacques held up his hand to break in. This was where I could help, he told me; surely if there was convincing new circumstantial evidence as to the existence of a previously unknown artist with these initials working in Seurat's circle in the 1880s then this picture would gain dramatically in interest and value. Furthermore, if an academic of my standing were prepared to back the picture as being by this newly-discovered artist with the initials C.H., the proposition would gain in credibility.

But what would be the benefit, I asked him, even if I did agree to this unethical proposal? What good would it do us in the longer run? This one-off picture would be sold, at a much inflated price perhaps, but that would be an end to it. St Jacques then explained that this was far from being the case as he had an extended strategy in mind. This was not the only canvas signed C.H. which had come into his possession; in fact there were a good twenty more to which he had access. He could envisage that with patient and careful planning, a gradually rising market for this newly created artist could be manufactured and sustained, all of which would make us a lot of money. But the first step was for me to put together some sort of certificate stating persuasively that I believed the picture I was now looking at was by a hitherto unknown artist with the initials C.H., for whose close association with Seurat in the 1880s there existed documentary evidence which I would be publishing in the not too distant future. What good would this do? I queried. It surely would not be persuasive enough to induce a buyer to pay a large sum "from cold" as it were. But St Jacques told me this was not the object of the exercise. The purpose was merely to adduce enough prima facie evidence to persuade a leading international auction house that this was a potentially important enough picture to include in a top Impressionist sale, where the art world's attention would be focused. Once it appeared, illustrated in colour in the catalogue, then St Jacques would arrange for it to be bought by one of his own agents for a healthy-looking sum, say £25,000. This was an investment well worth making for St Jacques as he would get most of his money back and it would start the ball rolling. Works by the artist C.H. would thereby acquire a proven commercial value, a track record to encourage other buyers at future sales. So, would I go away and think about it? Then, all being well, would I come back with the name of this newly-created artist whose initials were C.H.? If I agreed to this first stage, St Jacques promised me an immediate payment of 40,000 francs, with future percentages on sales to come.

Of course I agonised over the decision. I realised that I was contemplating an essentially criminal course of action, and my first reaction was to recoil in horror. The tragedy of the story was that such a tempting offer should be dangled in front of me at such a vulnerable moment, for it was just at this very stage that one of my gambling creditors, who had also supplied me with drugs, was threatening to go to the Institute authorities unless I met my obligations immediately. Such a move would probably have led to my dismissal as it would have been exploited by my opponents to secure this end. I could not face this possibility, to be left with no academic position and immediate dishonour. So I chose another sort of dishonour; and it must be confessed that at the same time I was attracted by the idea of playing a successful trick on the art historical establishment. In the end I acquiesced in the plan. When I reappeared the next morning at St Jacques' gallery and suggested that our man's name should be Claude Hartier, I had crossed the Rubicon. In fact I was rather pleased with myself: I had come across this name, in research on another matter, recorded as one of the entrants to the atelier of Gérôme in 1878. His date and place of birth were recorded also, but checking through further records revealed that he did not pursue his studies with Gérôme, and there is no more trace of him. Perhaps the real Claude Hartier gave up painting, or found more remunerative employment in designing ladies' hats; whatever the truth, he was the perfect basis for my mythical Neo-Impressionist. At this point, anyway, I passed on to St Jacques a certificate of sorts stating that in my opinion his picture was the work of Claude Hartier, that Hartier was a recently rediscovered Neo-Impressionist associate of Georges Seurat, and that I would shortly be publishing more information about him. It was enough to gain the picture entry into an important Impressionist sale in London. When it came up it realised, thanks to the agency of St Jacques, £26,000. People sat up and took notice, and the picture was reproduced in one or two magazines as the work of an artist who was a curiosity, with the potential to become something rather more substantial.

St Jacques came to me again, of course, for help with the second phase of the operation. In a way one had to admire his restraint. He argued, quite rightly, that it would be a great mistake to rush in immediately and release several Hartiers on to the market at once. Patience should be exercised, no matter how great the temptation to make a quick killing. Now was the time for a little consolidation of the academic situation to whet the appetite of the market for more works by this rare and undervalued artist. Ideally a book about Hartier should be forthcoming, but even St Jacques understood that it was unrealistic to expect me to produce that at short notice. However, a learned article in a respected journal was viable, and I was asked to organise it. I gave the matter some thought and reached the conclusion that it would be better if the author of the article were someone other than myself; not that any suspicion attached to my name, but it would be more convincing for the next academic contribution to come from a different reputable source, to broaden the base of Hartier studies. I set my mind to orchestrating this, to producing a second pioneer in the field. Given their proven antipathy to me and my work, my colleagues in Paris would not easily be gulled into undertaking a project of this nature; but I had my eyes on other candidates. There were certain British and American scholars who might be deceived into putting pen to paper on my behalf, particularly if they could be fooled into thinking that they were the ones engineering a personal art-historical breakthrough. It was up to me, however, to provide the new material which must fall as if by chance into their laps.

That month I was due at a conference in Stuttgart at which fate decreed I should come across an ideal candidate. As soon as I met Dr Ewan Connard I recognised that here was a man with a sufficiently high opinion of himself to be duped into accepting faulty or incomplete historical evidence for a proposition provided that proposition reflected enough glory and sensation on himself as its proponent. I showed him photographs of two more canvases signed C.H. from the St Jacques group, pictures which I claimed to have discovered in a private collection in France. I also alerted him to a letter which I said existed in the Bibliothèque Nationale - indeed I may even have given it a spurious reference number. I happened to have a transcription of it, to save Connard having to check for himself. It purported to have been written by Georges Seurat to Claude Hartier in 1884, and was replete with extravagant praise by the former of the latter. It all looked reasonably convincing, and Dr Connard was worked up into a state of great excitement. As I judged he would, he accepted the authenticity of the letter without checking it. He snatched away the photographs which, after making a play of reluctance, I allowed him to have. I managed to create the impression that, while I was in possession of this sensational material, I had been too stupid, or too unassertive, to realise its full significance and act upon it. I even succeeded in convincing Connard that I was flattered by the interest which he, such an eminent authority, was showing in my paltry labours. He told me - and this was surely an untruth - that he had been intending to write a brief piece on Hartier for some time; would I mind his incorporating some of the documentation I had just shown him? I said that it would be an honour, and he went away delighted with himself. Four months later the Burlington Magazine carried his articled entitled Claude Hartier: The Forgotten Neo-Impressionist, or some such absurd title. I marvelled at the vanity of men who claimed to be serious scholars, and congratulated myself on a task successfully accomplished. The article served its purpose admirably, and St Jacques was pleased. The Hartier snowball was rolling.

Having bided his time, St Jacques now decided the moment was right to release another Hartier on to the international market. This he did by sending one of his underlings, posing as a French private owner, to New York with one of the pictures. He entered it for sale at Parke Bernet as a private seller, revealing nothing about its provenance except that he thought his late father had bought it in the provinces before the war. It bore, however, a recently-issued certificate of authenticity from the acknowledged Parisian expert on the artist, Dr Louis Ranchec, and that satisfied the auctioneers. More to the point, it satisfied the buying public for it exceeded all expectations when it realised 120,000 dollars, this time to a genuine bidder no doubt encouraged by the recent Connard article and the general atmosphere of hyped-up acquisitiveness which surrounds all important Impressionist sales. I was 12,000 dollars richer, and when St Jacques telephoned me that evening to give me the news, he assured me that this was only the beginning. If we handled the sale of the remaining canvases intelligently we would find we were sitting on a veritable gold mine. In the summer another Hartier was released on to the international auction market and fetched £130,000, this time in London. Again I received ten per cent.

The whole Hartier phenomenon was gathering momentum. News reached me that one of Connard's students in London was proposing to devote his thesis to the artist. Connard himself had allowed him to do so, I suspect, when Connard discovered how difficult it was to prise further Hartier information out of me or any other French source. This was of course explained by the fact that there was no more information as yet in existence. It was a gap that needed filling, and St Jacques was alive to the deficiency. He told me in no uncertain terms that if the operation was to be sustained, more biographical and artistic details about Hartier would have to be forthcoming. I had proved myself in the past to be an able art historian, he said, but now I must become an adept writer of fiction. A full life story and scheme of artistic development for Hartier must be invented, as plausibly as possible, with a view to bringing out a substantial book on the embryonic master.

I took retirement from the Institute in June. It was a year early, and represented I suppose a subconscious withdrawal, a severing of ties with official art history. I settled down to the task of creating a backcloth for Hartier. I had already established him as a native of Normandy, and a lapsed student in the atelier of Gérôme. Starting from there I decided to invent, using a liberal historical imagination, the course of his life and work. As circumstantial evidence for his story I decided that I would have to bring into existence a certain number of other documents, like letters from Hartier's mother to her sister, extracts from Hartier's own journal of the early 1880s, and snippets from the diary of his mythical wife, whom I christened Christine Lesrel. This lady was introduced into the plot to account for two apparent problems in presenting a convincing analysis of her husband's artistic endeavours. Why was his life's extant work likely to amount to only twenty or thirty canvases? Because the dragon-like protector of her husband's memory went mad in the later years of her widowhood and put large numbers of his pictures on the bonfire. Why are there not more contemporary accounts of Claude Hartier? Because under his wife's irresistible influence he packed his bags and retreated from Paris at a young age, forbidden to show his work publicly until he could be guaranteed the reception which she felt was his due. For me the task of writing this biography was to be a demanding job, impossible to achieve without considerable ingenuity. In the meantime came news from St Jacques that he had sold another Hartier, this time privately through his own gallery to the American collector King C. Wattle. Again my own bank balance improved.

I stayed in Paris throughout August in my rented apartment. My intention was to work solidly through the holidays without outside distractions. But a curious thing happened. In my solitude I became victim to the most appalling depression. It was a reaction to many months' deliberate dulling of my moral sense, a gathering cloud of conscience and remorse which broke suddenly and dramatically over me. I was paralysed. With complete clarity the turpitude of my conduct was borne in on me, how it was motivated by the most demeaning resentments and jealousies, how its continuance would achieve only my total degradation. By this time all I had achieved was to put together a brief draft of a few pages outlining Hartier's life by reference to various extracts from mythical letters and journals; now I could add not one word. Beyond anything I wanted to bring the whole dreadful charade to an end. Every day it continued longer was an agony to me, and I was wracked with revulsion at myself for having allowed myself to be drawn into such depravity. I had prostituted my scholarship and dishonoured my vocation. What had my life been worth?

I sought to communicate my state of mind to St Jacques, but he was unreachable, lotus-eating on an Aegean island throughout the month. By the time he returned at the beginning of September I had reached the end of my tether, and I went to him immediately to tell him I could not continue. I would have returned the money he had already paid me, but of course it amounted to a sizeable sum and it was long since spent. Needless to say, I had no other resources. I was in an emotional, almost distraught, state and told him he was a crook. He only laughed at me and said I would get over what he called my "little attack of conscience". He argued that my career as a serious academic was finished whatever I did now, so why not be finished and rich rather than finished and penurious? I hated him for his cynicism, and for the way I had allowed him to corrupt me. I moped on in Paris for a time, not sleeping at night and brooding on my dishonour. Somehow I had to get away.

What prompted me finally to make the break and run suddenly to the south was a telephone call from St Jacques telling me that he wanted another expertise on Hartier. It was as if my protestations to him had never occurred, were not to be taken seriously. I packed my bags and disappeared leaving no forwarding address. For several weeks I moved between cheap hotels like some half-dead survivor of a shipwreck swept from rock to rock, until I arrived here in the hills overlooking the Mediterranean where I have found lodgings of a sort. St Jacques cannot find me here. That is my only consolation.

Now that I have written all this down I feel a little more at peace. I do not expect or plead for forgiveness from the person who may read this. I cannot deny that I have behaved reprehensibly, that my life's achievement such as it was is now utterly devalued. What is there left for me? I hope, however, that the reader of this document will at least understand the genuineness and profundity of my remorse. I have been through the horrors of hell these past few months. I have sought all manner of refuges, from alcohol to narcotics; the only measure of release from my anguish which I have achieved is in the thought that this confession at least sets the record straight. If in so doing it also points a finger of accusation at the original progenitor of the scheme, Raoul St Jacques, then it will not have been in vain. I do not know the full story of his acquisition of the original canvases nor of his formation of the plan of how to handle them, but I suspect the involvement of the restorer Théodore Gontier. One day they will be brought to justice; I feel that I myself have suffered enough. As I lay down my pen, my misery is overwhelming. My resources will enable me to live this life of baleful exile for another month or two, but thereafter I neither know nor care what will become of me.

Signed, Louis M. Ranchec.

Evan rose from his chair and laid the papers aside. He went to the hotel bedroom window and looked out. In the road three stories below he saw the lights of cars passing, then halting as traffic lights turned to red. A man and a woman, well wrapped against the cold, hurried home arm in arm. He marvelled that life could continue as normal when the very foundations of his own world had been rocked by the revelations he had just read. It was callous that the oblivious traffic did not grind to a halt, that horrified passers-by did not pause and look up in sympathy at his window now that this knowledge had come into his possession. One man was dead, that was terrible. What was worse was that another had not even existed.

A few hours later in California the fabulously wealthy widow who was Chairman of the Board of Governors of the San Pietro Museum of Fine Arts rose smiling from her seat.

"Well, Dr Connard, we've completed our deliberations and I guess you've got yourself a job. We hope you'll accept our invitation to become the new Director of our Museum."

"I should be honoured."

"There are just a few formalities to be gone through, then the appointment can be confirmed officially in four weeks. Then we can go public with it. Dr Connard, my co-board members and I look forward to welcoming a scholar of your calibre to San Pietro."

"And I look forward to justifying the confidence you have shown in me."

They walked out on to the terrace. There was a gorgeous sunset, and the air was still pleasantly warm. The champagne was waiting for them.

SEVENTEEN

Evan Conrad lifted the telephone to dial a number. He was back in his Paris hotel room, having flown up from Nice that morning. It was nearly twenty-four hours since he had read Ranchec's confession, and during that time he had done a lot of hard thinking, and reached a few conclusions.

His initial reaction to the Hartier story as delineated by Ranchec had been disbelief, sustained by the suspicion that the whole statement might be some sort of macabre practical joke. But the more he absorbed of Ranchec's tortured revelations, the truer they rang, the more plausible they became. Had not the man just committed suicide? Was not this document evidence of the clearest possible motive for taking his own life? Louis Ranchec had been living a lie and had been unable to face himself for doing so. It all added up. And if what was written on those sheets of paper was true, then a whole series of further consequences and implications had to be taken into account and considered. Not the least of these was that Evan himself looked pretty stupid, having been about to devote four years and a PhD thesis to researching an artist who never existed. He burned with shame and indignation, outraged at the turpitude of the whole venture, at the corruption of St Jacques, at the duplicity of Ranchec, willing accomplice to the besmirchment of Scholarship.

Evan had resolved that the untruth must be eradicated forthwith, that the fraud must be exposed. The good name of Art History and the integrity of the Art Market must be protected, and he, Evan Conrad, having been initially an unwitting party to the promulgation of the deception, would now take upon himself a crusade to set the record straight. Ewan Connard would need to be informed at the earliest possible opportunity of course. He would suffer a major embarrassment, but that did not weigh in the balance against the importance of the proclamation of the truth. But Evan's first duties were in Paris, he decided. Should he not go straight to the man chiefly responsible for the whole deplorable situation, Raoul St Jacques, confront him, and let him know the game was up? Fate had thrown into Evan's hands this damning evidence in the form of Ranchec's letter, just exactly the damning evidence which had eluded the mysterious M. Alexandre earlier in the week when he came to search the dead man's lodgings. Probably M. Alexandre was not a relation at all, speculated Evan; more likely he was another St Jacques minion despatched to clear away any compromising material which might be lurking. Perhaps he was even the same man who had stolen Ranchec's original notes on Hartier from Evan's hotel room. Well, he had failed in his task at the Leclaires, thanks to the infant Alain. And now Evan, his idealism roused and his personal dignity deeply insulted, would make sure that the guilty men paid.

So the newly self-appointed Elliot Ness of the art world had boarded the Paris plane that morning with his jaw set in a hard line of incorruptibility. But as he travelled he was prey to sudden doubts. The weasel-faced St Jacques, devious and unruffled, taunted him with his self-assurance. Evan remembered what sort of a man he was, the sort of person who would not be moved by morally-outraged accusations, even when backed up by Ranchec's written confession. He would laugh them off, deny them, or turn very nasty indeed. Perhaps on second thoughts St Jacques should be left till last and only approached when the weight of evidence against him was irresistible. To that end Evan decided that he would first visit the Bibliothèque Nationale and also pay a call on M. Théodore Gontier, the restorer, whose telephone number had appeared in Ranchec's original file. Gontier could nail St Jacques, and Evan meant to persuade him that he should. He was therefore now ringing him from the hotel.

"Could I speak to Monsieur Gontier, please?"

A slurred voice said: "Who wants him?"

"My name's Evan Conrad. I'm telephoning him to discuss certain important matters concerning the late Louis Ranchec."

"You're not the police?"

"No, not at all. I'm an art historian. But I need urgently to speak to M. Gontier."

"You're speaking to him." The admission was followed by a terrible wracking cough. "Merde! I am not feeling so good."

"I'm sorry. But what I've got to talk to you about is important. I'd very much like to come and see you."

"I regret, it's not convenient."

Evan steeled himself. His natural inclination was always to back away from confrontation, to avoid direct conflict of wills. But now he said: "I think you'd better make it convenient. You see I know about Ranchec and St Jacques and the Hartier business."

"You know? What do you know?" There was a perceptible difference in tone now.

"I know everything. In fact I'm about to take the matter up with the proper authorities." Evan paused, then ventured: "But it's my impression that St Jacques and Ranchec were the instigators of the fraud, and I thought you might be able to shed a little more light on this. Maybe you weren't so closely involved yourself?"

"What do you mean?" There was definite unease now, even a hint of fear. "This whole bloody business wasn't my idea, not at all."

"Look, we should talk. Perhaps I can help you."

"Oh, my God. I don't know."

"Where can I find you?"

More coughing, then with surprising lack of further resistance Gontier spilled out the address. Evan said decisively: "I'll be with you in an hour."

Such assertiveness and resolve were not Evan's natural attributes. But they were weapons which sprang readily to his hand roused as he was to such a pitch of righteous fury by the Hartier deception. What gave his anger that extra edge to triumph over instinctive diffidence and reserve was that his own dignity had been wounded: he was personally stung to have been a victim of the fraud. How dare they, these people, make fun of his own very serious academic ambitions? A huge outrage had been committed against the ideal of Scholarship, an ideal which Evan knew had to be protected at all costs. And a crime had also taken place against the principle of Fair Play in the Art Market; as far as he knew this was also a principle to be upheld with vigour. And if his resolve had needed any further strengthening it was provided now by his second telephone call, to the Bibliothèque Nationale. An unusually helpful gentleman informed him that according to his records the reference number which Evan gave him bore no relation to any Seurat letter held in the collection; indeed it appeared to have no connection with any item housed in the establishment. Might there not be some mistake? Yes, there might very well be some mistake, agreed Evan, and set off for the address Gontier had given him with a purposeful stride.

As he walked, he thought of Sylvie. Even in this turmoil she was never far from his mind: his first action that morning had been to telephone her apartment, but it had been a vain hope that he would actually find her there. She remained distressingly elusive, a ravishingly beautiful butterfly who flew at random into his orbit and out again. He had no idea of her present whereabouts, nor of her likely time of return. Was it really only three nights ago that he had achieved such intimacy with her? It seemed more like three months, so eventful had the intervening period proved. But surely the closeness they had enjoyed must mean something? She would not disappear again for as long as the last time? Questions, questions: just what she did not like. Evan told himself that in order to win her he must be as resolute in her pursuit as he was being in his crusade to expose the deceptions of St Jacques and Hartier. The problem was that when he contemplated the Hartier scandal, he was very angry indeed; but when he contemplated Sylvie he just felt weak at the knees.

Evan climbed the stairs to Gontier's apartment. The notice on the door said Théodore Gontier, Conservateur des Tableaux, and the man himself appeared, wheezing unhealthily, in answer to Evan's knock. Gontier was not an appealing sight; he was perhaps fifty-five, corpulent, with sparse curly grey hair and puffy features. Nicotine-stained fingers plucked a cigarette from grimy lips, and as he breathed a nervous greeting it became apparent that he had already drunk a considerable quantity of alcohol although it was only mid-afternoon. The room into which Evan was shown was a restorer's studio but bore evidence that it was also used as a bedroom and living room by its occupier. Canvases stood stacked unsystematically against the walls, and a variety of work tops were laden with chemicals, oily rags, paint tubes, derelict cups of coffee, empty whisky bottles, cigarette ends, and an arbitrary tooth brush standing alone in a mug. The floor was filthy. A stained sofa covered in magazines and articles of clothing offered the only possible place to sit, if one discounted the unmade bed in the corner. On an easel stood a small Corot-esque landscape of surprisingly good quality.

"Scotch?" enquired Gontier unsteadily, unscrewing a half-empty bottle with shaky hand. Evan declined. The thought of a man in this state attempting to restore a delicate work of art filled him with the same apprehension as the image of Roger Brady operating on his first patient the morning after one of his "benders".

Gontier filled his own glass and turned bleary, unhappy eyes on his visitor. "So what do you want me to tell you?"

"I know most of the story. I have read the full confession Louis Ranchec wrote before he died. I know that Hartier never existed, that the whole thing was concocted by St Jacques and Ranchec as a money-making enterprise. But I want to hear your side of the affair."

Gontier shook his head. "Jesus Christ! St Jacques won't like this. He always said Ranchec had too much to lose ever to spill the beans. Now the poor sod's dead, but he's got his revenge."

"How were you involved in all this?"

Gontier rubbed his eyes with the palms of his hands and did not reply for a moment. "Believe me, I wasn't really involved, I had no idea things would turn out like this. It's a nightmare. Look, I'm a picture restorer, a good one, at least a good one when I'm sober. I've done work for the Louvre, you know. I should never have allowed St Jacques to start this whole bloody scheme, I told him we'd all end up in jail."

"How did the whole scheme start?"

"I'll tell you how it started, and you'll see that it wasn't my idea. But St Jacques gave me a good profit on them, and it was a perfectly straight deal, there was no harm in it at the time."

"What did he give you a good profit on?"

"On the pictures, the pictures that were turned into Hartiers."

"Where did they come from?"

"They came from this girl. She came to see me, out of the blue, three years ago it was. She had twenty or thirty unstretched canvases, all rolled up. We spread them out on the floor over there to have a look at them. Yes, over there." He drank again, nervously, and appeared to lose the thread of his narrative.

"Go on," said Evan.

"Shit. It's a bloody awful business about Ranchec."

Suddenly for an awful moment Evan thought the restorer was going to cry. There was a fraught pause while he stared emotionally at his glass. Then he said: "Limoges."

"Limoges?"

"Yes, Limoges, she came from Limoges. She said she'd found the canvases in her uncle's attic, because he had just died and she was clearing out the house. She wanted advice on whether they were worth restoring. She said her uncle had painted them round the time of the Great War; they were quite pretty pointillist landscapes, and it seemed they were by this uncle because his name was Charles Herault, or something like that, and they were signed with the initials." Gontier screwed his eyes up in the effort of recalling events elusive in the alcoholic mists. He added: "They weren't bad, kind of pastiches really."

"So what did you do? Restore them?"

"No, it transpired she really wanted to get rid of them, so I bought them from her. I was a bit liquid then: I gave her 8,000 francs for the lot."

"How did St Jacques get involved?"

"I showed them to him when he came round to bring me a picture to clean. He was intrigued by them. He said what a pity they hadn't been done thirty years earlier, contemporary with Seurat rather than a generation after. We laughed a bit and I thought no more about it. But St Jacques was back a couple of weeks later and said held buy the lot off me at a good profit. The condition was that I should put the C.H. initials on to the unsigned canvases so that they were all signed. I agreed to it because I really needed the money then. But I only found out later what his plans were, how he'd got Ranchec working for him. I don't mind telling you, I was pretty shattered when I saw one of the bloody things coming up in New York and fetching $100,000."

"Didn't you ask St Jacques what was going on?"

"I did, I did," said Gontier miserably. "But I was hard up again and he offered to meet my debts. Shit, what a business."

"You were bought off," said Evan disdainfully. The sense of outrage rose within him again as the duplicity was confirmed. He recalled his own innocent enthusiasm as he embarked on the quest for an artist who did not exist. It was acutely embarrassing. What would his friends at the Institute say? And what about Ewan Connard? He should be informed at the earliest opportunity. Evan looked at Gontier with pity and contempt. His stream of expiatory confession seemed to have run dry, and as he refilled his glass yet once more it was hard to imagine a more wretched looking character.

"You'd better be careful, you know," mumbled Gontier. "St Jacques is a dangerous man to be on the wrong side of. I'm having no more to do with him, I'm washing my hands of the whole business. Herault, Hartier: it was a bad day for me that girl walked in through the door with those pictures."

"I'll tread carefully, but I'm going to expose him. This fraud cannot be allowed to continue. It's making a mockery of.... of everything."

"Well, don't bring me into it." Gontier was suddenly defiant. "I'll deny I ever spoke to you. Ranchec ended up at the bottom of a cliff, and I don't want to follow him."

"Are you suggesting that St Jacques...."

"I'm not suggesting anything. I just don't want anything more to do with it. I'm not doing any more work for St Jacques, but I'm sure as hell not going to give evidence against him. Keep me out of this!"

"What about the girl who sold you the canvases? Can I get in touch with her?"

"No. She left no address."

"You never saw her again?"

Unease returned to Gontier's bloodshot eyes. "Christ!" he exclaimed, and rose unsteadily to his feet. "Now I remember." He crossed to a small chest of drawers, fished about within and pulled out a small rolled canvas. "She came back to me six months later and dropped this off. She said it was an extra one by her uncle which she'd come across and that I might as well have it. I thought about selling it to St Jacques, but I put it away for the time being and then forgot it."

Evan took it from him. Exhausted by his exertions, the restorer slumped down on to the sofa again. He looked very ill. Evan spread out the canvas and saw it was a colourful pointillist coastal scene, measuring about 12 by 18 inches with the magic initials C.H. in the bottom right hand corner. Inspected closely in the light of what he had heard in the past 24 hours, it appeared a poorish pastiche. But it was no better nor worse than others he had seen in his time. He re-rolled the canvas thoughtfully, and announced:

"I think I should take this with me. It will be important evidence."

He anticipated a degree of resistance from the whisky-sodden figure to whom the declaration was addressed, but all he heard was a low snoring. Turning round from the light in which he had been examining the picture, Evan saw that he was indeed asleep. Why bother him? His skin looked disgustingly mottled, he was dribbling slightly, and his breathing was irregular. An image of degradation. Leave him be; Evan would take the picture now, remove it not as an act of theft but as a sort of Citizen's Arrest, a commandeering of crucial evidence. Nothing wrong with that, he told himself, as he closed the door carefully behind him, having placed the small rolled canvas gently into his briefcase.

What now? he wondered. The main thing was to set into reverse the whole process of deception which had created the Hartier phenomenon. It was bad enough that the Art Market should be sullied by this appalling hoax; but what was far worse was that academic disciplines had been compromised, that the integrity of Art History itself had been undermined. Scholars had, in most cases in good faith, put their names, their insignia of approval as it were, to completely false material. He must inform all the innocent owners who had given good money to possess pictures by Hartier, get King Wattle's example withdrawn from the sale, expose the immoral operations of St Jacques (would it mean a prison sentence? He rather hoped so.) Then he must see Ewan Connard, a retraction must be published in the Burlington Magazine. As far as possible the whole sorry episode, replete as it was with evidence of the worse side of human nature, must be written out from the records.

The canvas which he had concealed in his briefcase began to worry him. It was important to be able to produce it as proof of the crime which had been perpetrated, and he had some confused vision of its being produced in court at some future date; his first instinct had been to take it with him on the plane back to London first thing in the morning. But it was illegal to carry out from France any work of art without an export licence. That had been drummed into him by Rokeby's, and the last thing he wanted now was to be stopped for questioning at customs on that score. He might be unwittingly implicated thereby into the whole sordid intrigue. No, he had better leave the picture in safe hands in France for the time being. Where? Inspiration came to him: he would leave it with Sylvie. He would go to her apartment now, and if she was in he would explain everything in person. If she had not yet returned, it would still be possible to leave the canvas since, in a gesture of the vainest sentimentality, Evan had "forgotten" to post back through the letterbox Sylvie's key when he departed the last time. Its continued possession had been a comfort and a charm to him. He had taken it out to look at and to cherish at regular intervals over the past seventy-two hours. Now he could use it to gain entry in order to leave the picture and a covering note.

Of course Sylvie was still away. Evan moved through the shadowy flat as if in the most sacred shrine. He penetrated momentarily into that holy of holies, the bedroom, where her scent still lingered provocatively. For a second she seemed heart-stoppingly close. He left the canvas and a brief note on her dressing table; then he let himself out again and this time posted the key back through the letterbox. There was something pleasingly Arthurian about entrusting the weapon with which he intended to right momentous wrongs to the care of the lady who was mistress of his heart.

Ewan Connard arrived at the private view in St James's in a better than average mood. He had thrown off his jet-lag speedily and was savouring the imminence of the announcement of his glittering new appointment. Of course it was still secret, and it was tantalising not to be able to speak of it to people on an occasion like this, but the glory could wait. He took a glass of champagne and gave his attention momentarily to the exhibition. The proprietors of the gallery were an unlikely duo, one the elegant younger son of a British noble house and the other a former manicurist from Lewisham who had fallen on soft times, progressing from health-club ownership to art dealing in easy stages. They were united in their impeccable suiting, their smooth talking, and their prehensile social tentacles. The show they had mounted rejoiced in the title "Edwardian Summers: Aspects of British Impressionism 1890-1930", a piece of nomenclature which betrayed a greater concern for vivid marketing than for historical accuracy. There were a number of bright, banal scenes of children jostling each other on beaches and of ladies lying languidly in sun-drenched gardens, the pictures' ignorance of simple principles of draughtsmanship and resultant fudging of outline constituting in most cases their primary claim to being considered "Impressionist". Ewan overheard his aristocratic host describing a particularly lurid coastal landscape to his avid listener as "grotesquely underrated, it's like a Derain really", and averted his ears. It was more rewarding to look at the people than the pictures, and a surprisingly large crowd of art world personalities were present, together with a tempting number of youngish females. His hosts were indeed more renowned as socialites than connoisseurs; what the wares on sale lacked in draughtsmanship, the sellers made up for with a different sort of drawing power.

The ex-manicurist buttonholed Ewan. "How are you? So glad you could come, I haven't seen you for ages. Have you been away?"

"Just back from California, actually."

"Yes, I didn't think it was the old sun lamp. Been doing

something exciting out there?"

"Quite exciting, yes," smirked Ewan, "but I can't say too much about it at the moment."

"Mmm. We'll all be agog for revelations. Look, have some more champagne. Do you know Amanda Fyffe-Knightley?" Ewan perked up as he shook hands with a classic specimen of the Sloane Ranger. She gasped breathless greetings in return. The phenomenon of this type of girl fascinated him, and he settled to a closer study. It was his experience that in girls like Amanda the outward veneer of conventionality, silk scarves, pearls, and solid establishment thinking occasionally veiled volcanic sexual passion. There could be an element of thrilling paradox to be savoured between apparent straight-laced purity, an implicit denial even of the existence of sexual organs except in certain dogs and horses, and real enthusiasm for the job once the lights were out and the matter was in hand. But Ewan, unlike the unfortunate Jean-Pierre Grifon, understood that there was an art to achieving this exciting release from restraint, an art elusive to those not well-versed in the way of English womanhood. Most Sloane Rangers adored practical jokes, pranks, and high-spirited japes. The key was to present the whole enterprise in these terms, to create an atmosphere of jokey badinage rather than one which threatened serious intent. A pass should be made as "a bit of a laugh". If encouragement was received on this basis, the moment then came for a subtle change of gear, and final conquest might be achieved by stimulating the target's traditional wholehearted enthusiasm for any activity undertaken (like hockey at school on a wet afternoon, much more fun if you put your back into it) and channelling it into the sexual act. It was not the girl, who might well as in this case be nothing of a beauty, but the paradox which exerted the attraction.

"I'm a secretary at Rokeby's, actually," she volunteered in response to his inquiry.

"Oh, really? It must be an exciting time at Rokeby's with the Wattle sale coming up this week."

"It's brilliant. The only thing is the beastly telephone never stops ringing." Amanda giggled as an attentive waiter recharged their glasses. "That's enough, I'm getting really quite tiddly!"

"Oh, come on, I think you've earned a little relaxation after a hard day's work. No-one has enough fun these days, we should all get out and enjoy ourselves a bit more!"

"Jolly good idea!" Amanda giggled again and reached for her handbag. "You know what, I'm going to have a cigarette."

"A thoroughly good decision, you're getting the hang already," encouraged Ewan, leaning across with his cigarette lighter. Glancing down before she snapped her bag shut he was surprised to catch a glimpse of what appeared to be a bottle of Dettol.

"And what do you do? Sorry, I don't think I caught your name properly," inquired Amanda.

"Ewan Connard. I teach a little art history at the London Institute, amongst other things." He smiled self-deprecatingly.

"Super." Amanda paused for a moment, caught in shadowy remembrance of some barely-definable incident all but lost in the murk of time. "I was just thinking of Evan Conrad who runs our Impressionist department. He came from the Institute, didn't he?"

"He did indeed."

"So you worked under him?"

It was as Connard struggled with the task of setting straight this flagrant misapprehension without striking a note of pompousness inappropriate to a man about to prove himself one of nature's high-spirited fun-lovers that he was accosted by Dr Fabia Neate-Panker. She pecked him on the cheek and said in a proprietorial tone: "Ewan: wonderful to see you. I must snatch you away to meet someone who very much wants to talk to you. Do excuse us." Amanda was abandoned, an unlit bonfire whose ignition would have to be postponed. Fabia should not be alienated. He followed her obediently between braying guests to the other side of the room where he was introduced to an earnest and studious-looking American.

"Ewan, this is Rudi Grossner. Rudi wanted your advice on one of the Wattle pictures in the sale at Rokeby's."

"Yes, Dr Connard. I would deem it an inestimable favour if you could guide me. I act for a major mid-Western collector."

"Of course."

"You viewed the Wattle sale?"

"Yes, this afternoon as a matter of fact."

"My client is wild for the canvas by Claude Hartier. I thought I just must check with you as the world expert on the artist. Am I correct in surmising that this example is a good one?"

Connard had heard of the demise of Louis Ranchec; it had not escaped his notice that the Frenchman's passing left him pretty much undisputed as the new ultimate arbiter on Claude Hartier, by virtue of his Burlington Magazine article. It was a role in which he was not averse to being cast.

"Absolutely genuine, of course," he pronounced decisively. "Circa 1886, I would say, and not at all a bad one. Your client could buy a lot worse."

Rudi Grossner nodded in gratitude, and Fabia flashed a smile which spoke of unstinted admiration for Connard's prowess and expertise. Ewan decided that a little dinner was called for, followed by drinks in Manchester Square. There was a certain amount to celebrate: his accession to the position of world expert on Claude Hartier was the icing on the cake of his achievement in capturing the Directorship of the San Pietro Museum, and for this he owed Fabia a favour or two.

As they made for the door together, he was approached by a weasel-faced Frenchman.

"Dr Connard?"

"Yes?"

"Ah, it is a pleasure to meet you. My name is Raoul St Jacques, from Paris. Forgive me for introducing myself in this way, but I felt we should meet and talk as we have some interests in common."

"Do we? What are they?" Ewan was by now helping Fabia into her fur coat.

"Claude Hartier particularly. But I can see now is not the moment. Could I invite you to dinner one evening this week? What about Cecconi's, on Friday after the sale?"

"What is all this about?"

"I'd like you to write a book for me on Hartier. I think you will find the terms very - ah - persuasive. Telephone me at my hotel, here is my card."

"It seems to me that you are considerably in demand," observed Fabia, impressed, as they emerged out into Jermyn Street.

Ewan could not in all conscience bring himself to disagree. "Maybe so, but for now all I'm really looking forward to is a mutually-gratifying discussion of the early work of Pelizza da Volpedo. Will you join me?" As he put his hand in his coat pocket it closed conveniently about a long-forgotten packet of Raunch.

EIGHTEEN

"That is an incredible story," declared Freddy Fairbanks. He flashed a conspiratorial grin at Evan, the sort of breathtaking grin that had earned him his reputation as one of the most charming men in London. "You know, when the Frogs put their heads together they're capable of some pretty crooked deals, but this just about takes the biscuit."

Evan flushed with the righteous indignation which still beset him whenever he contemplated the full enormity of the outrage. He forgot for a moment the acute embarrassment of sitting opposite Freddy, here in the decorous club-like atmosphere of the latter's Rokeby office, in the knowledge that Freddy knew he knew about Renata; the details of the joint deputy chairman's private life, however closely they touched on Evan's own intimate past, were a separate issue and could be disregarded for the moment. The account that he had given Freddy of the steps by which the full duplicity of the Hartier scandal had been revealed to him was comprehensive, including a sight of the Ranchec confession and details of his conversation with Gontier. Nor had he omitted to mention the fact that the Seurat letter had never been part of the Bibliothèque Nationale collection. Guilt was established, and now Evan itched for action.

"We've got to do something at once," he exclaimed. "We must withdraw King Wattle's Hartier from the sale, and we must confront St Jacques. Or should we just put the whole matter in the hands of the police?"

Freddy blinked and grinned, if possible, even more disarmingly. "Now hold on a minute, old chap, you're being a little hasty. What we can't afford to do in a delicate situation like this is go crashing in like a bull in a china shop. Let's think carefully: there are a lot of different angles to this which have got to be considered."

"It seems pretty simple to me," said Evan hotly. "A crime has been committed, and the criminals must be brought to justice."

"Of course you're absolutely right, absolutely right. It would run completely counter to Rokeby's philosophy, to all that Rokeby's stands for, to condone any sort of criminal activity. Good lord, we gave a donation of £500 to the Art Fraud Squad this year, that's how seriously we take our responsibilities, and no-one feels more strongly about this than I do. But we have to consider how it affects a variety of innocent people, consider the interests of the Art Market, and the interests of our clients, which may be seriously damaged if we act too precipitately."

"But surely we should alert King Wattle?"

"No, I really think that at this stage that would not be wise. Most unwise, in fact. I mean, look at it this way: the sale of his collection is only a few days away. There's already tremendous interest, and the whole auction is coming nicely to the boil at the right time. It couldn't be better, it's got the feel of a real hum-dinging success, and that's good for everyone in the art market. But these things are precarious, you know, horribly precarious. The announcement that one of the pictures in the collection has been withdrawn as a fake could rock the boat just enough to tip the balance from success to failure. Buyers are fantastically suggestible, extraordinarily sensitive to the slightest straws in the wind. If the sale has the smell of success about it, they excite each other from extravagance to extravagance and the level of prices rises above all expectations. But once word goes round that there's something - even the smallest thing - not quite right, the whole chase can go horribly cold. Believe me, I've seen it happen. Lots would fail to meet their reserve, people wouldn't bid, and Wattle wouldn't make money. How could it possibly help to tell him - and the world at large - that his Hartier is a fake?"

"But.... it is a fake."

"A fake? Well, yes and no, but it's not an easy thing to define a fake. After all, Wattle's Hartier is as genuine an example as any other in the world. From that point of view there is nothing to be gained from upsetting him. Or the market."

"But what about St Jacques? He can't be allowed to go on the way he has. He's been committing crimes, he should go to jail."

"Up to a point, of course. But I've known old Raoul St Jacques for twenty years. He can be an absolute prick, of course, but he's an important dealer. And I happen to know (though this is entirely between you and me) that he's coming to the Wattle sale with about ten million pounds worth of bids from major Swiss clients. One can't disregard bidding power like that, you know. We'd be cutting our own throats to alienate him."

"But the whole thing's bound to come out sooner or later."

"Maybe, but far better later than sooner, and better not through our own direct agency. Certainly better not now, days before the most important Impressionist sale we've ever had."

Evan felt as though he was running through treacle. Freddy's cloying smoothness ensnared his every objection, no matter how cogent and strongly held. It was frustrating in the extreme, but more experienced aims than Evan's had been deflected by Freddy's barrage of eloquence, charm and persuasion. He vaguely sensed that he was up against a man reacting to the most powerful stimulus he could experience, the need to protect a vested interest. Further expostulation would be fruitless: clearly the racket was not to be exposed through Rokeby's, not if Freddy and the other members of the executive committee had anything to do with it. They needed beyond anything a successful sale out of the Wattle collection, and Evan must abandon all thoughts of progressing down this avenue. But there were other avenues, oh yes, and his resolve to clear up the whole dreadful business had not diminished. He must bide his time a little longer and approach the task from a different angle. Now he swallowed his fury and said submissively: "Well, of course I do understand that it's a delicate situation...."

Freddy leapt on his words enthusiastically. "I knew I could rely on an intelligent chap like you to take that attitude. And you must think of your own interests, too: it doesn't need me to tell you that if the Wattle sale is an out and out success, it will only reflect well on you."

Evan nodded, and Freddy was encouraged to adopt a more confidential tone: "I must say that I've been most impressed with your performance in the months that you've been here, and I've no doubt that you'll go a long way in this organisation. But there are moments when you must tread carefully, exercise discretion. I hope you won't mind my giving you this advice: I do so because I flatter myself I know you quite well, having identified your great potential and capabilities the moment we first met, and because I like to feel we've become friends." Here a further winning smile flashed across the desk. "And of course we do have certain other things in common in our private lives." This last remark was accompanied by a rather more roguish, man-to-man smirk.

"Oh, quite," mumbled Evan, covered in confusion and blushing deeply as he identified the reference to Renata. Such was Freddy's sublime self-confidence that he could even turn an apparent weakness

- in this case his wildly unsuitable liaison with Renata Crum - into an instrument for asserting his will. There was no arguing with him. Indeed prolonging the present topic of conversation would only lead to further embarrassment. Evan must admit temporary defeat and withdraw.

"'Ow was Paris?" enquired an unfamiliar man in Jean-Pierre Grifon's office as Evan passed by. "Did you 'ave an agreeable weekend?"

"Very, thank you," said Evan politely, letting himself into his boot-cupboard. A moment later he doubled back to check on the person who had just spoken to him. Good God, it WAS Grifon, but Grifon transformed by the loss of his jet-black locks, now cut to a militaristic brevity and coloured platinum blond.

"I see you are admiring my new cut of hair." Grifon spoke with considerable pride.

"Yes.... yes, very much." Evan shook his head in perplexity. Grifon blond, Grifon dark, Hartier genuine, Hartier fake: nothing seemed certain any more.

"The English girls, they are now - 'ow you say? - giving me the eye."

"Oh?" It seemed unlikely.

Grifon leered knowingly back at him. "You were right."

"I was?"

"About the blond hairs. The girls adore them."

"I'm pleased to have been of help."

"Have you noticed Victoria? She is looking at me often today. I think I shall ask her to 'ave lunch with me."

"You do that."

"Oh, by the way: while you were making your meeting with Monsieur Fairbanks, that lady from Paris, Mademoiselle Legrand, she telephoned you."

"What! Sylvie? She telephoned me? Can I ring her back?"

"No, I regret - she said she was in a callbox, and she had to depart on an aeroplane."

"Where was she going?"

"She did not tell me," reported Jean-Pierre with an infuriating shrug of his shoulders. "It is important?"

"It'll have to wait." Evan retreated miserably into his office. Sylvie. So near and yet so far. What balm to his troubled spirit the mere sound of her voice would have been, and yet he had been denied even that. In the chaos of the events of recent days the interlude of their intimacy seemed increasingly unreal. He needed to be reassured by contact with her; and telling her of his recent shattering experiences and discoveries might be one way of getting them into perspective. But what chance was there of that now? What was the destination of the plane she was boarding? It could be another continent, the other side of the world. It could be Bali, setting of their shared dreams. Damn Freddy for detaining him with his soft soap when he could otherwise have been in his office to take her call. Damn Hartier, for being the cause of his meeting with Freddy. Damn St Jacques, the direct progenitor of Hartier. Right, he resolved with renewed vigour, he would settle all their hashes once and for all. If Rokeby's were not to be the agency for the exposure of the scandal, he would pursue another line.

He lifted the receiver of his telephone and dialled the home number of Dr Ewan Connard.

"That is an incredible story," declared Ewan Connard.

He sat swathed in a particularly extravagant silk dressing gown on the elegant fauteuil to which he had been glued with mounting horror since Evan Conrad began his account of the Hartier fraud. Little had he suspected the appalling revelations about to spill out; he had greeted his former pupil with casual urbanity, ushered him into the drawing room and introduced him to Dr Fabia Neate-Panker immaculate in her Dior working suit, smoothly explaining away her presence in the Manchester Square flat at such an early hour with an unlikely but impressive sounding tale about a breakfast meeting to discuss a book on Italian Divisionism. Fabia had departed and he had sat down with Conrad for the chat about something important which Evan had urgently requested. Then the nightmare had begun. His first instinct had been, of course, that the revelations unfolding, the sequence of confessions and sensations, could not possibly be true, that they were the product of some fevered and malignant imagination. A mythomaniac was at large. However, the sight of the document written by Ranchec and Evan's detailed description of his interview with Gontier convinced him that the whole thing was possessed of a dreadful plausibility. The news that the Seurat letter did not exist in the collection of the Bibliothèque Nationale came as a further sickening blow.

"So you never saw the original of this letter Seurat allegedly wrote to Hartier?" demanded Evan implacably, turning a jagged-edged knife in the wound Connard was not yet prepared to admit to having sustained.

"Well, of course with a scholar of Ranchec's standing it wasn't necessary at that point to go routing around to check his every reference. It would have been tantamount to discourtesy. But hold on: we mustn't jump to hasty conclusions. There may very well be a perfectly legitimate explanation for all this."

"For this?" persisted Evan, brandishing Ranchec's written confession.

"Yes, even for that." Now if ever Connard's brain must move with lightning speed to justify its alpha status. It was an emergency calling for incisiveness and not a little imagination. The implications of the news that Hartier effectively did not exist were disastrous in so far as he was concerned. He would be a laughing stock, the man who wrote an article in the Burlington Magazine about an artist who was no more than the figment of an unscrupulous dealer's imagination. He had been taken for a ride, and the world would see that he had been taken for a ride. His professional standing, for so long on a thoroughly satisfactory arc of ascent, would forthwith plummet. Dullards like the regrettable Professor Throg would receive the news with glee. More pertinently, once the board of trustees of the San Pietro Museum of Fine Arts learned of the affair they might well refuse to confirm his appointment as Director. They could hardly be expected to support the candidature of a man who was shown to be at best a fool and at worst a charlatan. There was only one thing for it: the whole story must be suppressed. It could not be allowed to surface, not now of all times.

"But surely this confession is proof?" insisted Evan.

"It's evidence of something, but of what? I mean poor old Louis Ranchec seems to have become pretty unstable towards the end of his life. A drug addict, an alcoholic, a manic depressive, he's not the most reliable witness. And he clearly detested St Jacques. It could very well be that he put together this whole concoction just to damage St Jacques - and certain of his eminent colleagues in the academic world - from beyond the grave. Well, we shouldn't dismiss that possibility, anyway."

"Why should Gontier corroborate the story?"

"For the same sort of reasons, perhaps." Connard was warming to this explanation of events. The more he elaborated it, the more he liked it. "Didn't you say that Gontier was more than a little worse for drink? Another extremely unreliable witness, it seems to me."

"The fact that the Seurat letter doesn't exist in the Bibliothèque Nationale must be pretty conclusive, though," pleaded Evan.

"On the face of it, it's compromising, I agree. But the fact that it doesn't exist there doesn't mean it doesn't exist at all. Maybe there was a misunderstanding and it's actually held in another public collection; or even in private hands." His brain was seething with wild fantasies of manufacturing an original from a mythical private source. It could be done: anything to paper over the chasm which threatened to engulf him and drag his career to destruction forever.

"But surely you agree that if there's been a fraud it must be exposed? The integrity of scholarship must be protected."

"Of course it must. In due course there must be a thorough investigation."

Evan looked at him unhappily. "I can't bear to think of this deception continuing a moment longer," he said. "Rokeby's are being absurdly cautious about the whole thing, and I'd hoped you would be able to do something about it rather quicker. It's all so frustrating."

"Look, Evan, don't worry yourself about this." Connard's voice was calm and decisive. "I think you'd better leave this whole matter in my hands. Don't take any action on your own account. Rest assured, I shall check the whole story out most thoroughly. After all, it's a question of Scholarship, and I agree with you whole-heartedly, where Scholarship is concerned the most rigorous standards must be maintained. But ill-considered and foolhardy action must be avoided at all costs. We simply must not go making irresponsible accusations until we are absolutely sure of our facts. And by sure I mean one hundred per cent rock-solid certain."

Evan cast about for some further argument to marshal against this infuriating policy of laissez-faire, but Connard continued in a conciliatory tone: "Anyway, you've got a hell of a lot on your plate at the moment with the Wattle sale this week. Leave everything to me."

Evan admitted: "Well, of course, it's a busy time...." But he perceived the construction of yet one more brick wall across his path towards the exposure of the Hartier scandal. First there had been

Freddy Fairbanks articulating the unwillingness of the auctioneers to rock the boat; now here was the ambiguous and ultimately obstructive reaction of his erstwhile director of studies to any dramatic revelations. The art trade and the academic world had struck an uneasy alliance for the express purpose of frustrating him.

"Now we must keep in touch," said Connard rising from his chair and wrapping his dressing gown securely about him as if to protect himself from the unpleasantness he had just been forced to contemplate. "But remember, don't you do anything at this stage." His first priority had to be to make sure that nothing came out until his San Pietro appointment had been confirmed. That was paramount. Meanwhile he must consider the matter carefully, and if he could not invent some means for the permanent suppression of the story, he must create conditions under which its impact would be minimised. "Thank you so much for coming to see me about all this," he added.

Evan walked back towards Rokeby's in a state of some disillusion. The whole business stank. But what more could he do now? Where could he turn? Strangely and unexpectedly, he thought of Renata. Whatever her other faults, she at least could be relied upon to adhere unshakeably to principle, to maintain views which would not admit of compromise. She would appreciate the disgraceful nature of the outrage he had uncovered, and would encourage him to resist such a disreputable conspiracy. A dose of Renata's outspokenness, on occasion in the past so aggravating, might now come as strangely invigorating. Then again, was he perhaps getting the whole business out of proportion? For nearly a week now it had obsessed him, driving him from Paris to the south of France and back again, from Ranchec to Gontier, from Fairbanks to Connard. He was sick of the art world, its posturings and its deceptions. He wished he could turn his back on it, get away from it all. There recurred to him the golden image of Bali, the ultimate refuge, the final escape. A deserted tropical beach, swaying palms, flawless blue sky, and Sylvie. What did all this matter by comparison? As soon as he reached his office he rang her number in Paris. But it was a gesture of desperation and doomed to disappointment. Again there was no reply.

NINETEEN

On the day of the auction of the King C. Wattle Collection of Impressionist Pictures the main saleroom at Rokeby's offered a curious mixture of images. It was part theatre, part film set, and part cathedral. The serried ranks of chairs facing the rostrum implied the staging of a major event, possibly dramatic, conceivably religious. A gantry of cameras was assembled in one corner of the room, trained on the twin targets of the auctioneers' box and the podium where the pictures under the hammer would be displayed. At this early stage in the afternoon, with the sale not due to start till 7 p.m., the room was still the domain of technicians, lighting men, carpenters and telephone engineers all putting the finishing touches to their preparations. Television news would be recording the bidding on the more important lots, to be relayed to the waiting world later that evening. A battery of telephones was set up against another wall. Through these, manned by members of Rokeby's staff, bidders would be linked in from all over the world; from Japan, from Switzerland, from the United States, collectors would be spending millions of pounds without leaving the comfort of their drawing rooms or offices.

Not that there was any shortage of demand for seats from people who wished to attend the sale in person. Every space in the main saleroom had long since been booked, and there was even hot competition for places in the two secondary rooms whence, proceedings being viewed by closed-circuit television, bids would be relayed to the main auctioneer. It was one of those occasions which had captured the media imagination, as major Impressionist auctions sometimes do, and there had been newspaper and magazine articles previewing the collection in many different countries across the world. Freddy had not exaggerated when he had told Evan that the sale was coming nicely to the boil. Even Jean-Pierre Grifon, in the absence of anyone senior, had been pressed into service to give an interview to Norwegian Television about the auction; and while viewers in Oslo were unlikely to have understood much of the Gallicised dissertation which resulted, distracted as they undoubtedly must have been by Grifon's occasional on-camera employment of a greasy comb to settle aspects of his coiffeur, nonetheless it all added to the general atmosphere of excitement and anticipation, to the feeling that something very much out of the ordinary was taking place.

The heads of most of Rokeby's European offices had flown in for the occasion. Cyrille de la Guerre had arrived that morning and lost no time in communicating to as many colleagues as possible the news that he was - naturellement - the guest of the Ambassador at the French Embassy ("Claude, of course, is one of my closest friends"). To his fury, Flipsi von Tortrop could not boast a lodging of similar grandeur, and went to some considerable trouble to have his hotel upgraded at a cost to Rokeby's of an additional £85 a night. But what did that matter set against the millions to be taken this evening?

In the seclusion of the Boardroom, the three joint deputy chairmen sat down to discuss the arrangements for the momentous proceedings in prospect. Success of any kind was of course welcome; but in the present climate of relations between the three, no-one could afford to relax lest that success should reflect too shiningly on any one of them at the others' expense.

"There's one important point which I don't think we have yet formally confirmed," said Freddy. "It seems to make sense that I should be the auctioneer this evening. I've done most of the big picture sales in recent months."

Ron and Endymion bridled. It was no secret that Mr Terence was due to make his decision about the succession at any moment. The high-profile publicity which would attach itself to the individual who was the auctioneer at such a major event as the King Wattle sale would give that person an unfair edge over his competitors in the final run-in. Neither of them welcomed Freddy's automatic assumption that he was the man for the job.

"Wait a minute, Freddy," objected Luce, trying to mask his anger with a tone of sweet reason. "I don't see that it necessarily makes sense at all for you to do it."

"Oh?" said Freddy, affecting a considerable degree of surprise at this eccentric point of view. "What alternative can you seriously suggest?"

It was more of a challenge than a question, and Endymion rose to it. "I can suggest myself as a matter of fact. If you look at the most financially productive sales that have taken place in the past twelve months, I think you'll find that they were the two big French furniture auctions, both taken by me."

"Come, come," said Freddy, as if Endymion had just essayed a joke in poor taste. "You may be all very well with the furniture boys who know you and are prepared to put up with your little quirks. But for a big international sale like this one the situation demands someone a bit more imposing, someone with a bit more stature and authority."

"Well, that rules you out for a start."

"And you're certainly not doing it, you vicious old queen." Freddy felt that for his auctioneering ability to be called in question was akin to an insult to his virility.

Ron held up a moderating hand. Overheated temperatures must be cooled: once again it fell to him to assert the voice of reason over these two pathetically childish colleagues, quarrelling like small boys over a disputed toy. It was a pity Mr Terence was not present to witness this display of mutual pettiness, to have it confirmed to him once and for all how untenable the candidature of either man was for the Chairmanship when they could behave in such unmeasured fashion. As far as Ron was concerned, he certainly did not want Freddy to grab the limelight at such a crucial moment, but there were obvious similar dangers in allowing any latitude to Luce. If only he, Ron, were an auctioneer, that would clearly be the answer, but it was not a role to which he had ever in the past aspired. Now he said:

"Gentlemen, please. This sort of squabbling is not getting us anywhere. I suggest we...." He was interrupted by a knock at the door and, as if in answer to his prayer, the tall, slightly stooping figure of Mr Terence Rokeby shuffled into the room.

"Ah, so pleased to find you all together," he announced. "I was hoping to be able to speak to you in private."

All three faces turned to him in expectation, two still scowling like fighting dogs who have just been separated while the third set itself into a smile of studied obsequiousness. "Won't you sit here, Mr Terence?" suggested Wheale, guiding him to a chair.

"Thank you, thank you. I came in hoping to find you here because I have been giving matters a great deal of consideration, and I want to make an important announcement."

Everyone's adrenaline surged irresistibly in anticipation of long-awaited news. So the old fool had chosen this moment to declare his decision about the succession, thought Freddy. Well, about time: and surely there could be no doubt about the outcome. As chairman-elect, there would be no problem about his taking the sale, that was something. What an unlikely trio they were, all hanging on Terence's words: the pompous old pansy, the jumped-up office boy, and Freddy, the natural leader of men. Come on, come on, get on with it. Endymion also eyed Rokeby tensely, and into his mind was thrown suddenly the absurd image of Terence clad in a tunic, an unlikely looking Paris forced into an invidious decision between the three Graces paraded before him. On whom would the shaking hand bestow the apple? Ron, in a moment of rare imaginativeness, was also visited with a strange and vivid analogy. Involuntarily he conjured up in his mind's eye that point in the Miss World contest when the judges have reduced the field to three and the compere announces the result, but in reverse order.

Rokeby coughed, and looked round uncertainly. "As I say, I've been giving matters considerable thought over the past few days. After a lifetime in the business one looks back on various difficult decisions that one has had to make, and it's never easy to be sure. But I'm reasonably confident that I am doing the right thing now. I've reached the conclusion that I should be the auctioneer tonight."

The jaws of Freddy and Endymion dropped in amazement and disbelief. Before either of them could frame an adequately diplomatic protest, they saw Ron leaning across and shaking the old man by the hand.

"An excellent decision, Mr Terence," he was saying, "and one which I most heartily endorse. I have no doubt that in your hands the sale will be an enormous success."

"Thank you, gentlemen," said Rokeby, rising unsteadily.

"Is that all you want to tell us?" asked Freddy.

"Nothing else, no. I'll leave you to get on." Rokeby hobbled out.

"Well, that resolves the problem of the auctioneer," said Ron happily once the door had closed.

Neither Freddy nor Endymion could bring themselves to comment.

Back in the privacy of his own office Terence Rokeby lowered himself gently into his chair, poured out a small reviver, and shook his head. He picked up the well-thumbed copy of last Thursday's edition of the Sporting Life, and ran his eye yet once more over the story which had become distressingly familiar:

Catterick Casualties
Three runners fell in the 3.45 at Catterick yesterday where Nautilus was the only finisher. Thruster and Fairy Boy collided at the second fence throwing their jockeys who were both taken to hospital with severe concussion, while The Upstart went lame and had to pull out a furlong later.

"Renata!"

Evan had been idly kicking his heels in the saleroom, finding himself curiously under-employed that afternoon as the hour of the great Wattle sale approached, when he spied Miss Crum, an unexpected visitor to the august halls of Rokeby's. She appeared to be leaving an envelope at the reception desk, and Evan had glimpsed her suddenly from his vantage point at the top of the stairs which led down to the front hall. She looked up when she heard her name called, and Evan cantered down to greet her. He had felt genuine enthusiasm to see her again viewing her from above, but by the time he reached her a fumbling awkwardness impaired his eloquence. After all, he had not actually exchanged words with her since that extraordinarily unnerving lunch at Leatherby. And was he imagining it, or was there something different about her at close quarters, something distinguishing her from the old Renata?

"How are you?" he said lamely. "It's been ages."

"Well, thank you," she replied briskly. Although not the most observant man in matters of female grooming and couture, Evan registered that a change had indubitably taken place here. Her blond hair was cut chicly and swept back from her face, and she was wearing a fashionable jacket over designer jeans. Glancing down he noted that her shoes were of an elegance which contrasted sharply with the bundle of discoloured plimsolls which had previously constituted her choice of footwear. With a shock he realised that to the casual observer she appeared in no way out of place in the foyer of this élite auction house.

"What are you actually doing here?"

"Just leaving a note for Freddy." Her manner was cool and self-assured.

Evan blushed. "Oh, of course." There was a pause, during which she seemed to be making to leave, so he added urgently: "Listen, have you got time for a cup of coffee? So much has happened since we last met."

"OK, but I can only spare ten minutes. I've got a very important appointment."

"Let's go to the cafe round the corner. You see, there's something I'd very much like your advice on."

Settled in the Italian sandwich bar behind Rokeby's Evan launched into his now-familiar Hartier narrative. His exegesis was unrestrained and to a certain extent cathartic. Assured of a sympathetic ear, he spilled out his fury and his rage at the duplicity he was describing. He gave full expression to his frustration at the obstructive stances of both the Rokeby establishment and of Ewan Connard. How could people behave in such a way, he demanded? Was it not incredible that the judgement of apparently respectable senior academics could be corrupted so thoroughly by self-interest? What should his next step be? Did she not agree that he would be entirely justified in taking matters into his own hands, in going to the police himself about the whole sordid intrigue? He paused, awaiting the burst of invective which Renata would surely unleash against the appalling manifestation of disgraceful capitalist skulduggery to which he had just drawn her attention.

"What was the dealer's name again, the one behind it all?" she enquired with polite interest.

"That bloody crook! He's called St Jacques."

"Quite a smart operator," she mused. "A clever piece of marketing, you have to admit."

"Clever piece of marketing? It's criminal! People have been disgracefully duped."

"Of course there will always be some casualties in the ebb and flow of the free-playing market. You can't make an omelette, as they say. My God, is that the time? I must dash."

Evan was bewildered. "Where are you going?"

"I'm due at an interview in Berkeley Square in fifteen minutes."

"An interview? Are you applying for a post-graduate place or something?"

"Certainly not. You know, I think I've outgrown academic life; I'm probably throwing it in this term. It's terribly limiting, really, and I can't tell you how my horizons have expanded just recently."

"Since you met Freddy?"

"Yes, I suppose it was. I've come across so many new people.

For instance, Freddy introduced me to Alan Grover, who runs this agency, and they're keen to take me on. They say they need people like me, and I'm off there for my final interview."

"Agency? What sort of agency?"

"Advertising of course. Alan feels I've got an enormous talent for it. I must say I find it pretty stimulating, I get a real buzz from it. And you know it's amazingly creative."

Evan shook his head. He had completely lost his bearings.

He succumbed to a momentary yearning nostalgia for the days of WAMPRIC, even for the exile in the Amazon jungle which Renata had once threatened to impose on him. But these were outmoded ideas, no doubt, jettisoned with the Guatemalan peasant woman's poncho and the collection of plimsolls.

"I suppose we've all got to learn to make concessions," he said, but she did not hear him. She waved from the door in really quite a friendly fashion, and then she was gone.

"You know, King baby, what I can't understand about all this?" confessed the still unsmiling Thelma as Mr and Mrs Wattle walked up the main stairway of Rokeby's to take their seats for the great event in the main saleroom a quarter of an hour before it was due to start.

"What's that, honey?"

"Why the hell Rokeby's is holding this sale when you always said you were going to get Sotheby's to do it."

"Did I say that?" asked King, brushing against a table encountered at the top of the stairs and upsetting a pile of catalogues.

"You darn well did."

"Well, I guess they got some mighty persuasive guys in this organisation. And you gotta admit, honey, when you look round at all this, they're doing one helluva job." This was true if the achievement was to be measured in the size of the crowd attracted to the auction and in the degree of frenetic activity that crowd was displaying. People were milling around excitedly, jostling for standing positions, fighting for catalogues, exchanging animated opinions about the pictures shortly to be offered for sale. All manner of types were in evidence: dealers posing as male models, male models posing as dealers, Californian widows of untold wealth, gay mid-Western museum directors, inscrutable Japanese, beady-eyed Swiss, perspiring Germans, interspersed with a variety of attractive girls in shortish skirts whose role in the proceedings was ill-defined beyond contributing a touch of well-groomed glamour; all these people had to be pushed through before the Wattles could reach their specially reserved seats in the fourth row.

"Good evening," said King, returning a greeting.

"Who was that guy?" asked Thelma.

"Fellow called Saint Jack. Big dealer in Paris."

"And who's this young guy? He looks kinda familiar."

"Hey, honey, you remember Mr Conrad." Evan came over to say hello to them both, a little uneasy in his ill-fitting dinner jacket, evening dress being obligatory for the staff on gala occasions like this. Why was it always his fate to feel sartorially awkward whenever he encountered the Wattles?

"Oh, yeah. Hi there, Mr Conrad. I think we met in Zurich."

"That's right, Mrs Wattle. And also very briefly in Paris."

King Wattle twitched at the mention of the French capital, and said loudly with elaborate heartiness: "You know what, Mr Conrad? I was just telling Thelma what a great job you guys have done with the sale so far. The catalogue looks real scholarly, and there's one helluva turn-out tonight. Thelma, it was actually Mr Conrad who was er - instrumental in persuading me to sell here at Rokeby's. I'm sure glad I took his advice."

Evan coloured at the memory of the naked whale-like form of King Wattle entangled in a sheet, moaning on the floor of the suite at the Ritz. It was a sobering thought that, had he not witnessed this phenomenon, none of these eminent people would be gathered here tonight; the cameras would have had to look elsewhere for their prime-time television news footage, and the journalists would need other material to fill their column inches in tomorrow's pages. All this because one afternoon in November he had walked through one closed bedroom door. He said: "I hope we can justify your faith in us, Mr Wattle."

"You bet. How's it all looking from where you stand, anyway?"

"Oh, extremely promising. There seems to be a lot of interest from all over the world, and we're looking forward to some big prices. A few world records could go tonight, I dare say." Evan paused, registering his own words in horrified amazement. Here he was, uttering the sort of slick platitudes which served only to bolster the art market, that very art market whose foundations he perceived to be rotten, that art market which flourished on the trafficking in pictures by artists who did not even exist. He was perpetuating the charade, subscribing to the doctrine that nothing mattered so long as money was made. And here stood King Wattle, an innocent duped into acquiring one such picture, a man mercilessly taken to the cleaners by unscrupulous operators like Raoul St Jacques. Surely, even at this late hour, he deserved to be told, to be given the chance to say no, I don't want a fake to be offered in my name at a public auction. "Oh, Mr Wattle," he began, "there's one other thing I feel I should tell you...." But Wattle had turned his back on him, absorbed in conversation with a burly man wearing a toupée, and a very expensive suit.

"That's King's New York stockbroker," explained Thelma. "You won't get a word in for some time now. I know, I've tried. They haven't seen each other for five days so they got a lot to discuss. What did you want to tell King?"

"It can wait, it doesn't matter." Evan edged away. Mrs Wattle wasn't listening anyway, having been deflected into conversation with a large American lady on her other side. As he left her orbit, he heard her recounting in shocked and outraged tones how one of the Swiss servants had had a brainstorm and taken an axe to King's compact disc collection.

Down in the telephone operators' room Lance busied himself with preparations for his duties during the sale. It was his last week at Rokeby's, and for that reason it had come as something of a surprise to find himself now entrusted with the responsibility of co-ordinating the connections for all the telephone bids which would come through for the auction that evening. For one reason or another, none of the rest of the telephone room staff had been able to stay that night, so here was Lance, in sole control. It was an opportunity which, for reasons of his own, he welcomed. It was up to him to ring through at the appropriate lots to all those who had prearranged to bid on the telephone. Having contacted them, he then had to put them through to the various extensions in the actual saleroom, extensions which were manned by high-ranking Rokeby's staff, who would bid live as instructed by the caller. There was a list in front of him of the various numbers to be dialled, together with the times at which contact should be made. There were clients in Japan, Switzerland, Saudi Arabia, the

United States, and Rio de Janeiro; but the most important by far, apparently, was the fabulously rich Alfred B. Chestermonger of New Jersey, who was bidding on no fewer than eight of the eighteen lots. His call was to be put through direct to the line of Endymion Luce who would execute his bids in the room.

Lance smiled to himself. Fate had dropped into his lap the means for avenging himself once and for all on Rokeby's in general and Luce in particular.

Everything was now in order, and he had time to make a personal call to a London number. An American voice answered.

"Ray sweetie, is that you? It's Lance."

"Yeah, Lance, it's me." Ray hailed from Chicago, had come to London as an actor, and had fetched up as a waiter in a gay bar.

"Just checking you're there. I'll be ringing you later as arranged. Don't forget what you've got to do."

"Uh-huh, I won't. So long."

"Bye."

The clock stood at two minutes to seven. The bulk of the favoured throng with seats in the main saleroom had found their places, and there was a general murmur of anticipation. Behind the rostrum stood an array of Rokeby's staff, most of them trying to look more important than they were. Some, including a rather sour Endymion Luce, were positioned by their receivers ready to cope with the telephone bidders. Von Tortrop and de la Guerre stood shoulder to shoulder, studiously not speaking to each other. Evan clutched his catalogue and had to admit to a slight sense of nervousness, a not entirely unpleasurable curiosity as to how the sale was going to turn out, even despite his acute reservations about one element in its contents.

"Your moment of glory," breathed a whisky-scented voice next to him. Evan turned to see the bulky form of Gervase Hopkins, clad in a dinner jacket that had definitely seen better days and a shirt with frayed cuffs. "Hope it's not too exciting. I've brought something to calm my nerves," he continued, gesturing to a hip flask.

"Quite a large crowd tonight," observed Evan.

"Look at them all: either disgustingly rich or nauseatingly pretentious. Some are both."

"You don't approve?"

"It doesn't matter whether I approve or not. The ritual must go on. All these people gathered together to witness the sacred ceremony of the Pursuit of the Impressionist Picture. It's almost religious, isn't it?"

"I suppose it is in some ways."

"It's a sort of modern Holy Grail when you think about it. The Impressionist Picture is probably the ultimately desirable status symbol of late 20th Century Society. If you've got one you automatically have conferred on you the twin badges of artistic sensibility and financial substance. What more can anyone aspire to?"

"You don't think these people really appreciate what they're buying?"

"New money likes colour. All they want is colourful pictures, it's as simple as that. That's the limit of their aesthetic feeling." Hopkins shook his head with all the weariness of a man whose spirit has been broken in trying to off-load Salomon Ruysdaels on a clientele whose real ambition was the ownership of garish Impressionist landscapes.

Attention was now distracted by the next stage in the rite, the arrival of the auctioneer. Like some crazed elderly clergyman brought out of retirement to preach in Westminster Abbey, Terence Rokeby mounted his rostrum with unsteady step, clutching his gavel and auctioneer's book. Willing hands supported him, guiding him into position. "Good luck, Mr Terence!" called Ron Wheale. Freddy scowled in Wheale's direction. Mr Terence tapped the hammer lightly for a modicum of quiet and announced in a reedy voice: "Good evening, ladies and gentlemen. Welcome to Rokeby's. We begin with lot one, the small Cézanne." He blinked momentarily as the television arc lights were switched on, and then suddenly he was away: "Two hundred thousand pounds.... and twenty.... forty.... sixty...."

The Cézanne sold for £850,000, above the top estimate, which augured well for the rest of the sale. Evan marvelled that here were people actually prepared to pay the extraordinary sums which he had arbitrarily and theoretically imposed on these pictures, indeed prepared to exceed his wild and random guesses. There was gratifyingly intense competition for the succeeding four lots, and then at lot six Endymion Luce entered the bidding from the telephone. He had been connected to Chestermonger, and now battle was joined with a vengeance. First came a tiny Renoir, estimated at £400,000 to

£600,000; Luce finally triumphed at £1.5 million. Next there was a Pissarro with a similar pre-sale estimate which Luce bought for £1.7 million. And at lot eight a Monet, optimistically predicted to reach £1.5 million, was knocked down to him at £3.5 million. Whatever the bidders in the room threw at him, Chestermonger, via Luce, would top. It seemed that nothing would shake his determination to acquire the pictures he wanted. Evan had the impression that even if the bidding reached 20 million, Chestermonger would go to 21. And at each success Luce smirked to himself, all eyes being drawn to him, in a manner which made Freddy wish to smash his teeth in with the receiver then force it down his throat. Bloody pansy, anyone can bid spectacularly with other people's money, thought Freddy; there's no reason for him to look so pleased with himself.

A special peak was attained at lot 12 when King Wattle's best Monet came under the hammer. The estimate was £3 to £4 million, and, after a thrilling duel with Raoul St Jacques, Luce finally emerged triumphant at £7.5 million. As a perspiring Terence Rokeby eventually brought his gavel down, the entire room burst into spontaneous applause. This phenomenon took Evan by surprise. What exactly, he asked himself, were they applauding? Was it perhaps the adeptness of the auctioneer? Or the bravado of the bidders? Or the sheer size of the sum of money involved, in the way that the audience in TV quiz shows clap the week's star prize? Or was it perhaps some obscure tribute to the artist who had actually painted the picture? Somehow the last possibility seemed the least likely.

And now Evan held his breath, for lot 13 was being held up on the podium, a pretty little Neo-Impressionist landscape which, according to the Rokeby's catalogue, was the work of Claude Hartier. The outrageous estimate he had originally placed on the picture was £200,000 to £300,000. Surely a work painted by an imaginary artist whose identity had been established by a non-existent letter could not be worth that sort of money? Slowly the bidding advanced; it paused at £190,000, already a world record for the artist, then an anxious-looking American dealer, whom Evan understood to be called Rudi Grossner, raised his catalogue. When Evan saw that he was now opposed by Endymion Luce on the telephone, he realised that something extraordinary was going to happen.

"Three hundred and twenty thousand, three fifty, three eighty.... gasped Rokeby, bobbing from one bidder to the other like a manic tennis umpire. "Four hundred, and twenty, and fifty, and eighty, five hundred, and fifty, six hundred.... Six hundred thousand pounds, any more? At six hundred thousand pounds, six hundred thousand." Bang. Luce had won again, and Grossner looked mortified, almost as if he were going to cry; he had obviously reached the outermost limit of the enormous bid he had brought with him, confident that it would be enough to secure the picture for his client, and now he had failed.

By the time the hammer had come down on the last lot and Terence Rokeby had been practically carried, exhausted but delighted, from the rostrum, the total proceeds amounted to the best part of 35 million pounds. Alfred Chestermonger, through Luce, had bought more than half of it in monetary terms. It had all been the most glorious, spectacular success, and the room was a seething mass of excitement and comment. The great news was the Impressionist market was alive and well. ITN attempted to set up an instant interview with Terence Rokeby, but Freddy stepped up smartly and intercepted the request. Unfortunately, he explained, Mr Rokeby was too tired now to give further interviews, but he as deputy chairman would happily fill in. He was just congratulating himself on this coup when he looked round and to his fury glimpsed Luce giving an interview to the BBC. "No, I can't reveal who I was bidding for," he heard Luce announce in a mincingly self-important tone, "but I can at least tell you that he's American, a major collector, and absolutely delighted with his purchases."

Down in the telephone room Lance tidied everything up for the last time. He somehow felt he would not be coming back into Rokeby's again, that possibly in the morning he might not be the most popular man in the firm if he did. He slipped into his overcoat, then made a final call to Ray.

"Ray, sweetie, you were wonderful, a dream. I listened in the whole time. That silly old queen Luce was completely taken in, he really thought you were Alfred Chestermonger. And didn't you love the way he said to you at the end: 'Thank you so much, sir, it was a privilege talking to you.'?"

"You sure no-one will find out? No trouble for me?"

"No, no, not a chance. Talk about convincing, you deserve an Oscar. I wish I could see Luce's face when the real Chestermonger rings him to complain that Rokeby's never made contact with him.

Then it'll be Flapperama! Rokeby's could end up having to pick up the tab for 20 million pounds worth of purchases. What a scream, silly gang of sods they are. I certainly won't be around for the fireworks, I can tell you. Fancy a little drinky later? You certainly earned one."

"Yeah, why not. See you down the club?"

"See you there."

After the sale Evan stood alone for a moment in his place behind the rostrum, shell-shocked by the barrage of money he had just seen let loose. The last bidders were funnelling out of the main doors and the porters were beginning to clear up. There was a flatness now after the intense excitement. He heard his name being called, and turned to see the earnest figure of Rudi Grossner approaching. He looked very serious.

"Oh, Mr Conrad, excuse me. I wonder if I might have a word?"

"Of course."

"I have to know: are you aware of any more Hartiers available for sale?"

Evan coloured with embarrassment. This was it. What a fool he had been not to take a stronger line immediately, to allow himself to be browbeaten into tacit consent to the Hartier deception. He saw it all now: Grossner was in reality an undercover fraud squad officer of Interpol, moving in for the kill, the recent sale having convinced him that matters could not be permitted to continue any longer. His own failure to speak out implicated him in the guilt, and there would be hellishly awkward moments in the witness box at the ensuing trial. What a mess.

"Look, Mr Grossner, I know why you're asking...."

"You do? You can help me?"

"Well of course under the circumstances you can count on my full co-operation. It's my duty, I understand that."

"Your duty? No, really, this is overstating matters. But you see my client is a very wealthy man and he's wild for Hartier. He's desperate to own one. I just telephoned him to tell him I was only underbidder on the picture tonight - I'd already gone well above the limit we'd agreed - and he was mad at me for not buying it. He wants one, and he wants one now. So if you know of any private owner who might have one to sell quickly, I'd be prepared to pay a very good price."

"Oh.... Oh, I see.... So you're not...."

"Not what?"

"No, it doesn't matter."

"But you say you can help me?"

"Yes. I mean no. I'm afraid I don't know the whereabouts of any more Hartiers."

"Oh, Mr Conrad, please try. I'm desperate, I want to help this client real badly. I'll be frank, he's one hell of a rich guy, and I can't afford to lose him. Will you at least think about it? Here's my card, give me a ring at the Ritz. I'll be there for a coupla more days if you have any more ideas."

Evan finally adjusted his view of the pleading figure before him back from Grossner, the secret agent of the forces of law and order, to his true guise as Grossner, the commercial agent of a mid-Western collector, and said, in order to be rid of him, that he would keep the matter in mind, let him know if anything cropped up. Grossner's gratitude was intense: "Remember, I got immediate access to £250,000 itching to be spent, no questions asked. Just say the word."

Evan watched him go, then slowly followed out of the saleroom as the porters stacked the last chairs and the television technicians dismantled their final pieces of equipment. It was over. King Wattle could count his millions, the world's press could run their stories of another art market bonanza, Terence Rokeby could savour his greatest triumph as an auctioneer. Most people were happy, although Evan himself could not in all conscience share in that happiness. The whole thing was rotten, but what could he do? In a mood of hopelessness he descended the stairs of the great auction house, debating whether or not to treat himself to a taxi home. Then he glanced across to the reception and saw her standing there. It was Sylvie.

"Eevan! Thank God, I did not miss you."

They embraced. She was swathed in fur, and her cheeks were flushed. She looked delicious. "What are you doing here?" asked Evan.

"I've been working on this job here in London, and we finished half an hour ago, so I thought I would come to see you at your work. It was a big sale tonight, yes?"

"It was a big sale tonight, you're right. But it's finished now, and anyway your being here is far more important than any sale."

"It's good to see you."

"Let's go and have dinner," said Evan decisively. "You must come. We're going to get very drunk."

"That should be fun." She laughed in the conspiratorial way that turned his knee-joints to water and reminded him that there were more important things in life than the art market.

TWENTY

"So, Monsieur St Jacques. You want me to write a book?"

"Yes, on Claude Hartier"

"Hartier?"

St Jacques beamed back at Connard through his little probing eyes. He reached over to refill his wine glass and said: "You must agree that after what happened tonight in Rokeby's there will be a certain degree of - how shall we say - curiosity about this artist, a hunger for more information. And after the sad loss of Dr Ranchec yours is the obvious name to fill the gap."

"Of course this is a flattering suggestion, but.... "

"And I think there is another thing. Perhaps we both have a common interest in seeing Hartier properly handled, properly presented to the public."

"What makes you say that?"

"Come, Dr Connard. I think you know that Dr Ranchec had his critics, even his adversaries. Men who for base ulterior motives sought to disprove his research on Hartier, to claim that it was false, even to make the public believe that he was a far less important artist than you and I know him to have been. You understand me?"

"I think I do. Of course my interest in Hartier is only very tangential...."

"Now don't be so modest. Everyone knows of your brilliant and much-discussed article in the Burlington Magazine. It was the work of a pioneer. As a result of that your name will be tied to that of Hartier for all time."

Ewan tried not to flinch too conspicuously. "Surely an exaggeration?"

"No, no, it is not. But now that the first champion of Hartier is gone, he needs a new defender. Can I count on you?"

"Well, I'd like to help. But there could be difficulties."

"Nothing insuperable, surely?"

Connard took a deep breath. "A letter in the Bibliothèque Nationale could be difficult to find. It's an important one."

"That can be arranged."

"Do you think so?" Ewan's enthusiasm betrayed him.

"Oh, certainly. I think it will be found that the letter was wrongly identified as being in the Bibliothèque Nationale. It was never in that collection. However, I know well the private collection in which it can be seen."

"That sounds excellent, but...."

"Tell me what else worries you."

"It's none of my business of course, but I happened - entirely by chance you understand - to hear that there is a restorer in Paris (was his name Gontier?) spreading some unhelpful stories about aspects of - of the condition and provenance of some Hartiers. He seems a threat to.... to scholarship in this instance."

"Ah, Dr Connard, you need have no anxieties in that regard. I have had a word personally with Gontier. He now accepts he was entirely mistaken. He will be making no more comments on the matter: I have persuaded him that it is in no-one's interest."

"That's satisfactory."

"I think we have a deal, do we not?" St Jacques raised his glass.

There were still hideous problems to be negotiated, not least the one posed by Evan Conrad, but with the burgeoning optimism of a man not built by Nature for setbacks Connard concentrated on the widening circle of light he perceived at the end of the tunnel. On balance he felt moved to raise his own glass too.

"And so," exclaimed Evan as he let them into his basement flat, "the whole business stinks. They're all crooks. Don't you think they're all crooks? Tell me you agree they're all crooks."

Sylvie divested herself of her coat and lay back indolently on the sofa. She said huskily: "You know what I sink you need."

"What?"

"You need a holiday."

"I need a holiday with you," breathed Evan.

"Me, I have not had a holiday for two years, not a proper holiday. But it's true, you know, I have some weeks free now, this job in London is finished. So we go together, that is decided, yes?"

"My darling, I would go with you anywhere."

"Mmm, your lips are very hot. So we got to Bali at last, chéri?"

"Mmm. To Bali, yes please."

"Shall we telephone to the travel agent now?"

Evan laughed. "Right now. The only thing is, what do we use for money?"

Sylvie broke away from his embrace suddenly and stood up. "I show you: I brought something for you." She delved into her capacious bag and produced a cardboard cylinder; the nature of its contents perplexing Evan, he stood up as well to see what she was unpacking. With a flourish she unrolled the 12 by 18 inch canvas on the table.

"Voilà: I guarded it for you and now I have brought it to you. Is it very valuable?"

Despite everything, Evan found himself making instant calculations. "You may find this hard to believe," he told her, "but if this evening's results were anything to go by a Hartier like that's worth at least £200,000, perhaps more."

"Then we must sell it at once."

"Sell it?"

"Mais pourquoi pas? Let's take the money and go. Who's going to stop you? Not those men in Paris, you know too much for them to make trouble. And think what a holiday we could have in Bali on that. Chéri, we could almost live the rest of our lives there on it."

As she sank into his arms and Evan closed his eyes, he was momentarily visited with a vision of golden beaches and swaying palms. But she could not be serious, surely, could she? She could not expect him to be party to the appalling Hartier fraud, to sell a picture which didn't even belong to him. And he couldn't imagine Rokeby's allowing him the several weeks' leave which would be necessary in order to undertake the trip which she envisaged. No, it was sheer fantasy.

Much later that night he awoke and watched her sleeping next to him, wanton, warm, and infinitely desirable, and he thought he had never seen anything so beautiful in his life. It was then that he remembered Rudi Grossner in his room at the Ritz.

Freddy was apoplectic. His eyes bulged with anger and, although it was only 11 a.m., his cheeks assumed a positively post-prandial ruddiness. He was alarming in this state. He looked as though he might well commit physical assault if he did not suffer a coronary first.

"You took the bloody call. Why the hell didn't you recognise it wasn't Chestermonger? Good God, you've been claiming yourself as his bosom friend for long enough."

"How was I to know what that despicable little shit Peerman was up to?" Endymion's back was to the wall, and his voice rose in a whine of self-justification. "He must have found some verminous accomplice to impersonate Chestermonger, and he did it damned well, I can tell you. Anyone would have been taken in."

"I damned well wouldn't," claimed Freddy. At his side sat Ron with a grimly censorious expression intended to convey that he wouldn't either.

"Anyway," continued Luce, "we haven't asked who was to blame for the far more basic error which allowed the whole situation to develop."

"What was that?" Freddy and Ron looked up with suspicion. The atmosphere inside the boardroom was electric with mutual hostility and thinly-veiled panic.

"I must point out that I was the one who identified Peerman's inadequacies as a telephonist and gave him the sack four weeks ago. So what I want to know is, what the hell was he doing in sole command of the switchboard on such an important occasion? That's your responsibility, Ron."

"My responsibility?"

"Yes, you're ultimately responsible for telephone exchange rotas, aren't you?"

"I don't think you've absorbed this management base diagram," countered Ron huffily, extracting an elaborate graphic from his file. "As you will see, the responsibility chain module has lateral as well as vertical mobility with the result that...."

"It's a bloody balls-up," interrupted Freddy. "It's a bloody disaster. If Wattle sues us to pay up all the money we took in bids last night, it'll bankrupt the firm. That won't look too good for any of us in this room. What did Chestermonger say on the telephone this morning? He's not interested in any of the lots he's meant to have bought - claims they're far too expensive. He's even thinking of suing us as well, for falsifying his financial position by giving out that he spent 20 million pounds last night on impressionist pictures. Says it presents a damagingly profligate image at a delicate time."

"Christ!" exclaimed Luce in despair.

"What happened when you spoke to Wattle just now?" asked Ron.

"Of course I didn't let him know the scale of the problem," answered Freddy. "I just suggested there might be some difficulty in extracting payment on one or two lots, some delay anyway."

"How did he take that?"

"Not well at all. He turned nasty, in fact, the fat shit. He actually had the impertinence to say that he held me personally responsible as held signed the sale contract with me in Paris."

A perceptible wave of relief radiated from the other two at the news of Freddy's emphasised implication in the débâcle. There was a sudden realisation, arrived at simultaneously by all three of them, that for better or worse they were in it together. Much though each one of them might wish individually to emerge guiltless from the disaster, leaving his other two colleagues firmly in the mire, this was not to be.

Ron said firmly: "There's no denying it's going to cause a stink, this story, but what we've got to do is think positively, find ways of containing the damage."

"You're right," said Luce. "And I've been thinking: perhaps things aren't quite as bad as they seem. I mean all those lots knocked down to Chestermonger at large prices had underbidders, people who were genuinely interested in acquiring them and were prepared to pay all but the final bid for them. They must all be approached immediately and done deals with: the sales clerks will have a note of their names."

"That's true." For the first time since the meeting began Freddy looked a little less red in the face. He went on with mounting enthusiasm: "If we move quickly we won't be shouldering anything like the full liability. If we're lucky, we can unload most of the lots like that, at one bid below the price they actually reached. In fact, we'd only be talking about a loss of 10 per cent or so."

"And that would be covered by the 10 per cent buyers' premium, so we wouldn't be in a net loss situation at all," confirmed Ron. For a moment they had almost convinced themselves that the hole was plugged, that there was nothing to worry about after all.

Then Luce said: "Still, the story will get out. One can't suppress something like that, and the publicity will be hideously damaging."

"Let's fight fire with fire then," declared Freddy, determined that spirits, his own least of all, should not be dampened now.

"What do you mean?"

"What we need is a sacking. People like that, shows decisive action on our part. There's no point in trying to hide the error, but let's get some credit by being seen to move quickly to identify the problem, eradicate it, and punish the person who made the mistake. Yes, a well-publicised sacking."

"And who do you suggest should be sacked?" inquired Luce defensively.

"That's the question. It should be someone quite senior, senior enough for it to mean something. But not so senior as to shake shareholders' confidence. Not our level of course."

"Of course not." Wise heads shook in agreement. Then there was an uncertain pause. Finally Endymion said:

"It's got to be Conrad, you know."

Freddy looked at him meditatively, then nodded. "I think you're right. Conrad's got to go."

"I never entirely trusted him, I must say," added Luce. "The way he sewed that sale up in Paris, it was all too good to be true."

"Of course it was too good to be true. He never followed the details through then, and he certainly didn't check the details out last night. As head of the Impressionist Picture Department, he must bear total responsibility for the Chestermonger error. It's the department's job to verify the credentials of prospective bidders. The verification just wasn't carried out. It's deplorable that he was so lax, deplorable!" Freddy was warming to his theme, driving himself back into a state of fury as he contemplated the palpable shortcomings of Evan Conrad.

"It's a disgrace, don't you agree, Ron?"

Did he agree, Ron asked himself? He was conscious that he was now facing a crucial decision, one with conceivably disastrous effects. Naturally he could see the force of the argument put forward by Endymion and Freddy, that Conrad should be sacked. Such a course of action would certainly have the desirable effect of deflecting blame for the Wattle débâcle from the three people seated in the boardroom. But could Ron afford to allow this blow to fall on Conrad with impunity to himself? The chances were that Evan knew Ron's dental secrets. Might he not in vengeance after his sacking blurt them out, exposing Ron to the ridicule he had so long dreaded? In his anguish he sucked his teeth distractedly, and Luce, impatient at the delay in their reaching a unanimous agreement, turned on him:

"You know damned well Conrad's got to go, so you may as well accept it. And for God's sake stop blowing through your dentures in that absurd fashion!"

Ron opened his mouth to speak but no words came. That the world, in the form of Luce and Fairbanks, were fully apprised of the existence of his false teeth, was a concept too big to admit of immediate assimilation. The enormity threatened to overwhelm him.

But gradually one aspect of the situation was clarified at least. If his guilty secret was out, then Conrad had no hold on him.

"Got to go, of course," croaked Ron weakly.

"And the sooner the better," echoed Endymion.

"Let's call him in now."

After they had seen Conrad, Freddy said: "I think we'd better put Terence in the picture. We'll have to tell him a bit about the problem, but there's no point in worrying him with too many details. We must emphasise that everything's under control, that the culprit's been identified and dealt with."

Terence came into the room and sat down to listen to the account of the morning's developments. His eyes were bloodshot after his night of triumph; occasionally his hand shook involuntarily, mimicking the action of a falling hammer. There was a strange air of suppressed excitement about him which suggested that his attention, was wandering.

At the end of it all, Rokeby murmured dreamily: "Who is Conrad?"

"Don't worry, Terence, it's under control."

"Good, good."

"I trust you approve the steps we've taken?"

"Certainly, excellent."

They looked at him expecting him to leave now, but he sat on in silence beaming back at them. Then he cleared his throat and announced:

"That sale last night.... did me a power of good, you know. Woke up this morning feeling ten years younger. Invigorated, yes, that's it, invigorated." He paused to savour the word. "Anyway, the long and the short of it is I feel it would be wrong for me to pull out now when I've obviously got a few good years left in me. Not fair to the firm. So I'll be staying on as Chairman. Felt you chaps should be the first to know. Probably find my decision quite a relief, eh what?" The horrified silence which greeted his observations was interpreted by Rokeby as consent. "Anyone got a bottle of bubbly handy? Rather the moment to crack one, don't you think?"

Bewildered, disorientated, and feeling slightly sick, Evan Conrad tottered down the steps of the grand front entrance to Rokeby's for the last time. A light drizzle was falling but he did not notice it. He wandered blindly through the streets of Mayfair, miserable and uncomprehending. His sacking had been swifter than his hiring, and even less expected. It was not clear to him exactly what he was supposed to have done wrong, but there could be no doubting the finality of the message. His connection with Rokeby's was severed. The enormity of the injustice was overwhelming; he was perplexed by the sheer force of the blow which Fate had dealt him, numbed and bemused rather than angry.

But one thing kept him going, one ray of light on which he must at all costs keep his eye. He had woken that morning in the arms of Sylvie Legrand, and he had arranged to meet her at her hotel for a drink at 6 that evening. No matter what happened in the intervening period, they could not take that away from him. The image of her loveliness was untarnished, their mutual tenderness remained unsullied. That was what counted. And now at least he was a free man, owing no loyalty to Rokeby's and fettered by no obligations of employment. What did people do on occasions like this? Sacked senior executives of whom he had read in the newspapers generally brandished their golden handshakes and announced that they were off on long holidays to consider their futures. What was to stop him making that trip to Bali with Sylvie? Nothing now. Nothing except money, that was. The trouble was that in his case there had been no hefty golden handshake. His employment at Rokeby's had been relatively so short, and events had moved during that time at such a pace, that he had never actually signed a contract. It had been vaguely agreed that the first year would be a period of trial, anyway. In retrospect, he had been foolish not to protect himself, but how could he have known? So money was a serious problem, a bitter obstacle to the idyllic retreat with Sylvie which beckoned.

As he walked an increasingly insistent idea assailed him. At first he tried to suppress it as unworthy, then to reject it as unworkable, but it wouldn't go away. He was haunted by the image of Rudi Grossner. How long would it take in a taxi back to his flat and then straight on to the Ritz? An hour, perhaps, to collect the Hartier canvas and transport it to Grossner. A minute for Grossner to write out a cheque for £250,000. Another quarter of an hour to Sylvie's hotel. They would have a blissfully extravagant dinner and plan in detail their trip of a lifetime. Compared with that entrancing prospect, what did his treatment at the hands of Rokeby's matter? With every step past the glittering facades of Mayfair shops and galleries, the more dominant became the vision of Grossner, pen poised over his cheque book, and the weaker grew the faint voice of conscience whispering that the action he was contemplating represented a criminal desertion of principle which would reduce him at a stroke to the level of Raoul St Jacques.

He was actually at Grossner's door in 53 minutes.

"Hi, Mr Conrad, good to see you. My, you look wet."

"It's raining outside, but that doesn't matter - I came as quickly as I could. You see, I have a Hartier here."

"You have? What are you drinking, scotch on the rocks?"

"Yes, yes, thank you. So here it is, in this parcel."

"Sure."

"Don't you want to see it?"

"Oh, yeah. Nice little thing." Even through his own feverish excitement, Evan perceived a disturbingly detached tone in Grossner's voice. The man's manner contrasted markedly with the pleading figure he recalled from 24 hours earlier.

"What do you think?"

"How do you mean?"

"What'll you give for it? I thought £250,000, but I suppose I might accept - I mean I think the owner might accept an offer a little less."

"Well, that's mighty good of you to think of me. But of course I don't need it now."

"You don't need it now? But I thought your client was desperate?"

"He was, right enough. But then you fellows came back to me this morning, said I could have the Wattle picture after all, the buyer had defaulted or something. Of course I leapt at that. My client's delighted."

"Oh, I see."

"So it all worked out fine."

"Yes, I suppose so."

"Just fine. Your very good health. To Hartier."

Evan drank disconsolately. "Look, he wouldn't like another Hartier would he? Your client, I mean."

"What, this picture? Oh, I don't know: I doubt it, not now. What's the story on this one, where did it come from? It's OK, is it?"

"Certainly it's OK. It comes from...." Evan faltered. Where had it come from? He could hardly announce its provenance as being the studio of the restorer who had been responsible for faking all the other Hartiers in existence. "It's.... it's anonymous, I'm afraid."

"No, I think we'll have to pass on this one. My client's got the Hartier he really wanted, he's happy now. But he does need a great Signac, though. Any ideas?"

Crushed. Evan took his leave, a quarter of a million pounds poorer than he had anticipated.

He felt sick again, and it was worse this time. He felt sick with the effort of trying to suppress what he didn't want to think about, the horrific implications of his abortive visit. Christ Almighty, had he been mad? He had no ground left to stand on: in going to see Grossner he had sacrificed entirely the moral advantage he had held over the perpetrators of the Hartier scandal. How could he expose them now, having revealed himself to Grossner as being prepared to traffic in the very goods which he knew to be fraudulent? He had become one of them, no better than St Jacques. As he stumbled out into the dripping evening, the realisation of his personal corruption seeped into him as inexorably as the rain.

Sylvie. He was already late for his appointment with her. He tried to pull himself together and hurried through the rush-hour crowds to her hotel.

Unfortunately he was hardly meeting her in the condition of personal opulence which he had envisaged for himself. He found her in the bar, looking ravishing. He kissed her, and then, mindful of the absence of any cheque in his pocket, ordered a Coca-Cola rather than of glass of champagne.

"You 'ad a nice day?" inquired Sylvie.

"Not exactly," admitted Evan, and told her in as much detail as he could bear.

"So you no longer work for Rokeby?"

"Nope."

"And Bali - what is it that you propose?"

"Of course I'd love to go with you sometime. But the money's the problem, really."

She laughed her husky laugh. "Yes. it was a crazy idea. Maybe it's for the best."

"For the best?"

"You see, there's been another plan. I 'ave the chance for three weeks in the Caribbean. It's a nice invitation."

"Oh."

"I can leave tomorrow."

"Who would you go with?"

"Oh, Guy and some others."

"Guy?"

"Ah! Here he is! Guy, we are over here!"

The man caught sight of them and approached their table smiling in such a way as to reveal a set of perfect white teeth. He was tall, bronzed, and horribly good looking. He wore a jacket casually draped over his shoulders, in the top pocket of which undoubtedly lurked a pair of expensive sunglasses.

"Evan, I present my colleague, Guy Romero. Guy is my producer."

"Oh.... how do you do."

"Enchanté."

Of course, what else? Guy was charming, glamorous, and a film producer. Here was confirmation of all Evan's worst suspicions. Guy slid in to take the place next to Sylvie, opposite Evan, effectively isolating him. After the fever of the afternoon's activities, the dash to the Ritz, the frenetic and doomed attempt at salesmanship, a paralysis descended, a complete inability to cope with the present situation. Guy made most of the conversation, politely addressing the occasional remark to Evan; but gradually, with the inevitability of the receding tide, their talk began to exclude him, embracing people and incidents of which he had no knowledge. Sylvie laughed enchantingly at Guy's jokes; Guy ordered another round of drinks; Evan mournfully demolished a bowl of cashew nuts. Then with one last effort Evan stood up and declared that he felt the time had come to make a move for dinner. No sooner had he spoken with such decision than Guy had risen and shaken him by the hand, and Sylvie had kissed him politely on both cheeks.

"Of course, you have to go. I understand," she said.

Evan opened his mouth to explain that this was not what he meant, that his plans for the evening definitely included her, that.... but the appropriate words refused to come. Guy and Sylvie suddenly looked right together, natural. They looked as though they belonged to each other, in the way that Rokeby's belonged to people like Freddy Fairbanks, and the San Pietro Museum of Fine Arts belonged to Ewan Connard. You couldn't argue with the order of things, not when you were as tired and as damp as Evan Conrad.

Forlornly he drifted out of the hotel and into the rain once more. An aimless determination to keep moving propelled him through the sodden streets, down forgotten alleys, past sleeping arcades, until by chance he found himself on the Embankment. Here he halted, leaning over the Thames to stare into the river's murky depths.

He had lost everything, hadn't he? Sylvie. Rokeby's. Even Renata. And now he sensed he had lost something even more important: in the bewildering six months since he had been swept out of the institute into the art trade, he had lost his innocence.

He thought for a moment, then very deliberately he opened the briefcase which he still carried with him and withdrew the rolled-up canvas secreted within. Here was the symbol of his guilt, of his shame, of his compromise with corruption. He drew back his arm and flung the offending object with all his strength into the night, towards a watery doom. A gust of wind caught it, blowing it upwards and back, flapping like some demented bird. It hovered momentarily above the traffic in the road behind him, lurched, then plummeted down. In one horrific split second Evan envisaged it plastered to the windscreen of some passing juggernaut, obliterating the driver's view and precipitating widespread carnage. He shut his eyes, beyond all hope.

When he looked again the traffic was still flowing freely. The canvas was nowhere to be seen. Released from his final connection with Hartier, Evan breathed more easily. So there it was. The flat off the Fulham Road would have to go now, of course, without the Rokeby's salary. Perhaps Roger Brady still had a room to let? And would the institute take him back? He'd have to find another thesis subject, but he could make a new start. As he splashed through the puddles to the tube station, he suddenly remembered that little-known follower of Puvis de Chavannes who had always rather interested him, the one who had died young. What was his name? He'd look it up tomorrow.